"Let's take a little to...

Jill took Mitch's hand and led him out into the darkened store. It was deserted. The doors were locked and the lights were dimmed. The intimacy of the store shot his pulse up. His gaze lingered on her sexy strut. She hadn't done anything and already he could hardly stand the tension.

She paused in front of a tall bookcase filled with various bottles and jars and pulled him close to her, so that their thighs touched. Her perfume mingled with the spice and floral scents surrounding the display.

"Good sex is a feast for the senses," she said, her voice hushed. "Men respond most strongly to the visual, so we have a number of items to enhance that visual experience. Costumes. Videos. Props." A wave of her hand indicated the different displays, from the movies to an arrangement of body jewelry.

"There are the other senses, too. Smell. Taste. Touch," she continued.

He had to touch her. Now. He slipped a hand behind her back trying to pull her to him, but she resisted. Was this to be a continuation of the demonstration she'd given when she'd handcuffed him to the display? His heart pounded in anticipation when she leaned in close and whispered in his ear.

"Take off your clothes, Mitch."

Blaze™

Dear Reader,

Some characters are so much fun you never want to leave them. In this book, my first Harlequin Blaze novel, I'm delighted to revisit Jill Sheldon, whom I introduced in my November 2002 Temptation title #902, *It's a Guy Thing!*

As soon as brash, fun-loving Jill stepped onto the pages of *It's a Guy Thing!* I knew she was the perfect heroine for Blaze. And I think she's found the perfect hero in Mitch Landry, a man of hidden passions who can capture Jill's heart.

I had a lot of fun writing this story; I hope it's fun for you, too. I love to hear from readers. You can e-mail me at CindiMyers1@aol.com, or write to me in care of Harlequin Books, 225 Duncan Mill Road, Don Mills, Ontario M3B 3K9, Canada. And be sure to look for other exciting Blaze news at www.tryblaze.com.

Happy reading,

Cindi Myers

Books by Cindi Myers

HARLEQUIN TEMPTATION
902—IT'S A GUY THING!

JUST 4 PLAY

Cindi Myers

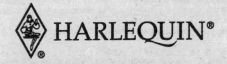

TORONTO • NEW YORK • LONDON
AMSTERDAM • PARIS • SYDNEY • HAMBURG
STOCKHOLM • ATHENS • TOKYO • MILAN • MADRID
PRAGUE • WARSAW • BUDAPEST • AUCKLAND

To my wonderful editor, Wanda Ottewell.
Thanks for all your encouragement and support.
And special thanks to Terri Clark, the title goddess.

ISBN 0-373-79086-4

JUST 4 PLAY

This edition published by arrangement with Harlequin Books S.A.

® and TM are trademarks of the publisher. Trademarks indicated with
® are registered in the United States Patent and Trademark Office, the
Canadian Trade Marks Office and in other countries.

Visit us at www.eHarlequin.com

Printed in U.S.A.

1

JILL SHELDON BELIEVED in Happy perfume, Miracle Bras and in not letting a day go by without having fun. So when she'd seen the Help Wanted sign in the window of Just 4 Play, she'd known that was the job for her. What could be more fun than working in a toy shop?

Okay, so Just 4 Play sold sex toys and lingerie. People needed more fun in their sex lives too, didn't they? In the six months since she'd joined the staff at Just 4 Play, Jill had had plenty of good times, on the job, and off. After all, life was too short not to have fun.

"Should the musical condoms go with the other condoms or in the novelty section?" she asked as she and her co-worker, Sid Crawford, unpacked the latest shipment of merchandise one Wednesday afternoon.

Sid frowned, his eyebrow ring shifting toward his nose. "With the novelties, I think. And rearrange the display so it looks really full. This might be the last shipment we get for a while."

"Why is that?" She squeezed a condom package and grinned as a tinny rendition of "Bolero" filled the air.

"It'll take a while to get all the accounts shifted over to the new owner's name."

She set the condoms next to a box of edible underwear. Maybe she'd shelve them with the massage oil and bill the set as a total sensual experience. "I'm going to miss old Grif." She sighed, and paused for a moment in memory of the late Griffeth Landry, former proprietor of Just 4 Play. He'd died suddenly last month when he was struck by lightning while playing golf. All his gold fillings had melted, welding his mouth shut, a final irony for a man who had a mouth every bit as big as his heart.

"Yeah, Grif was cool." Sid nodded, his pink Mohawk swaying with the movement.

"So what's his nephew like?" Jill asked.

Sid shrugged. "Don't know. Haven't met him."

"Oh come on. You must know something. What's his name?"

"His name's Mitchell Landry, but that's all I know."

She set aside a bottle of bubble bath and came over to lean on a tower of boxes next to Sid. "Where's he from? Does he live here in Boulder?"

"Don't know."

"What does he do for a living?"

"I have no idea."

"How old is he?"

Sid held his hands up in front of his face to ward off this barrage of questions. "I swear, I don't know anything about him. Honest." He slit open another carton. "You sure are nosy."

"I like to know things. Haven't you ever heard knowledge is power?"

"Right. When have you ever been powerless?"

She crossed her arms over her chest. "Never. And I don't intend to be. Ever."

"Guess you're going to have to stay in the dark until Mr. Mitchell Landry decides to grace us with his presence."

"He can't be too old if he's Grif's nephew." She smiled. "Maybe he's young and good-looking. Maybe I

could even help him try out some of the merchandise.''
She held up a pair of fur-lined handcuffs.

Sid shook his head. ''You're incorrigible.''

''I just know how to have fun.''

''Yeah, but you gotta be serious sometimes.''

This from a man with pink hair, who owned more
jewelry than she did. ''Life's too short to be serious,''
she said. She slit open another carton and pulled out a
sequined bra top. Rhinestones and faux pearls winked in
the fluorescent light. Her eyes widened. ''Get a load of
this!''

''What's it supposed to be? Some kind of costume?''
Just 4 Play specialized in elaborate costumes for those
patrons who enjoyed acting out their romantic fantasies.

''I think it's a harem girl.'' She reached into the carton
and fished out a pair of filmy harem pants. ''Isn't it
gorgeous?''

Sid shrugged and went back to unloading boxes. ''Bet
it's not as popular as the French maid or Nurse Betty.''

''I don't know, Sid. It's pretty sexy, if you ask me.''
She turned the bra top this way and that, watching the
gems sparkle. ''I think I'll put it on the mannequin in
the front window.''

''That's a good idea. That black leather is going to
dry out in the sun.''

She scooped up the harem pants and started toward
the back of the store. ''Hey, where are you going?'' Sid
called. ''We still have another pallet of boxes to unload.''

''I want to try this on. Model it for a while.''

''Just make sure the customers know you don't come
with the merchandise.''

She grinned over her shoulder at him. ''Depends on
the customer.''

"Girl, you're all talk and you know it."

She stepped into the dressing room and drew the curtain. So maybe she wasn't as wild as she made out to be sometimes. Half the fun was pretending. Just 4 Play was all about fun and fantasy, so what harm was there in flirting with the customers a little? She liked to think they left the store a little happier than when they'd come in and if sexy clothes and double entendres did the trick, why not?

The bra top fit snugly, accentuating her cleavage. The filmy harem pants, which she put on over a pair of pink satin panties, hung low about her waist, the shimmery gauze billowing around her legs, fastening at her ankles. She smiled at her reflection in the dressing room mirror. Not bad. This was going to be a top seller.

Now if the right man would buy it *and* the pirate costume...

She laughed. Grif and Sid had teased her about the Errol Flynn getup she'd convinced them to order. "What woman wouldn't want to be swept away by a swashbuckling pirate?" she'd argued. Apparently not enough, since the costume had been gathering dust on the costume rack for six months. Still, one day, she would find a man to wear that outfit for her.

The problem with most of the men she met was that they were too serious. She'd start out thinking they were going to have a little fun and the next thing she knew, they'd be looking deeply into her eyes and talking about marriage and kids and all kinds of complicated things like that. Whatever happened to all those commitment-phobic men she'd read about? Why did she always end up with the other kind?

She shook her head and stepped out of the dressing

room. "So what do you think?" she called to Sid. She raised her arms and twirled around.

He turned and surveyed her critically. "Rebecca of Sunnybrook Farm goes to Arabia," he said.

"Aww, come on. Don't I look a little bit exotic?"

Sid shook his head. "Sorry, sweetheart, but those big blue eyes and upturned nose, not to mention the blond curls and freckles, make you look like you just stepped off the bus from the Iowa cornfields. You'd be better off with the schoolgirl costume."

She did her best to glare at him. "It's just because I'm short. It's hard to look seductive when you're only five-two."

"Hey, don't knock it. A lot of guys go for the wholesome look."

"Wholesome is for milk." She was about to stick her tongue out at him when the bells on the front door jangled and a customer walked in.

People had a lot of different attitudes when they came into Just 4 Play for the first time. Many were nervous, jingling change, giggling, even blushing. Some knew what they wanted and headed straight for it, not bothering to look at any of the other merchandise. A few apparently thought they were entering some kind of hobby shop and, realizing their mistake, quickly retreated. Couples came in holding hands, talking quietly as they studied the displays, using the shopping trip as a prelude to a more intimate encounter.

But the man in the business suit who walked in now had an attitude Jill hadn't encountered in a customer before. From the top of his well-cut brown hair to the toes of his spit-shined wing tips, this guy was completely serious. His expression was one you'd expect to see on a banker who had just turned down your loan, and his shoulders—nice and broad, she noted—were squared like a gladiator about to do battle.

Talk about uptight, Jill thought as she glided toward him. She smiled to herself. Nothing like a challenge to get her afternoon off to a good start. By the time she was finished with Mr. Stuffed Shirt, he'd be smiling and ready to have a little fun. Judging by his sour expression, the guy hadn't had nearly enough Vitamin F in his life lately.

"Welcome to Just 4 Play," she said, coming up to him and purposely standing too close. "Are you a virgin?"

His eyes—a gorgeous chocolate-brown—widened. "I beg your pardon?"

She moved a little closer, her arm brushing up against his. She breathed in his spicy cologne. Aramis. A scent she'd always found particularly sexy. "Is this your first time to visit the store?"

"Yes." He took a step away from her and glanced around. He frowned as his gaze rested on a life-size blow-up doll wearing a red satin bikini. "I see everything I've heard about this place is true."

"Oh." She took his arm and gently tugged him farther into the shop. "Good things, I hope. Are you looking for anything in particular? Something for you and your wife?"

"I'm not married."

She smiled. So he wasn't married. How nice.

He was still looking around the room, frowning, as if he didn't approve. Well, they got people like that, too. But Jill figured since he'd walked through the door, he had to be a little bit interested. The trick was to play to that interest, until you found out what the customer really wanted. "Something for you and your girlfriend, then."

That actually got a jolt out of him. He moved out of her grasp. "I don't think my girlfriend would be interested in anything you have here."

"She might surprise you." They had stopped in the section of the store devoted to lingerie and costumes. "We have some very nice lingerie. Nightgowns and teddies. Our garter belts are very popular as well." She held up a lacy black number. "Picture her in this, with some silk stockings and stiletto heels."

A faint flush of red showed on his tanned cheeks. "That's not why I came in here."

Jill grinned and laid the garter belt aside. Who was it who said still waters run deep? She bet Mr. Starched Shorts here would be a real tiger if he let himself go a little. "Maybe you'd prefer something more sensual." She took his hand and led him toward a display of massage oils—a good place to start for novices. As they passed the front window, sunlight caught the rhinestones on her bra top, scattering reflections.

"What is that you're wearing?" her customer demanded.

She paused and held up her hands, giving a little belly-dancer shimmy. "This is part of our fantasy costume collection. Would you like to see others?"

The man's gaze swept over her, more intimate than a caress. She fought the urge to cross her arms over her breasts, shielding herself from his intense gaze. He definitely needed to learn to lighten up. "People actually wear those things somewhere besides Halloween parties?"

The amusement in his voice relaxed her. "Of course. Couples enjoy acting out their romantic fantasies. For

instance, the man might dress as a cowboy, complete
with leather chaps. Or our construction worker tool belt
is very popular." Her grin widened. Her customer would
look *very* nice in that particular costume. "Or a woman
might dress as a French maid, or a nurse." She leaned
closer, lowering her voice to a sexy purr. "What's your
fantasy, sir? I'm sure we've got something to help you
fulfill it."

His eyes locked to hers, warning her she'd asked the
wrong question. Or the right one. The raw emotion she
glimpsed before the polished facade moved into place
once more hinted at a man with unplumbed depths. A
man who kept his feelings in chains, waiting for the
woman with the right key to free them....

She looked away, her cheeks warm, like a child who'd
seen something she wasn't supposed to see.

He stepped back. "I'm not interested in fantasy at the
moment, I—"

"We also have some wonderful instructional books
on sensual massage." Telling herself she was silly to let
a stranger make her lose her cool, she took his hand
again and tugged him toward an old-fashioned wardrobe
filled with brightly colored bottles and jars. "And we
have these flavored massage oils. They're very popular
with both men and women." She unscrewed the cap on
a tester bottle of cinnamon massage oil. She felt him
watching her, and shivers of awareness danced across
her bare skin.

"Did you know they've actually done surveys showing that one of the most arousing scents for men is the
smell of baking cinnamon rolls?" She dabbed a bit of
the oil on the inside of her wrist and held it out to him.
"Doesn't that smell wonderful?"

His fingers around her wrist were strong and warm.

Long, sensitive fingers, the kind that could bring a lot of pleasure to a woman, if he knew how to use them. And something told her this man knew how to use all his assets. He brought her wrist to his nose and inhaled deeply, eyes closing for a second. His lips were so close to her skin she could feel the heat of his breath and her knees began to turn to jelly. She wanted to pull away from his grasp, but couldn't find the strength. What was going on here?

He opened his eyes and his gaze locked with hers once more, intense and searching. Serious, as if her flirting act hadn't fazed him one bit. He looked right past her frivolous costume and teasing manner, to a part of herself she never let anyone see.

She jerked away from him, startled. Now where had that come from? What was he doing looking at her that way—and why? "Um…maybe you'd better tell me why you came in here and I'll see if someone can help you," she said, avoiding his gaze. And the someone wouldn't be her. She replaced the bottle of oil and rubbed her bare shoulders, trying to banish chill bumps. She was used to being the one in control and she didn't like it that a stranger could take over a situation so quickly.

"I'm looking for the manager," he said, his voice portraying no hint that anything out of the ordinary had passed between them.

"Sure. That's Sid. He's in back unloading new stock." She straightened, forcing confidence back into her voice. "Tell me your name and I'll go get him."

"It's Landry. Mitchell Landry. I'm the new owner of this place."

2

MITCH'S JAW TIGHTENED as a rosy glow warmed the salesclerk's cheeks. She had the most exquisite skin… much of which was displayed to advantage in that harem girl getup. And those eyes—violet-blue and wide as a child's as she stared at him now. He almost smiled. It had been a while since he'd struck awe in a woman.

"I…I'll get Sid," she stammered, and hurried away with a rustle of silk and satin. He watched her go, intrigued. He hadn't expected such a combination of class and sass in a place like this.

But then again, when he'd learned Uncle Grif had left him a sex toy shop, he'd halfway expected to discover a dimly lit building on the "wrong" side of town, where people in black leather skulked among racks of dirty movies.

Instead he'd found this perfectly respectable-looking building in the heart of Boulder's business district. Well, respectable as long as you didn't notice that the antique armoire held an assortment of whips, handcuffs and other bondage gear, or that the walnut secretary showcased a collection of vibrators in crayon colors.

And what was with the costumes? He studied a mannequin who wore a lacy apron that barely covered her breasts, a black lace garter belt, black thong underwear, fishnet hose and spike heels. He wondered what Lana would think if he suggested she wear something like that.

He shook his head. Who was he kidding? Lana Montgomery didn't even like to leave the lights on when they were in bed. She definitely wouldn't approve of her boyfriend owning a shop like Just 4 Play. Her father and the other members of the bank board weren't exactly thrilled when they heard about it, though he'd managed to placate them with his talk of plans for the future of the building.

"Mr. Landry?"

Mitch turned and stared at the man moving toward him. This *person* had a four-inch tall pink Mohawk rising above his shaved head like a rooster's comb. The hair and the two-inch heels on his motorcycle boots made him tower a good eight inches over Mitch's own six feet. The man was dressed in black leather pants and vest, with an alarming array of silver rings and diamond studs glittering from both ears, his nose, eyebrow and lips. Mitch wasn't surprised when he opened his mouth to reveal a silver barbell piercing his tongue. "Hi, I'm Sid Crawford, the manager of Just 4 Play. Man, it's good to finally meet you."

Sid had a firm handshake and a smile that transformed his rough features from menacing to charming. Mitch almost laughed. Apparently nothing was as it seemed at Just 4 Play. "Nice to meet you, Mr. Crawford."

"Call me Sid. We aren't into formal around here."

Mitch glanced at the snake tattoo winding its way up Sid's left bicep. "No, I can see this isn't a very formal kind of place."

"So I guess you've had a chance to look around." Sid rubbed his hands together. "What else would you like to know?"

"I'll want to look at the books, of course."

"Sure. They're right back here." He followed Sid to the checkout counter in the center of the store. The manager pulled out a thick sheaf of computer printouts. "Business is real good. You don't have anything to worry about there."

Mitch's eyes widened when he read the final figure on the computer report. "This is the income for one month?" he asked.

"Oh, no, man. That's for one week."

Mitch blinked. He'd had no idea… "Who buys all this stuff?" he asked.

Sid tugged on his left earring. "Lots of people. We get a lot of married couples in here. You know, looking to spice things up. College students experimenting. Single women. Lots of single women." He grinned. "You attached?"

"Uh, not exactly." He'd been dating Lana Montgomery for several months now, but he wouldn't say they were exactly attached, though maybe in the future….

"It's a great place to meet chicks," Sid continued. "We get all kinds of people really—gays, straights, people into S&M or fetishes. You name it, we've got something to make them happy."

The rustle of silk distracted him and out of the corner of his eye, he watched the blond salesclerk sashay past. She certainly was an attractive little thing.

"So, dude, I'm sorry about your loss."

"Loss?" Mitch glanced at the books again. Was there a loss on here somewhere?

"Yeah, Grif was an awesome guy. We're really going to miss him."

"Oh, Grif. Yes, he was…awesome. Thank you." Actually, in the family, his father's brother had been known mostly for his young girlfriends, eccentric habits and outrageous taste in clothing. He and Grif had never been particularly close, though they'd stayed in touch. The last time they'd seen each other, Grif had accused his nephew of being "a regular stick in the mud." Was willing him Just 4 Play Grif's idea of a joke?

"I'd better give you this, too." Sid rummaged in the drawer under the cash register and fished out a key.

Mitch accepted the key. "What's it for?"

"It's the key to Grif's office." Sid nodded toward a door at the back of the room. "I think most of the stuff in there is personal. Grif had a sort of apartment fixed up. He liked to stay over sometimes, rather than driving back to his place in Denver. But there might be some business stuff in there, too."

Mitch pocketed the key. "Thanks. I'll take a look at it later."

The blonde moved past again, carrying a cardboard box. Mitch couldn't help watching her walk across the room. She had the most distracting sway in her hips....

"And you met Jill already." Sid nodded toward the blonde. She'd stopped before an armoire and was busy unpacking bottles from the carton and lining them up on the shelves. She ignored them, but the tension in her shoulders told Mitch she was listening to every word that was said.

"Yes, I've met Jill," he said. "She was giving me a *personal* tour of the store."

A pyramid of plastic bottles fell with a crash and Jill knelt to gather them up. "Let me help you." In three strides, Mitch was beside her, helping her gather up the bottles. He read the label on one. "Kama Sutra Sensation. Have you tried this one?"

The go-to-hell look she gave him might have

wounded a lesser man. "Why didn't you tell me you were the owner instead of letting me go on like that?" she asked.

"You didn't exactly give me a chance." All the bottles reclaimed, he offered his hand.

She hesitated before taking it and allowing him to pull her to her feet. "I must say, I was impressed with your sales technique," he said. "You shouldn't have any trouble finding another job."

"Another job!" She shoved the bottles onto the shelf and faced him, hands on her hips. "You're going to fire me just because I didn't know you were the new boss?"

"Not fire you. But you'll need to find another job when I close the place down."

"What do you mean, close?" Sid hurried over to them.

Mitch looked around at the costumed mannequins, the cabinets full of condoms and oils and lingerie and fetish toys, finally letting his gaze come to rest on Jill's pixie face, all flashing eyes and pouting mouth. "Uncle Grif might have gotten a kick out of this place, but now that he's left it to me, I intend to close it and use the space to open a restaurant." He nodded toward the reshelved massage oil. "I think most people are more interested in Kung Pao than Kama Sutra, don't you?"

"You'd better take a look at those books again," Sid said. "This place makes way more money than any restaurant would."

"Oh, I don't think this has anything to do with the money, Sid." Jill crossed her arms over her chest and glared at him.

"No, it isn't about the money." Mitch looked her in the eye, resisting the temptation to let his gaze drop lower, to her very enticing cleavage. "It's a personal decision."

Sid frowned. "Come again?"

"Mr. Landry doesn't think we're respectable," Jill said. "He's embarrassed."

"Ohhhh." Sid nodded and clapped him on the back. "Go take a look at those books again, dude. You'll get over your embarrassment, I guarantee."

Mitch shoved his hands into his pockets. "I have a younger sister, and business associates. I'll admit I don't care to have them know I own a business that sells ten kinds of dildos and fur-lined handcuffs."

"Twenty," Jill said.

He blinked. "Twenty what?"

"We have twenty kinds of dildos." She took a step toward him, backing him up against the armoire. "And we have hundreds of satisfied customers. Just 4 Play provides a needed service in the community."

"By selling musical condoms and Ben Wa beads?"

"No, by selling fantasy. And fun." She leaned closer, until the tips of her breasts almost brushed against him. "Something you apparently haven't had enough of in your life."

"Life is about more than fun." He forced himself to ignore the enticing aroma of jasmine that surrounded her. "I have work to do. Responsibilities." He straightened. "And a reputation to protect, whether you agree with that or not."

She stepped back, a scornful expression on her face that might have been more effective if it hadn't made him think of the *I Dream of Jeannie* reruns he'd seen on *Nick at Night.*

"Just 4 Play has a reputation too," she said. "And it's not as bad as you seem to think. You haven't even been here an hour and already you're making judgments. You ought to at least give us a chance to show you what this place, and our customers, are really like.''

He shook his head. ''I'm sorry, I can't do that. The architects are all ready to draw up the plans and I've started the paperwork for the construction loan and building permits.''

Sid's shoulders slumped. ''So when do we shut the doors?''

''You have a month.'' He waved his hand at the shelves of bottles, boxes and gadgets, avoiding Jill's angry face. ''You'd better start marking things down.'' He checked his watch. In thirty minutes, he had to meet Lana at the bank. ''Now if you'll excuse me, I have to go.''

Jill caught up with him at the door. ''Isn't there anything we can do to change your mind?'' she asked.

He shook his head. ''Not a thing. I'm the kind of man who, when I make up my mind to do something, it stays made up.'' He hadn't put himself and his sister through school and started his own real estate business by being wishy-washy.

''You say that as if it's a virtue.''

Her words caught him off guard. He studied the toes of his shoes for a moment, then looked up at her. ''I guess if you think life is all about fun, it isn't,'' he said. He nodded goodbye and opened the door.

He thought he'd gotten the last word, but right before the door shut, her voice drifted to him. ''If you don't have fun, you don't have a life, Mr. Landry. Too bad no one ever taught you that.''

JILL SLAMMED THE DOOR SHUT on Mitch Landry, then turned and punched Blow-Up Betty right in the stomach. ''I can't believe he would do this to us!''

Betty swung back and forth on her stand until Sid moved over to steady her. "Careful with the merchandise, sister."

She brushed by Sid and began to pace. "I mean, how can he waltz in here, take one look around and decide to shut us down?"

"He's the owner. He can do anything he wants." Sid walked over to the cash register and slumped onto the stool behind the counter. "I guess we'd better start looking for other jobs."

"I don't want another job." Jill didn't stamp her foot, but she wanted to. This was one of those times when an all-out temper tantrum would have felt good. "I want to keep this one. There must be something we can do."

"You heard the man. He's got the architects working already. In another few months people will be ordering up fried rice where the costume rack is now." He picked up the paper and opened it to the classified ads. "There must be something in here I could do."

Jill hurried over to him and grabbed his arm. "Sid, you don't want to get another job."

His eyebrow ring rose. "I don't?"

"No. If you get another job, they'll make you change your hair. Or get rid of your jewelry." She leaned closer, her voice almost a whisper. "They'll make you wear a suit. And a tie."

Sid put a hand to his throat. "A tie?" He shook his head. "There must be something I can do where I don't have to wear a tie."

"Not and still have the title of manager. Even the manager of McDonald's wears a tie. Plus, anyplace else you go to work, you're liable to have to be there at eight o'clock, or even earlier."

"Eight in the morning?" Just 4 Play opened at

11:00 a.m. and closed at 10:00 p.m. For a night owl like
Sid, 8:00 a.m. might as well be the middle of the night.
He laid aside the paper and gave her a stricken look.
"What can we do?"

"We have to change his mind."

"How? We only have a month." He looked around
the store. "By then we might be sold out of everything."

"We'll simply have to show him how important this
place is—that we provide a much-needed service for
people."

Sid frowned. "How can you do that? I mean, let's
face it, we're not exactly the food bank. Plenty of people
get along fine without candy pants and nipple rings."

"Only because they don't know what they're missing." Inspiration sent tingles up her spine. She grinned.
"I've got it!"

Sid leaned away from her. "Got what?"

"I know how we can convince Mitch Landry not to
close the store."

"How?"

She plucked a jar of body chocolate from a display
on the counter and began rolling it back and forth in her
palms. "I think a little seduction is in order." She
looked at Sid. "I'll make sure our Mr. Landry gets acquainted with the delights of some of our merchandise."

A pleasant warmth curled up from her stomach as the
idea took hold. Really, it was a brilliant plan. Mitch Landry wasn't a bad person, merely uninformed. He had a
great body and definite masculine appeal. It might even
be fun to strip away some of his stuffy attitude and inhibitions, not to mention that suit and starched shirt.

Sid looked skeptical. "You think that would really
make any difference?"

She set the jar of chocolate on the counter. "Sure it

would. Once he's having so much fun with the stuff we sell, it would be hypocritical to close us down.''

''You think he'd care about that?''

''You heard the man. It's not about money for him, it's about reputation. Responsibilities. He's got integrity up to his eyeballs.'' She gave a mock salute. ''No, I just have to find a way to get him to loosen up.'' Half the fun would be knowing where to start.

Sid shook his head. ''I don't know, Jill. I don't think it's a good idea for you to get personally involved.''

''Oh come on, I'm a big girl. It's not as if I plan to get serious with the guy. We'll just have a little fun.''

''He might not feel the same way. He struck me as the type who takes everything seriously.''

She shrugged off the truth of Sid's words. Seducing Mitch Landry would be a dangerous game, but nobody had ever mistaken her for a coward. ''I'll be doing him a favor by showing him how to lighten up.''

''And if it doesn't work?''

She leaned on the counter, chin in her hands, and smiled to herself. ''Then I'll have a hell of a lot of fun trying, won't I?''

3

MITCH WAS FIVE MINUTES LATE to meet Lana, but he wasn't worried, because she was guaranteed to be ten minutes late. It was one of the things that annoyed him about her. That and her tendency to be arrogant, but he supposed that came from always being at the top of the social heap.

Still, in any relationship, you had to overlook certain things. Lana had other qualities he admired: she was attractive, well-dressed, intelligent and elegant. And she had the kind of connections he needed to establish himself as a businessman in this town. Not that he'd ever date a woman solely for her social status, but it was an added plus when you were trying to get ahead.

She breezed through the double doors of the bank lobby right on schedule, at ten after. Mitch rose from his chair and went to meet her, leaning down to kiss her cheek. "Careful," she cautioned, pushing him back. "I just had my hair done."

Why that should make any difference, he wasn't sure. It wasn't as if he was going to run his fingers all through her hair in the course of a hello kiss. Not that he could anyway, she kept it so firmly pinned in place.

"Lana, darling, you look lovely as ever." Morton Montgomery emerged from his office to greet them. He patted his daughter's shoulder and shook Mitch's hand.

"I've got all the paperwork ready for you. Why don't you come right in and we'll go over it all."

Mitch followed Lana and her father into an office whose predominant theme was dead animals. Mounts of bighorn sheep, deer, elk, moose and even a mountain lion occupied most of the wall space. Mitch took a chair with his back to the lion and smothered an expression of distaste.

"So have you had a chance to check out the property yet?" Mort asked as he settled into a full-grained leather executive chair.

"I was over there this afternoon. I must say, it's not at all what I thought it would be."

Mort pursed his lips and nodded. "Still, not the sort of place you'd want your name associated with."

"What sort of place is it?" Lana looked at him, a pleasant expression on her perfectly made-up face.

Mort cleared his throat. Mitch resented the warning. He'd already agreed Lana didn't need to know the nature of the business he'd inherited. "Nothing special." He waved away the question. "A restaurant will do much better in that location, I'm convinced." His throat tightened only a little at the lie. He *had* been convinced a restaurant was a better financial venture until he'd seen the books at Just 4 Play. So convinced he'd sold most of his other real estate around town in order to put everything into this new enterprise. But who would have thought there could be so much money in sex?

"We've already had an appraisal done." Mort handed across a folder. "And here's the preliminary paperwork for the construction loan. You'll have no problem qualifying for the funds you need. All we're waiting on now are the architectural plans and the permits from the city."

"I should have everything ready in thirty days." He closed the folder and returned it to the banker.

"Excellent. I think this is going to be an excellent investment, Mitch. Something we can all be proud of." Mort grinned. "So do you two have plans for the evening?"

"We have reservations at the Boulderado." Lana picked up her purse and stood. "We need to leave now, or we'll be late."

On the way to the restaurant, Mitch only half listened to Lana's account of an annoying client who'd visited her CPA firm that day. He was replaying the conversation in Mort's office. Why did it bother him that Mort had said the restaurant was something they could "all" be proud of? Wasn't Mitch the one who was doing all the work? Wasn't he the one who'd earned the right to be proud—or not? Or did Mort think a simple business loan gave him control over the project—and over Mitch?

The maître d' at the Boulderado welcomed them with a smile and escorted them to their favorite table in the atrium. "Should I have the wine steward bring your usual?" he asked.

"Yes, James, that will be fine," Lana said as she settled into her chair.

James started to leave, but Mitch stopped him. "Wait. Instead of the merlot, let's have a chianti."

James and Lana both stared at him. "But we always have the merlot," Lana said.

He nodded and spread his napkin across his lap. "Tonight, I'd like something different."

"Yes, sir." James hurried away.

Lana regarded him with a half smile on her lips. "Feeling feisty tonight, are we?"

"Something wrong with that?" He kept his voice

light, but there was no mistaking the challenge in the words.

"No. It's just not like you to be so…different."

The truth of her words wounded him. Maybe Uncle Grif had been right. Maybe he was a stick in the mud. Well, that didn't mean he had to stay that way. People changed. He could change without sacrificing his integrity in the process.

He started by ordering broiled trout for dinner instead of his usual prime rib. Lana compressed her lips into a thin line, but said nothing. Mitch sipped the excellent wine and regarded her over the rim of the glass. Her dark hair was drawn back from her face and gathered in a low knot, the kind ballerinas wore. He supposed people would say she had a classical beauty—fine features, with deep-set green eyes and a Roman nose.

"Is something wrong?" She looked puzzled.

He shook his head and picked up his fork. "No, nothing's wrong."

"Then why were you staring at me?"

He forced a pleasant smile to his lips. "Maybe I simply enjoy looking at you."

She dismissed the compliment with a frown and began cutting up her prime rib with the precision of a surgeon. "I saw Jerry Brenham at lunch today. He says the Canterbury Apartments are going on the market next week. If you call him now, you could make a bid before anyone else."

"Actually, I'm thinking of getting out of the rental market altogether."

She raised one perfectly groomed eyebrow in question. "But why? The Boulder rental market is one of the most profitable in the country."

"Yes, but I'm tired of being a landlord." At least with

his own restaurant, he wouldn't have tenants calling him up in the middle of the night to complain about a lack of hot water or the noisy neighbors.

"You should hire a management company. Then you wouldn't have to deal with tenants."

"I like being personally involved in a business. That's why I decided to open a restaurant."

She dabbed the corner of her mouth with her napkin, careful not to smear her lipstick. "I can't imagine why. Half the fun of having money is being able to delegate the work to someone else." She stabbed at a piece of beef. "Then you can go out and make *more* money."

It always came back to money with Lana, didn't it? he thought. They'd met at an investment seminar. He'd been attracted to her from the first because she was so different from him. She had a grace and ease in social situations he wanted to emulate, and a cool reserve he felt could help him keep a tighter reign on his own sometimes tumultuous passions.

The fact that she was the kind of woman who would have never looked at him twice when he was a struggling scholarship student in college made the challenge of winning her that much more exciting. And now here they were, if not engaged, then certainly "in a relationship." But a relationship based on what—business?

They had dinner every Wednesday at the Boulderado, and attended the theater or a concert every Friday. He usually stayed at her condo two nights a week. She never stayed at his place; she said she couldn't be comfortable there.

Why hadn't he realized before how boring and predictable his life had become? He looked at his plate. Right down to the same New York cheesecake every Wednesday night for dessert.

"Mitch, why are you so quiet? Haven't you been paying attention to a word I've said?" Did he imagine a note of annoyance in her voice?

He pushed his plate away. "I don't want to talk about business tonight."

She frowned. "Then what do you want to talk about?"

He leaned back in his chair and studied her across the table. "Why don't we talk about us?"

Her eyes widened and she looked away. She balanced her knife and fork precisely in the center of her plate and folded her napkin neatly beside it. "I'm listening."

And what did he have to say? How could he describe this restlessness he felt? "Lana, do you ever think about doing things differently?" he asked.

"Doing what things differently?" She sipped her coffee.

Decaf, extra cream, no sugar, Mitch thought.

"Anything. Everything." He leaned toward her and lowered his voice. "For instance, sex."

Her eyes widened and her cheeks flushed. "What are you talking about?"

"I mean—do you ever think about...experimenting. Dressing up in sexy clothes or using some massage oil or...something."

By this time her cheeks were the color of ripe apples and her lips had almost disappeared as she compressed her mouth into a thin line. "Really, Mitch. Why would you want to do any of that?"

"I don't know...because it might be fun. Because maybe we've both been a little too...repressed."

She stared at him. "What's gotten into you?"

"Nothing's gotten into me. I just think my life has

grown a little…boring. I don't see what's wrong with wanting to try something different.''

''I'm sorry if you think I'm…repressed.'' She jerked her napkin from her lap and deposited it on the table.

''Lana, I didn't mean you—''

''I think I'd better leave now.'' She stood and clutched her purse to her chest.

''Lana, I—'' The apology froze on his lips. He couldn't say he was sorry, because he wasn't. What was wrong with a couple talking about these things?

''Don't bother to get up. I'll call a taxi.'' She gave him a last wounded look and hurried past him.

He told himself he should go after her. That's probably what she wanted. But why should he pursue her? If Lana wasn't even willing to listen to his point of view, what did that say about their relationship? He'd thought the safe, orderly routine they'd fallen into was what he wanted, but he realized that wasn't enough anymore.

So no, he wouldn't go after her. Actually it was a nice change sitting here alone, sipping his wine and thinking.

Mostly he thought of Jill. How different she was from Lana. Or from any other woman he knew. She was frank without being crass, funny without being phony. She looked like the girl next door and dressed like an erotic temptress. He'd only met her this afternoon but he already felt like she knew more about him than most people. She'd picked up right away on the reason he wanted to close Just 4 Play, and hadn't been the least bit impressed with his position or power. She hadn't cared if he owned a whole city block of businesses or if he was a scholarship student at the university.

He smiled, remembering the way she'd asked ''What's your fantasy?''

But his smile faded as her other words came back to

him. Was she right? Was he too uptight? Had he forgotten how to have fun?

She couldn't know how little room in his life there'd been for fun. From the time he was seventeen, he'd been looking after his mother and little sister, Meg. He'd worked and gone to school, and been there for every band concert and school program of Meg's. Now that Meg was a premed student, she didn't need him so much—except to pay the bills. And that meant he had to devote himself to business. To meeting the right people, making the right investments. He'd worked hard to develop a certain reputation. For Meg's sake, as well as his own, he couldn't let something like owning a sex toy shop cast a shadow over everything he'd worked for. People judged you more harshly when they knew you came from nothing. If too many people thought that way, you could end up with nothing again.

He'd have time for fun later. Right now he had to take care of his responsibilities.

Which brought him back to Jill. She was one of his responsibilities now too. And Sid. He would let them know he'd treat them fairly. He'd give them a generous severance package and help them find other jobs. Maybe he'd even offer Jill a job in his new restaurant. It would be nice having her around. Maybe one day, she'd even come to think of him as a friend.

JILL WAS SURPRISED TO FIND Mitch hard at work in Grif's office when she arrived at Just 4 Play the next morning. At least, from the looks of the papers spread out on the desk in front of him, he'd been working; when she knocked on the door frame and stepped through the open door, he was staring into space.

When she came into the room, he glanced at her, then straightened. "Good morning, Jill."

"Good morning. I see you're here early."

"I've been here since nine. That's not exactly early."

"It is around here. We do most of our business in the evening, though the lunch hour is good, too. People like to pop in and pick up a few things."

"That gives a whole new slant on the idea of a quickie."

The remark startled a laugh out of her. Yesterday, Mitch hadn't struck her as a man with much of a sense of humor. Which just went to show, first impressions aren't always accurate. "Finding anything interesting?" She nodded at the paperwork on his desk.

He glanced down at the folder in front of him, then closed it. "Tell me, what did you think of Grif?" he asked.

"Grif?" The question surprised her. Why was he interested in her opinion of his uncle? "I liked him," she said. "He was a fun guy."

"That's it? A fun guy?"

"Yeah. I mean, he knew how to enjoy life." *Unlike some uptight people I could name.* She leaned against the desk. "I'll bet he was your favorite uncle, huh?"

Was the hurt that flashed across his face grief, or something else? He pushed the file away. "Did you need something?"

So much for getting to know each other better. Good thing she wasn't the type to give up easily. She flashed him her most dazzling smile. "I've been thinking about what you said yesterday." She moved around to sit on the edge of the desk. Her skirt rose up on her thigh, not an indecent amount, but enough that she was sure he noticed. She'd purposely dressed more conservatively today, in a simple skirt and sleeveless knit top. Sometimes what a man couldn't see was more enticing than what was right out in the open.

His color heightened as he glanced at her, then he jerked his gaze away. "What in particular were you thinking about?"

"What you said about most people being more interested in Kung Pao than the Kama Sutra."

"Oh?"

With one syllable, he lobbed the conversation back to her. But that one word told her a lot. He was interested all right, but determined not to show it. "I think, in general, people do tend to think about food more than sex, but maybe that's because we eat three times a day. I mean, food is always there, practically right in front of us."

"But most people don't have sex three times a day."

She smiled. "No, I think it's safe to say most people don't have sex nearly that often."

He nodded, still somber as a judge, though she thought she caught a hint of amusement in his voice. "If they did, it would severely interfere with work."

"In that case, it would probably be outlawed altogether. We mustn't let anything get in the way of the economy."

He laughed, and she counted that a minor victory. "So what are you trying to say?"

She picked up a pencil and smoothed her fingers along its length. "That sex is more special than food. That we shouldn't take it for granted. And if dressing up or playing with toys or using other things makes sex special for people, then that's a good thing, don't you think?"

He sat back, leaning away from her, his pose casual, but the tension in his shoulders letting her know he was aware of her in the way a man is aware of an attractive woman. "What's wrong with the old-fashioned way? A man and a woman, no props?"

She looked directly at him for the first time since she'd come into the office, her expression serious, chasing the mirth from his eyes. She wet her lips, her voice low, seductive. "With the right man and woman, that can be wonderful."

He held her gaze, not flinching. "Then they don't really need places like this."

"No." She leaned closer. The spicy scent of Aramis sent a warm tickle through her midsection. "Do you like cake?"

He blinked. "Cake? I guess so. It depends on the cake."

"Chocolate cake. Devil's food. With so much chocolate, it's almost black. Sinful." She wet her lips. "With chocolate buttercream icing an inch thick."

He swallowed. "And your point is?"

"Just 4 Play is like the icing on that cake. The cake is good without the icing, but it's so much better with it." She dropped her gaze to his lips. All this talk of sweet indulgences made her wonder what it would be like to kiss him.

Apparently she wouldn't find out today. "That doesn't mean I have to be the one to sell the cake." He sat forward again, his voice firm, the spell between them broken. "Or the icing. Or sex toys and lingerie."

She frowned. "You'd rather sell Chinese food. Something people can get at half a dozen other places in town."

"But not this Chinese food. I have a five-star chef who's going to create a special menu. We're not talking your average dollar-a-scoop buffet."

She crossed her arms over her chest and swung one leg impatiently against the desk. "It's still something ordinary. Expected." Why did it disappoint her so much that he'd settle for something anyone could do?

"Men have built fortunes providing people with ordinary services," he said.

She leaned forward, pinning him to the chair with her gaze. "But it's the risk-takers who've really made a difference in this world. Besides, you'd have more of a chance of making a fortune sticking with Just 4 Play. But of course, that wouldn't be respectable."

He frowned. "You say that like it's a bad word."

"Only if you're willing to settle for the ordinary, instead of the extraordinary."

"So you're saying Just 4 Play is extraordinary?"

"It could be. How are you going to know if you don't stick around and find out?"

"I guess I'll take that chance."

She slid off the desk and looked down at him. "I think you've forgotten what it means to really take chances," she said. "If you ever knew."

She turned and left, but not before glimpsing the hurt that flashed through his eyes at her parting words. Good. She'd made at least one point. And planted the seeds for further victories. She would convince Mitch Landry to see things her way. And maybe she'd show him what he'd been missing living his safe, conventional life.

4

MITCH PACED IN FRONT of his desk, debating whether to go after Jill, to tell her exactly what he thought of her unsolicited opinions and her attempts to change his mind. This was his business and he could do anything he damn well pleased with it. Why should he care what a salesgirl he'd known less than two days thought of him? He had half a mind to—

"Shit!" Pain shot through his leg as he banged against the corner of the daybed that sat against the back wall of the office/apartment. He frowned at the offending piece of furniture. The bed was covered in a fleece throw decorated with rows of bright yellow smiley faces. Another example of Uncle Grif's appalling tastes.

He sank down onto the bed, head in his hands. No, in this case, he *was* the one who'd behaved appallingly. He'd dismissed Grif as a crass playboy who'd devoted his life to golf, women and the sex toy business.

Going through this office this morning, Mitch had discovered another man entirely. He found a whole file drawer devoted to the various charities Grif supported— a mentoring program for adolescent boys, a shelter for abused women, a spay and neuter clinic for indigent pet owners. The thickest file in the drawer sent a pain through his chest.

He looked up, at the folder still sitting on the corner of the desk. From here he could read the hand-lettered label on the tab: Mary Landry Mental Health Education Foundation.

Loud, tasteless, fun-loving Uncle Grif had funded a program to educate the public about mental illness and the mentally ill. He had named it after his sister-in-law, Mitch's mother, who had spent her last years in and out of institutions, struggling for a normalcy she could never quite attain.

Mitch felt ambushed by grief for a man he'd never really known. A man he'd never have the chance to thank.

Had Uncle Grif left him these things to show how wrong Mitch had been in his judgment? Or as a way of saying he understood?

He stood and opened another folder on the desk. This one held tax forms. Despite his happy-go-lucky reputation, Grif had been a sound businessman. Just 4 Play was on solid financial footing and had increased profits every year in the three years since it had opened.

But money didn't equal respect. In yet another folder, he'd found paperwork showing the Chamber of Commerce had turned down Grif's application for membership, with a curt letter stating Just 4 Play did not enhance the family-oriented reputation they wanted to project.

He pushed aside the stack of files and stretched. A glance at his watch showed it was after noon. A good time to go out for a bite to eat. As Jill had pointed out, he had to eat three times a day, though sorry to say, he wasn't having sex three times a day. Not even three times a week. And from the way Lana had acted last night, he'd be lucky if she ever had sex with him again.

Then again, would that be such a loss?

With this disturbing thought, he emerged into the main part of the store. As Jill had said, lunchtime business was brisk, with people lined up two deep at the register and more browsing in various parts of the store. He spotted Jill in a back corner, rearranging items on a pegboard.

She glanced toward him, then quickly looked away. The deliberate snub annoyed him. Just because they disagreed on how he should run *his* business didn't mean they couldn't be civil. As her boss, it was up to him to set an example. He decided to ask her if she wanted him to bring anything back for her lunch.

She was standing on tiptoe to hang something on one of the pegs when he reached her corner. "Hello, Jill."

"Hello, Mitch." She reached into another carton, not looking at him.

"What do you have there?" He nodded to what looked like a ball of fake fur in her hand.

"Fur-lined handcuffs." She held up what he could see now was two circlets of black fur joined by a silver chain.

"Okay. But why fur?"

"It's more comfortable. See?"

Before he could react, she snapped one cuff around a pole on the display and another around his right wrist.

"Hey!" He struggled against the restraint. "What do you think you're doing?"

"Just showing you how comfortable they are." Her innocent smile failed to mask the evil gleam in her eye.

He refused to give her the satisfaction of thinking she'd bested him. He studied his cuffed wrist. The fur against his skin was cool and silky. "People actually think this is sexy?"

"It's not the cuffs themselves that are so sexy. It's the element of danger." She moved closer, her voice softer, confiding. "Of risk. Of having to trust your partner completely."

She was so close now he could see each individual eyelash, and the smattering of freckles beneath the powder on her nose. He held his breath, half-afraid she'd hear the hammering of his heart and know how she'd affected him.

"Here. You look uncomfortable." She grasped the knot of his tie and tugged it loose, then began to loosen the buttons of his shirt. She moved slowly, focused on the task, her fingers lightly grazing his skin as she parted the starched cotton.

He grabbed her wrist with his free hand. "What are you doing?" His gaze met hers, the blue depths of her eyes pulling him in even as his mind warned him to keep his distance. "Get me out of here before someone comes along and sees us." His voice was tight and husky, the voice of a stranger.

"Oh, no one's paying any attention to us." Her lips curved in a slow smile. "I thought you wanted to understand the appeal."

She stepped back, just out of his reach, and picked up a small whip, with a fringed leather tassel at the tip. "The cuffs are like this cat-o'-nine-tails. It's not really designed to harm." She flicked it across his chest, the tassel barely brushing against him. "You can use it to tickle. Or perhaps more firmly." She wielded the whip with more force this time, though still barely grazing him. "The idea is to heighten sensation."

All thought of his surroundings faded as he watched her. His skin felt feverish, his nerves raw, tingling with awareness of her—of the smooth skin of her arms brushing him as she reached for something on a shelf, of the curve of her breast outlined by the clinging knit of her sleeveless top, of the bottomless blue of her eyes as she watched him.

He reminded himself she was doing this on purpose. She was deliberately trying to make him feel vulnerable. Trying to prove some point. He wouldn't be swayed so easily. He forced a lightness into his voice that he didn't feel. "Do you always break in new bosses this way?"

"I thought you wanted to understand." She trailed the whip across his throat, tickling, teasing, stealing breath and coherent thought. "To see what it is that attracts people to these things."

"Are you into this kind of thing? Bondage?" Heat pooled in his groin and desire lent an edginess to his voice.

She stroked the handle of the whip down her throat, a half smile on her full lips. He bit back a groan, determined to maintain control. "Maybe." She leaned closer, engulfing him in the scent of jasmine. "That's what it's all about, isn't it? The experience?"

He reminded himself that they were not alone. At any moment now, someone might come down the aisle and wonder what was going on. It was important to keep his cool. Retain his dignity. And to not let Jill know she was getting to him. "I think you've made your point," he said, his voice perfectly even, emotionless.

"No. I've only just begun." She smiled, a secret, seductive look.

"I can see this is getting out of hand." He struggled once more to free his wrist from the cuff. But underneath the fur was solid steel. He was held fast.

"It's about so much more than sight. That's why sometimes people use blindfolds. To heighten the other senses." She took a black satin blindfold from the shelf and brushed it down his cheek. He glared at her, warning her she was taking this too far.

Still smiling, she laid aside the blindfold and reached for a small red bottle. "The sense of smell is important." She opened a bottle and held it under his nose. A spicy fragrance replaced the aroma of jasmine.

"Or taste." She touched her finger to his lips and he tasted cinnamon.

"And hearing." She swished the whip past his ear. He flinched, even as heat coursed through him.

"Touch." She trailed the whip down the center of his chest, the fringes dragging across his chest hair, tugging gently.

He fought to control his breathing, even as his body strained toward her. He couldn't remember wanting a woman more—needing her with an urgency that defied logic. If he wasn't held fast by the cuffs, he might have pulled her down right there in the aisle. He tried to read the expression in her eyes. Is that what she wanted, too, or was she only teasing him? Getting back at him for wanting to close the store?

"What about you?" he demanded. "What do you want?"

She blinked, and stepped back. "Wh…what do you mean?"

"Is sex the main goal for you? The sensual experience? Or do you want something more?"

She turned away, and replaced the whip on its hook. "I don't see why that should matter to you."

Her defensive tone told him more than the words themselves. "It does matter, doesn't it?" he said softly. "There has to be a connection with that other person. If you don't have that, everything else is just…make-believe."

"Whoever said there was anything wrong with make-believe?" With one quick movement, she released him. She snatched up the cuffs and replaced them on the pegboard. "Not every encounter is life changing," she said.

He rubbed his wrists and watched her as she busied herself moving things about on the display. Her head was bent, the hair parted on either side of her neck to reveal a triangle of white flesh. He fought the urge to kiss her there. "I think we're all looking for the life-changing encounters," he said. "Even those of us who don't want to admit it."

With difficulty, he turned and walked away, shaken by what had just happened, but determined not to show it. What did it mean that a woman he scarcely knew could touch him so? Was it the novelty of the experience, the charged atmosphere of this place? Or something more? Something that threatened to unman him, to destroy the control he'd worked so long to perfect?

"I SAW WHAT YOU DID." Sid's disapproving tone stopped Jill as she walked past the front counter after the noon rush had subsided.

"What are you talking about?" She pretended ignorance.

"I saw you and Mitch back there." He nodded at the security mirror angled toward the corner.

She flushed. She'd forgotten about that mirror. "He wanted to know what the handcuffs were for, so I showed him." She trailed her hand along the edge of the counter, avoiding Sid's eyes.

"You did a lot more than that."

And might have done more if they'd been alone. "So?"

"So, haven't you ever heard of sexual harassment? He could sue you!"

She laughed. "And tell a whole courtroom that I tied him up and teased him with a whip? I don't think so." She smiled, remembering the raw desire in his eyes. "Besides, I think he liked it."

"Liked it or not, you could end up in big trouble playing games like that."

"Oh, Sid, you worry too much. It was all in fun."

"It looked deadly serious from here. In fact, I'd say you're lucky looks *can't* kill, or you'd be laid out in the back room right now."

"I'm still standing, aren't I?" She leaned back against the counter, edgy with frustrated desire. The problem with a slow seduction was that Mitch wasn't the only one left aroused and unsatisfied. "Besides, what have I got to lose? If I can convince Mitch to keep this place open, you and I get to keep our jobs. If I don't, well then I'm out the door anyway, so I might as well try."

"But seducing the boss—it's a crazy idea!"

She laughed. "Unconventional maybe. Smart even. But not crazy."

"It *is* crazy. And it won't work. You heard him yesterday—his mind is made up."

"People can change their minds. Even men."

"Not men like him."

"I guess you're an expert on change, Mr. How-Many-Girlfriends-Is-It-This-Week?"

He stuck out his lower lip. "I have every intention of being faithful, as soon as I find the right woman."

"So you're saying the right woman will convince you to change your tomcat ways?"

He nodded. "When I've found the right woman, I won't need anyone else."

She laughed. "That's what I love about you, you're such a romantic."

His expression relaxed. "Speak for yourself, Miss I-Want-To-Be-Swept-Away-By-A-Knight-In-Shining-Armor."

"That's a pirate. I want to be swept away by a pirate."

"Whatever. I don't think Mitch Landry has ever been within sight of a sailing ship."

"Don't be so sure. My point is, if the right woman can make you mend your ways, then the right woman can make Mitch Landry change his mind about closing Just 4 Play."

"And you think you're the right woman?"

"Let's just say I'm a woman who always gets her man."

"Hmm. Well, if I were a betting man, I'd put my money on the man getting you. I think you're in over your head this time, Jilly girl."

She shook her head and walked away, ignoring the doubts nudging at her. For a moment with Mitch, she'd almost forgotten the rules of the game. Rules she'd established. Fun was the object. A mutually satisfying, sensual experience. A good time had by all. No need for messy complications.

Mitch's talk of "connections" and "life-changing experiences" had shaken her. Sure, those things were for some people, but not for her. What did Mitch know? Maybe he thought he'd seen some secret longing in her eyes, but he was wrong. She was attracted his body. To his mind, even. But that was as far it went. Anything else was just his imagination.

5

MITCH SAT IN HIS CAR, trying to calm nerves that felt as if they'd been filed with sandpaper, trying to make sense of what had just happened. He couldn't remember ever feeling so vulnerable and out of control, so exposed while fully clothed, or so incredibly aroused.

It was more than being caught off guard and tied up. More than the props Jill had used in her little ''product demonstration,'' more even than the admitted excitement of knowing that at any moment, they might be discovered.

No, something about Jill herself made his temperature rise and his mind lose track of where he was and what he was supposed to be doing. Something in the contrast between her innocent looks and her seductive words fired every synapse and sent common sense running for cover. The way she made him feel was based on instinct, not reason. The thought that anyone could reduce him to that sent a new tremor through him.

''Damn it, this is crazy!'' He hit the steering wheel hard with the heel of his hand. He wasn't some pimply teenager ruled by hormones. He was a businessman—and he had no business getting involved with a woman he scarcely knew. A woman who had the power to distract him so much.

Thwarted desire replaced by a more garden-variety frustration filled him as he started the car and pulled out into traffic. He'd intended to head over to Qdoba for lunch, but he found himself driving up University Hill, toward the only apartment building he still owned, where his sister, Meg, lived with another premed student.

Meg answered the door dressed in scrubs, holding a can of soup in one hand. "Hey, Mitch!" She stood on tiptoe to hug him, then stepped back and held up the can. "You're just in time for lunch."

"How about I take you out instead?"

She tossed the can over her shoulder. It landed on the sofa and bounced twice before coming to rest against a pillow. "Let me put my shoes on and you've got a date."

Fifteen minutes later, they sipped iced tea on the patio at Qdoba. "So what's up?" Meg asked, reaching for a tortilla chip.

"Nothing's up." He rearranged the salt and pepper shakers. "I remembered you don't have classes Tuesday and Thursday mornings and I thought I'd stop by and see how you're doing."

She shook her head. "Since when do you leave work in the middle of the day to socialize? Especially with your sister?"

He pushed the salt and pepper aside and contemplated his hands, palms down in front of him on the table. They were plain, unremarkable hands, no rings, nails clean and neatly filed. No scars or calluses. Hands with no character at all.

"Earth to Mitch." Meg snapped her fingers under his nose. "C'mon, what's up? You look like you lost your best friend."

He sighed and looked up at her. Strands of her dark curly hair fluttered in the breeze from the ceiling fan overhead. She wasn't wearing any makeup and she looked about sixteen. He couldn't imagine her ever delivering a baby or performing surgery on anyone.

She looked like their mother—a small, helpless woman. Except Meg wasn't helpless. She pointed a tortilla chip at him. "You might as well tell me, 'cause you know I'm going to worm it out of you, or else I'll nose around behind your back until I find out everything. You can't keep secrets from me, big brother."

"Did you know Uncle Grif funded a foundation to educate the public about mental illness? And he named it after Mother."

"I think I remember hearing something like that. Why?"

He sat back, shoulders slumped. "I just found out. I never knew that about him. Why would he do something like that?"

"I think he had a soft spot for Mama. And I know she was fond of him. She always looked forward to his visits when she was in the hospital."

"I always thought he was just a loudmouthed playboy who spent all his money on gin, girls and golf."

She tilted her head to one side, her expression sympathetic. "And now you're beating yourself up because you were wrong." She reached out and touched his arm. "Hey it's okay. Even *you* are allowed to screw up sometimes. It proves you're human, like the rest of us."

"Great bedside manner, Doc. I feel all better now."

"You'll get over it. Grif must not have held it against you, since he left you his business."

A business Mitch hadn't even known existed until the will had been read. Maybe this was Grif's way of having the last word.

Their lunch arrived and conversation stalled as they focused on their burritos. Mitch had found that even big

problems looked smaller when considered in the aftermath of any meal that included plenty of hot sauce and
melted cheese.

"So how did you find out about the mental health
foundation?" Meg asked just as he'd taken a bite of
burrito.

He swallowed and reached for his tea. "I was going
through his files at...at the business he left me."

"Oh, yes. The mysterious business." She speared a
forkful of beans. "Just what *is* this business, anyway?"

"Nothing important." He ignored the scowl she sent
his way and poured hot sauce onto his plate. "I'm going
to close it and open a restaurant on the site."

Meg shrugged. "Sounds like a lot of work to me, but
you're the big businessman."

He looked away, pretending great interest in his meal.
He hoped he wasn't making a mistake with this restaurant. He'd had the idea for over a year now, ever since
he first met Chef Ping. When he found out Uncle Grif
had left him a prime piece of downtown real estate, it
had seemed like a sign he should go ahead with the
project. Now he wondered...

"How's Lana?"

"Lana?" He looked up, startled. "Uh...she's okay.
Why do you ask?"

"No reason. I just haven't heard you say much about
her lately. I wondered if you were still seeing each
other."

"We're still seeing each other." More or less.

"I've heard more enthusiasm for the daily special at
the student union. Has some of the bloom worn off the
romance?"

"Why would you say that?" He stabbed at a piece of
tortilla. "Just because I'm not raving about her every

minute doesn't mean I don't want to continue dating her. A relationship doesn't have to have fireworks all the time." He scowled at her. "There's more to life than sex, you know."

"Whoa, whoa, slow down there." She put up her hands. "Who said anything about sex?"

He opened his mouth to protest, but she shook her head. "No, if you and Lana are having problems in the bedroom, I don't want to know." She dunked a chip in hot sauce. "But you might want to think about seeing other people for a while. I mean, I'll admit I'm prejudiced, but I think you've got a lot to offer a woman, and I'm not sure Lana really appreciates you."

He was trying to come up with a suitable retort when his phone rang. Still frowning at his sister, he jerked the phone from his pocket and flipped it open. "Hello?"

"Hi, uh, Mitch? This is Sid." The manager's voice sounded strained. "Uh, sorry to bother you, but you need to get back to the store, right away."

"What is it? Is something wrong?" Mitch's stomach clenched. Had they been robbed? Was some fundamentalist group staging a protest?

"I'm not sure. Uh...there's this woman here. And uh...she keeps asking for you." He lowered his voice. "She's kind of upset."

"Oh, hell."

"What is it?" Meg leaned toward him, her eyes questioning. "Is everything all right?"

He covered the phone with his hand. "It's the manager at Uncle Grif's store. There's a woman there demanding to see me." He put the phone to his ear again. "What does she want?"

"I don't know. Uh...she says her name is Lana. Lana Montgomery."

MEG HAD HEARD OF PEOPLE turning green, but she'd never actually seen it before—until now. Actually, Mitch's face went through an alarming array of colors, from ashy-white to fiery-red, before settling on this green-tinted phase. He snapped the phone shut and shoved up from the table so hard his chair almost fell over behind him. He grabbed the chair, saving it from crashing to the floor and signaled the waiter for their check. "I have to go," he croaked.

Meg tossed aside her napkin and stood also. "I'll go with you."

He shook his head. "No. You stay here and finish eating." He tossed a twenty on the table and headed toward the door.

She followed. He stopped at the exit and glared at her. "Meg, you can't come with me."

She ignored him and headed for his car. He hurried after her. "What do you think you're doing?"

The minute he unlocked the car, she opened the door and slid into the passenger seat. "Something's going on and I intend to find out what it is," she said.

He fit the key into the ignition and scowled at her. "Get out of this car."

She fastened her seat belt and returned the scowl. "Make me."

He growled and started the car. "All right. But you're staying in the car."

She turned to look out of the window so he wouldn't see her smile. Men were so predictable. Even her brother.

Mitch negotiated Boulder traffic with reckless speed, and screeched to a halt in a No Parking zone in front of a pink brick building. Meg looked up at the marquee over the building's door. Just 4 Play. Her smile broadened. She'd heard of this place. In fact, one of her girl-friends had recommended it. When Mitch jumped out of the car and went inside, she laughed out loud. So this was his secret inheritance. Oh, that was rich. Her straight-arrow brother had been saddled with a sex shop. This she had to see.

When she walked through the door, Mitch was leaning over the counter, deep in conversation with a petite blonde. The blonde pointed toward the back and he took off.

Meg walked over to the counter and picked up a pe-nis-shaped key chain. Now there was a conversation starter. "May I help you?" the blonde asked.

She laid aside the key chain. "I'm Meg Landry. Mitch's sister. We were having lunch when you called."

"Oh, I didn't call. The manager, Sid, did." She held out her hand. "I'm Jill Sheldon."

They shook hands. Meg looked around, at the candy-colored condoms, the blowup dolls, massage oils, how-to books and what looked like a belly dancer costume. Her grin widened. *Oh brother, what are you into now?* She turned to Jill. "So what's going on? Why did Mitch rush over here in the middle of lunch?"

Jill made a face. "A woman came in here this after-noon, took one look around and started hollering for Mitch."

"A woman? Who?"

"One of those society types. You know, fancy suit, fancy hair, fancy attitude." Jill's expression said Miss Fancy had left her singularly unimpressed. "She said her name was Lana Montgomery."

Meg shaped her mouth into a perfect O. "I take it Mitch hadn't gotten around to telling her about this place."

Jill leaned across the counter, ready to dish dirt. "Who is she?"

"Mitch's girlfriend. Or maybe ex-girlfriend now." She picked up a jar of body paint and studied the list of suggested uses. "Something tells me Lana's not the type to approve of a place like this."

Jill straightened. "I suppose she thinks there's something wrong with healthy sexuality. With helping people to improve their relationships and learn about their bodies—"

"Hey, I didn't say I didn't approve." Meg set aside the body paint. "To tell the truth, Lana's always struck me as somebody laced up a little too tight."

Jill glanced toward the closed office door. "Like Mitch."

"Well, yeah, big brother can be a little...intense. But he's really a great guy."

Jill raised one eyebrow. "You wouldn't be a little biased, would you?"

She grinned. "Not at all." She nodded toward the office. "So what happened before I got here?"

"Sid took this Lana chick back to the office. I think he was going to fix her some tea. If we're lucky, he slipped a tranquilizer into it."

"That would probably help." She walked over to a vibrator display and picked up a bright green model. No sense letting this shopping opportunity go to waste. "I've been thinking about getting one of these. What would you recommend?"

"We have some really nice models." Jill emerged from behind the counter and joined her at the display. "We have every color, size and shape you can think of." She began opening drawers and taking out boxes. "Somewhere in here is your perfect BOB."

Meg picked up a bright purple model. "Bob?"

"Your battery operated boyfriend." She glanced toward the office door. "Let me tell you, sometimes they're a lot less trouble than the real thing."

MITCH DIDN'T HAVE TIME to worry about Meg right now. He had to deal with Lana. What the hell was she doing here? How had she found out about the place? And what was he supposed to do with her now?

He paused outside the office door and forced himself to take deep, calming breaths. She was probably upset; fine, he had seen her upset before and he could deal with that. The main thing was to remain calm. After all, he'd done nothing to be ashamed of.

He grasped the doorknob firmly and shoved open the door, a placating speech already forming in his mind. But the scene before him froze him in his tracks.

Lana and Sid sat side by side in front of the desk. Sid's head was leaned toward Lana, an earnest expression on his face as he listened to her pour out some tale of woe, his pink Mohawk almost touching her perfectly coifed hair. The teacup looked like something from a child's toy tea set in his large hand.

"Thank you for being so understanding, Sid," Lana was saying.

Mitch made a strangled noise in his throat and they both looked up. Lana tensed and her expression grew stormy. "Mitch, how could you!"

He walked into the room and leaned against the desk, his pose deliberately casual. "How could I what?"

Two lines made a deep V between her brows and her mouth puckered in an expression of distaste. "How could you run a...a...smut shop?"

"We prefer to think of ourselves as purveyors of ac-

cessories to enhance people's pleasure and well-being.''
Sid's tongue-stud clacked against his teeth, giving him
a slight lisp.

Lana stared at him, her mouth going slack. A rosy
flush crept up her neck. ''Um, yes.''

She turned back to Mitch. ''Why didn't you tell me?''

''Because I knew you'd react like this. Besides, I intend to close the place down and open a restaurant.''

Sid looked pained. ''I told her.'' He rescued her teacup from her hand. ''Let me get you some more tea.''

''I don't want more tea.'' She clenched her fists in
her lap. ''I want an explanation.''

Why hadn't he noticed before how shrewish she could
be? He frowned. ''I don't see that it's any of your business, Lana.''

''How can you say that? Don't you realize I have a
reputation in town? What will people think when they
find out the man I'm dating owns a place like this?''

The man I'm dating. Was that all he was to her?
Someone to escort her to dinner or to the theater, nothing
more? ''Maybe they'd think you were lucky,'' he said,
only half-joking.

Sid brought more tea. ''Lots of respectable people
shop here,'' he said. His expression was grave as he bent
over Lana. ''The mayor's wife has even been here before.''

Lana's eyes widened as she accepted the teacup. A
trembling attempt at a smile even rose to her lips.
''You've been so kind,'' she said, her voice breathy.

Sid ducked his head, looking humble—or as humble
as a six-foot-plus tattooed and pierced man in leather
can look. ''My pleasure, ma'am.''

Lana turned back to Mitch, her smile vanished. ''This

is why you've been talking about…about sex and experimenting and being bored.''

He shoved his hands into his pants pockets. It was either that or give in to the temptation to shake some sense into her. ''I was only suggesting we had gotten into a rut.''

''Well…fine. If that's what you want then…fine.'' She set down her cup so hard tea sloshed onto the desk. ''You can find someone else to play your…your sex games.'' She grabbed up her purse and stormed out.

''Lana, wait…''

''I'll just make sure she's okay.'' Sid took off after her.

Mitch crossed his arms and stared at the vacant doorway. He should have been the one to go after Lana, but he couldn't bring himself to move a muscle. Whatever they'd had between them was over now. The only emotion he could muster was relief.

He sighed and straightened. That took care of Lana—now what to do about Meg? He had little hope she'd actually stayed in the car. Even as a toddler, she'd never minded very well.

He spotted her with Jill on the other side of the store and made his way over to them. ''What are you doing in here?'' he asked.

She held up a large purple vibrator. ''I had some shopping to do.'' She pressed a button and the purple plastic penis waggled like a hula dancer. ''Isn't it cute?''

6

ALL THE BLOOD RUSHED to Mitch's face. He grabbed the absurd toy and switched it off. "I told you to stay in the car."

She raised one eyebrow. "Since when have I ever done what you tell me?" She grinned. "Nice place you have here, bro."

His face felt hot. He was embarrassed—and embarrassed that he was embarrassed. Yes, Meg was a grown woman, but he couldn't stop thinking of her as his little sister.

She picked up a pink vibrator. "I think I like this one."

"The koi," Jill said. "A good choice. The fish's little fins provide excellent clitoral stimulation."

He wanted to put his hands over his ears. He didn't want to hear this. He turned away. He didn't want to see it, either. Behind him, Meg and Jill laughed, apparently in on some hilarious joke.

The bells on the front door jangled and Sid came back in. "I managed to get her calmed down a little, I think. At least enough to drive home without having an accident."

"What was her problem?" Jill asked.

"She doesn't approve." Mitch walked over to the counter and pretended an interest in a magazine lying there. *Piercing Times.* Who knew there were so many different places one could puncture the body?

"In my experience, when someone has such a negative reaction to something, it's because they're really more attracted to it than they think they should be." Jill laid the pink vibrator on the counter and leaned toward him. The scent of jasmine teased him and a sudden memory of her, whip in hand, flashed across his mind.

He shifted his stance, turning slightly away from her. "I don't think that's Lana's problem."

"Don't be too sure." Meg joined them at the counter. "Maybe there's really a wild woman inside that repressed, proper shell."

He shook his head. "No." If anyone was in a position to know that, he was. Lana didn't even like to make any noise when she climaxed.

"What are you going to do now?" Meg asked.

He shoved aside the magazine. "Nothing."

"Nothing?" Jill tilted her head to one side and studied him.

"If she's that upset about me owning this place, then it's probably best we don't see each other anymore."

"So you're going to let her go, just like that?" Jill shook her head. "One little disagreement and you're through?"

Why was she taking Lana's side? "You don't know anything about it," he snapped. "And it's none of your business anyway."

"I think it's more than 'one little disagreement.'" Meg joined them at the front counter. "I think things haven't been right between them for a while now—if they ever were."

He glared at her. "Stay out of this."

She shrugged. "I'm just saying you're better off without her. I never thought she was your type."

"Oh?" Jill turned to Meg. "What sort of woman do you think *is* Mitch's type?"

"Well now, let's see." She furrowed her brow. "Someone a little more laid-back. Someone who can help him loosen up. Take his mind off business." She grinned at him. "Someone who can help him have a little fun."

There was that word again—as if life was always one laugh after another. "Stop talking about me as if I'm not even here," he demanded.

Jill gave him a long look, her gaze starting somewhere around his knees and traveling upward, as if she was measuring him for an outfit—or picturing him without one. He felt warm and resisted the urge to fidget. Instead he looked straight into her eyes, intending to stare her down.

Her lips curved in a slow smile. "Yes, I'd say someone needs to help Mitch loosen up a little." She leaned closer, until her breath tickled his ear. "Wouldn't you know it? That happens to be my specialty," she whispered.

MITCH APPARENTLY HAD MASTERED the art of looking cool and collected on the outside, but Jill knew she was getting to him. His eyes darkened, his breathing came faster and a pulse throbbed at his temple, inches from her lips. He might pretend to be unmoved, but Mitch Landry kept a lot of passion reigned in beneath his businesslike facade. Meg was right. Miss Fancy-Pants Lana Montgomery was too much of a cold fish for him. A man like Mitch needed a woman who wasn't afraid to get a fire going.

She breathed in deeply, and felt her own pulse quicken as the scent of Aramis swept over her. Oh, yes. Now that Mitch was certifiably free from entanglements with any other woman, she was going to have a wickedly wonderful time showing him the delights of a walk on the wilder side of life.

"Don't you have work to do?" His eyes narrowed.

She stepped back, but slowly, reluctantly, telling him with her body and her eyes that things would be so much better if only he'd allow her to move closer. "Why yes." She turned and picked up the koi vibrator. "I need to ring this up. Let's see now, what is our family discount?"

He glared at his sister. "You're not really going to buy that."

She grinned. "Why not?"

"Because." His face burned. "Don't you have to be twenty-one to buy something like this?"

"Eighteen." Sid, who had been standing by the front window, looking out, spoke up. "Twenty-one is for alcohol." He turned to face them.

"Besides, I *am* twenty-one." Meg laid a credit card on the counter. "I know it's hard for you, bro, but I'm all grown up now."

His shoulders slumped and he smiled weakly. "When did that happen?"

Meg laughed. "Not only that, I'm a medical student." She picked up the vibrator and pointed it at him. "What I don't already know about anatomy and sexuality, I fully intend to learn."

Mitch wrapped his arm around her shoulder and pulled her close. "Be careful where you point that thing, it might be loaded."

Jill laughed. Just when she'd begun to think she had

Mitch all figured out, he surprised her with a remark like that. She always did like a man who could surprise her.

Sid joined them at the counter. "Maybe somebody should call Lana later. Make sure she got home all right."

"That's thoughtful of you, Sid, but I can promise you Lana isn't home weeping into her pillow." Mitch shook his head.

"Then where is she?" Jill asked.

"My guess is she's over at Guarantee National Bank, complaining to Daddy about what a creep I am."

"You don't think he'll withdraw your building loan, do you?" Meg asked.

"That would be one way of keeping this place open," Jill said to Sid.

Mitch frowned, letting her know he'd heard this remark. "He couldn't stop the loan even if he wanted to. The board's already approved it. But I think Mort Montgomery is a better businessman than that. He won't let Lana tell him what to do."

"So you're still planning on turning this into a restaurant?" Jill sagged onto the stool behind the counter.

"What made you think I'd changed my mind?"

"I was hoping since you didn't have Miss High Society to impress anymore, you'd ditch the crazy scheme to turn this into the Kung Pao Palace or whatever."

"Then I guess that shows you don't know me very well." He leaned on the counter, his face very close to hers. "I don't let a woman tell me what to do, either."

"Not ever?" She laid her hand over his. "Sometimes it can be a lot of fun."

He pulled away and straightened. "I'm not here to have fun. I'm here to run a business."

She shook her head. "The two don't have to be mutually exclusive, you know."

"Contrary to what you believe and what my sister says, I do know how to have fun. But I think there's a time and a place for everything."

"All right, then tell me—what do you like to do for fun?"

He blinked. "Why should I tell you?"

"Why not tell her?" Meg challenged. "Or can't you think of anything?"

"I do plenty of things for fun. I go to the gym. I go out to dinner…"

"Working out at the gym is just another kind of work," Jill said. "And everybody has to eat. Just because you do it in a restaurant doesn't make it fun."

"I can't help it if your idea of fun and mine aren't the same."

"Face it, Mitch, you've forgotten how to have fun." Meg turned to Jill. "He's been so busy looking after me and working to support us, he hasn't developed any hobbies. He doesn't play sports. I can't even remember the last time he took a vacation."

"Everybody works hard when they're starting out. I'll have plenty of time for fun later."

"How many headstones do you think that's carved on?" Jill asked. *"He said he'd have time for fun later?"*

"All right then, if you're such an expert, what do *you* like to do for fun?"

"The better question is—what don't I like to do? I like to hike or ride my bike. In the winter I ski or ice-skate. I like going to the movies or just going over to Pearl Street Mall and watching the tourists." She ticked off these activities on her fingers. "I like kayaking and swimming and dancing—I love to dance. And then of course, there's my all-time favorite fun-time activity.''

''What's that?''

She grinned. ''Sex!''

''You would name that one.''

''Oh, don't be such a prude. Or don't you think sex is fun?''

He reddened slightly beneath his tan. ''Sex can be fun.'' His eyes met hers, their intensity making her heart race. ''It can also be very serious. When two people love each other, it can be serious as hell.''

She slid off the bench and backed away, wanting to look away from him, but unable to. ''Who said anything about love?''

''Don't you believe in love?'' His voice held the same mocking tone she'd used with him.

She glanced at Meg, who was examining a packet of condoms on a display against the far wall as if she'd never seen anything like them before. Sid was standing by the front window, staring out at the street.

Mitch moved closer, trapping her between him and the counter. ''It's not a difficult question, Jill.'' His voice was low, vibrating through her, raising prickles of awareness on her skin. ''Do you believe in love...or don't you?''

''I...I believe in love.'' She dug her nails into the edge of the counter and willed her voice not to shake. ''But I don't believe it's as common as people want to believe. You can have great sex with someone and not necessarily be in love.''

He smiled, a slow, seductive salute that sent heat washing over her. ''Good sex maybe. But great sex...for that I think you really do need love.''

Who said women were the sentimental romantics of

the world? Between Mitch and Sid, she was surrounded by men who didn't have a clue. Love was fine for songs and romance novels, but the real thing came along less than once in a lifetime. Some people never experienced it. And that was okay. You could have a lot of fun and good times without complicating things with talk of love. "You talk like an expert on the subject," she said. "And yet you let Lana walk out the door with hardly a protest."

He glanced toward the door, then his gaze fixed on her once more. "Meg's right—Lana and I weren't in love. I knew it, but sometimes it's easier to stay in a familiar situation than to try and get out there and find a new one."

Jill shook her head. "You don't need love, mister. You need someone to shake loose the cobwebs. Someone to inject a big dose of Vitamin F into your life."

"And you're that someone?"

"I'm exactly the person for the job." She leaned closer, until they were almost touching. "In fact, I have a proposition for you."

He raised one eyebrow. "What kind of proposition?"

"You've got what, about four weeks until work is supposed to start on the restaurant?"

"That's right."

She wet her lips. "Then give me that time to prove to you that this store provides an important service for people."

"And how would you do that?" His voice was low, husky.

"By teaching you more about the merchandise here. Providing a few hands-on demonstrations, shall we say." She smiled. "By teaching you how to have fun with sex."

Then she did something she'd been wanting to do ever since he'd first walked in that front door. She pulled him to her and kissed him the way a man ought to be kissed—by a woman who knew what she was doing.

7

AHA. THIS WAS DEFINITELY the way to shut Mitch up. He thought he knew so much, with all his talk of love and being serious. She'd show him how to live in the moment, to let go of reason and surrender to the physical side of things.

At first he stiffened up on her, so that it felt like kissing a mannequin. But as she molded her body to his and traced the tip of her tongue along the contours of his lips, he began to loosen up. Like a plastic store dummy coming to life, he warmed to her touch. His arms encircled her and pulled her more tightly against him. His mouth opened to accept her exploring tongue.

And then his own tongue invaded her mouth, thrusting and withdrawing slowly, teasing along the edge of her lips before advancing once more. He tasted sweet and salty, better than a top-shelf margarita, and packing more of a punch. Any hesitancy had left him. He kissed her now with a forcefulness that made her light-headed and breathless.

All right, so she'd made her point. She'd shown him he was attracted to her physically, whether he wanted to admit it or not. That was enough lessons for one day. She tried to pull away, but he crushed her to him, sliding his hand down to cup her bottom while he suckled at the corner of her mouth. She felt his erection against her stomach, hot and heavy.

She choked back a moan and clung to him to keep from sliding to the floor. The rest of the world was out there somewhere far away, but all her senses focused on this moment with this man. She felt the scrape of his beard against her cheek as he turned his head to fully capture her mouth once more, heard the pounding of her pulse in her ears and the rush of breath in her lungs as she panted. Every breath filled her head with the intoxicating scent of his cologne, and the more subtle musk of sex and desire. She felt as if she were melting from the inside out, common sense and control burned away by the heat of passion. Another moan escaped her and the last vestige of sensibility surfaced to mock her. What was she doing swooning over this guy like some starstruck sorority sister? She was supposed to be the one in charge here, remember?

She tried once more to pull away, but his arms tightened until she could scarcely breathe. "Oh, no, you started this," he murmured, his breath tickling her ear.

The jangling of the string of bells on the door saved her from having to come up with a coherent reply. Arms that had held her fast now pushed her away. She staggered back and grabbed on to the edge of the counter for support.

The world came back into focus. Meg watched her from the other side of the counter, deep dimples on either side of her mouth as her eyes danced with laughter. Sid was near the door, talking to the customer, a biker in leather and chains. Or maybe he was a stockbroker? You never knew these days.

Mitch was standing not two feet away, studying her, eyes narrowed, arms crossed, a chill fast descending between them.

She looked away and brushed imaginary dust from the countertop. "It's time for my lunch break," she said.

"And I have a shift at the hospital this afternoon." Meg stepped forward and held out her hand. "It was nice meeting you, Jill."

They shook hands. "Same here," Jill said. "Maybe I'll see you again some time."

Meg smiled at Mitch. "Oh, I think I'll be seeing you again very soon."

When Mitch and his sister were gone, Jill gave up on her jelly legs and sank down onto the stool behind the counter. So what had just happened here? Besides a mind-blowing kissing session. Whatever else she had against him, she had to admit that Mitch Landry was one hell of a kisser. Which begged the question—if he was that good at the preliminary moves, what was he like in the bedroom itself?

The thought sent a new wave of dizziness over her and a bolt of heat straight to her groin. She shifted on the hard stool and took a shaky breath. So they'd set off some physical sparks. This was a good thing. She could use that attraction to make him see how wrong he was to close Just 4 Play. It was nothing she hadn't antici-pated.

Liar! her conscience shouted.

Okay, maybe she had felt a bit overwhelmed there for a minute. She was a little out of practice. And Mitch had surprised her. Who would have thought Mr. Serious Business had the makings of a sex god?

Never mind. He only *thought* he was in charge. In no time at all, she'd make him see how wrong he was.

SOMEHOW MITCH SUMMONED the strength to stroll out of Just 4 Play as if he didn't have a care in the world, while every cell in his body was screaming at him to get back in there and finish what he'd started with Jill.

And what exactly had he started? He'd recognized her kiss as the power play she'd intended, and the knowledge had annoyed him at first. Then he felt her soft curves pressed against him and reasoned there was nothing wrong with trying to beat her at her own game.

But somewhere between trying to show her who was boss and proving he was man enough to take what she had to dish out, he forgot his objective and starting enjoying the game a little too much. She moaned and he grew hard. He pulled her closer, craving the softness of her breasts against him, the firmness of her ass beneath his hand. He wanted to bury himself in her, to hear her cry out in passion.

He wanted her to want him, not because he was someone she could conquer or control, but because she needed him with a fierceness that went beyond simple lust or physical desire.

"I thought Jill was very nice."

Meg's words pulled him back from such dangerous daydreams. He glanced at his sister, who was looking at him with that irritatingly superior expression of a woman who thinks she knows what a man is feeling. He focused his gaze on the road in front of him, though he was scarcely aware of the traffic. "There's nothing nice about her," he snapped. "She's like a piranha. Or one of those black widow spiders. The kind of woman who uses men for what she wants."

"You talk like that's a bad thing." Meg laughed. "Honestly, bro, if you could see yourself right now. You look like a general getting ready for battle."

He tightened his grip on the steering wheel. "Maybe because I feel that way."

She leaned across the seat and lightly touched his arm. "Hey, lighten up. It looked to me like you enjoyed that kiss."

Enjoy didn't do justice to how he felt about that kiss. Excited maybe. Aroused. Turned on to the power of ten. And underneath it all, like the extra bite of hot peppers on an entree, he felt the sting of fear. Jill wasn't like any other woman he'd met. She made him think things…feel things. She had the power to make him lose control. That alone was enough to send him running for cover.

"I meant what I said back there." Meg pulled him out of the fog once more.

"About what?"

"About you. You *don't* have enough fun. Even a lowly premed student knows that's a ticket to an early grave." Her voice softened. "I worry about you, Mitch."

"I'm fine." He forced himself to relax his shoulders and gave her what he hoped was a reassuring look.

"You're really okay with Lana leaving?"

He almost laughed. What did it say about him that he'd already forgotten about his girlfriend of the past year? "I guess I've seen it coming," he said. "It's kind of a relief, though I suppose admitting that makes me a jerk."

"An honest jerk, though." She laughed again. Meg was like that, seeing the humor in any situation. He smiled. He was lucky to have her around to keep him from taking life too seriously. "I was just teasing," she said. "You could never be a real jerk."

"Maybe you're prejudiced," he said. "Maybe I have hidden depths of jerkiness you'll never know."

He pulled into the lot of her apartment. As she climbed out of the car, she stopped and looked back at him. "I like Jill," she said. "I really do think she's a nice person."

He frowned. "I don't know about that."

"I think you know more than you're letting on." She gave a little wave. "Take it easy, bro." She slammed the door shut, then blew him a kiss, her lips forming the words "I love you."

"I love you, too, sis," he whispered.

He turned the car around and headed back toward the store, thinking about love, and how little he really knew about the subject. He'd loved his father, but it wasn't something they'd ever talked about. And then his father was gone.

He had probably loved his mother once, when he was younger. Before she got sick and became a stranger to him. Then he'd settled for loving a memory of her. The emotion he felt for the real woman he was responsible for was closer to pity, mingled with resentment.

Meg was the only person he could say he truly loved now, with the no-strings-attached, no-holds-barred emotion he sensed love ought to be.

As for romantic love, he could only think of it in the abstract. He had meant what he said to Jill, about needing love for sex to be really powerful. Not that he had firsthand experience, but he believed it. Good sex involved the body, but to his way of thinking, great sex needed an emotional component. Something that had been missing from his life so far. Jill could talk about fun and good times, but he was ready for something more. Something she obviously couldn't give him.

So where did that leave him—besides frustrated and still wanting her? Should he take her advice and concentrate on having fun, damn the consequences? Maybe so. If he and Jill couldn't be lovers in every sense of the word, there was no doubting they could set off fireworks in the bedroom. One kiss had left him hornier than any seventeen-year-old.

Why not take her up on her offer to "demonstrate" the merchandise in Just 4 Play? He had no intention of changing his mind about closing the store, but that didn't mean he couldn't enjoy himself for the next few weeks. And he had no doubt he *would* enjoy himself with Jill.

Maybe she had the right approach after all—go for physical pleasure, no strings attached. Consider it an experiment. One he'd be a fool not to make.

THE NEXT MORNING, Jill smoothed the leather miniskirt over her hips and smiled at her reflection in the mirror. Decked out in dog collar, metal-studded black bustier, miniskirt, black silk stockings and stiletto ankle boots, she was every man's fantasy. She picked up the cat-o'-nine-tails and flicked it at the mirror. Or every man's nightmare, depending on his point of view.

She turned away from the mirror and added a studded bracelet to each wrist. This dominatrix getup was one of their hottest sellers and she could see why. There was nothing sexier than a heady dose of power. All the leather and chains didn't hurt either.

She peered out the door of the ladies' dressing room. Good. Mitch was at the front counter with Sid, looking over an inventory list or something. She opened the door a little wider and sauntered toward the two men, hips thrust forward, swaying provocatively.

She pretended to ignore them as she strolled past, though she had to bite the inside of her cheek to keep from smiling when all conversation stopped. She walked over to the paper goods department and began straightening the greeting cards, humming to herself as she worked.

She hummed louder as she heard Mitch approach. He stopped three feet away, as if not wanting to get too close. Even so, her nipples rose to attention at the first whiff of Aramis.

"No time to go home and change after last night's costume party?"

She slowly turned to face him, eyes wide and innocent. "I'm sorry, Mitch, I was thinking of something else. Did you say something?"

He assumed his typical frown, but not before his gaze darted to her not insignificant cleavage framed by the leather bustier. "What are you supposed to be, a biker chick?"

She unclipped the cat-o'-nine-tails from her belt and struck a pose, hip cocked. "The Deluxe Dominatrix is one of our bestselling fantasy costumes."

"I hardly think it's appropriate for a place of business."

She laughed. Mitch was always at his stuffiest when he was nervous. "I'd say it's very appropriate for this particular place of business." She opened her arms wide and slowly turned in a circle, making sure he got an eyeful. "Apparently many men find a powerful woman to be a big turn-on." She flicked her whip at him. "Do you feel that way, Mitch?"

"I think you ought to be selling the merchandise, not wearing it."

She wagged the whip at him. "Customers can't appreciate the full effect of a costume unless they see it on," she said. "So you see, I'm doing my part to unload all our inventory before the chopstick dealers and soy sauce sellers move in." She leaned closer. "Besides, I wanted to get you in the mood for your first lesson tonight."

He took a step back. "What are you talking about?"

"I'm going to teach you how to have fun with sex, remember?"

"I don't recall agreeing to your proposition."

She trailed the whip down his arm. "Not with words, maybe, but your kiss told me you were definitely interested."

His eyes darkened, and a faint flush rose up his neck. "Let me make sure I understand this. You're promising four weeks of wild sex, with no strings attached?"

"Just give me a chance to show you how good a walk on the wild side can be."

He took another step back, out of reach of the whip. "Feel free to do your damnedest then. But for now, I suggest you put that costume on a mannequin."

She pretended to consider this "suggestion." "Well, I suppose I could do that." She grinned. "But then I'd have to walk around naked, since all my clothes are at home."

Jaw clenched, a pulse throbbed at his temple. Without another word, he turned and stalked to the front door.

"Where are you going?" she asked.

"To my other office. My *real* office. To get some work done." He left, the door bells jangling wildly behind him.

Jill looked at Sid and shrugged. "What's his problem?"

Sid shook his head. "Not a good day to mess with him, Jilly. I asked him if we could reorder some of our bestsellers, things the customers have been asking for, and he almost bit my head off."

"He *has* been a grouch this morning." A romp under the covers was obviously just what he needed.

"Maybe he's upset about Lana," Sid said. "From what she told me, they'd been dating quite a while before she came in here that day. He could be having second thoughts."

"Oh, I'm sure that's not it. He made it pretty clear things were over between them." Her stomach tightened. But were they, really? Did Mitch still have feelings for Lana? Was he in love with her? She flicked the whip at the condom display. "If he misses Lana, then he ought to go after her and tell her, instead of moping around here and making us miserable, too."

Sid sighed. "I guess love is one of the most complicated things there is."

"So are calculus and foreign politics, which is why I don't get involved in any of them."

Sid straightened and closed the ledger. "You don't fool me, Jilly. I know you're a romantic at heart. One day you'll meet a man who'll prove it to you."

"I don't need a man to prove anything to me." She trailed the fringes of the whip along the edge of a display case. "Except that he knows when not to take things too seriously." Anyone could see Mr. Serious Businessman Mitch wasn't the man for her. Not on any long-term basis. As long as she kept that in mind, everything would be fine. Wouldn't it?

8

MITCH SPENT AN UNPRODUCTIVE afternoon at his downtown office, trying to focus on quarterly reports and rental agreements, the words a black-and-white blur on the page before him. The image of Jill in the dangerously distracting leather outfit was imprinted on his retina, the feel of her body against his tattooed on his skin.

When the point on his mechanical pencil broke for the third time in an hour, he shoved his paperwork aside and leaned back in his chair. So he'd let a sexy woman get under his skin. So what? He'd play her little games, have a little fun, and get her out of his system. Then he could get back to focusing on what was really important right now: securing his future. A future that did not include being the owner of a sex toy store.

In the meantime, he and Jill had a date, didn't they? He checked his watch. He had time to grab a bite to eat, shower and change before Jill got off work. Maybe put clean sheets on the bed. The thought made him harder than he already was. Yeah, definitely clean sheets. He didn't want Jill to think he was a slob.

When he walked in the door of Just 4 Play a few hours later, a young woman with vibrant red hair was behind the counter, adding up a stack of checks. "Who are you?" Mitch asked.

She grinned, revealing the silver tracks of braces.

"I'm Tami. You must be Mitch. Sid told me you might drop by."

He nodded. He vaguely remembered the name from the payroll reports Sid had given him. "Good to meet you, Tami." Great, one more person he was putting out of work.

"I'm just closing up," she said. "You want to take the deposit?"

"No. That's all right. Just do…whatever you normally do." And what was that? He'd have to find out. Except, why bother if the business wasn't going to be open much longer? He walked past her, into his office.

He smelled Jill before he saw her, the exotic aroma of her perfume sending a rush of heat through him. He switched on the light and she was there, perched on the edge of his desk, her long legs encased in black stockings, the tabs of a garter belt peeking beneath the hem of the short leather skirt. She twirled a pair of handcuffs from one finger. Not the fur-lined kind the store sold, but a real pair. "It's about time you got here. I was ready to call your cell phone."

"You didn't think I'd forgotten, did you?" He moved past her to collect the stack of mail from the desktop, studiously avoiding looking at her silk-encased thighs.

"No, you wouldn't forget. But I wouldn't put it past you to chicken out."

His laugh was a harsh explosion of breath. "Do you think I'm afraid of you?"

She put her hand flat against his chest and slid her palm up to cradle his neck. "No. But you might be afraid of yourself. People who keep such tight control of their emotions often are." Her voice was low, her breath warm against his cheek.

He concentrated on keeping his voice even, his tone

light. "Let me guess—you majored in psychology in college."

"Let's just say I know a lot about men." She grasped the knot of his tie and tugged to loosen it. "Are you ready for your first lesson?"

He was ready all right. He'd been ready since yesterday, when she'd made her ridiculous proposition and given him that mind-erasing kiss. He'd been on fire for her ever since, but was determined not to show it. He put his hand over hers. "Let's go back to my place."

"Oh, no. If I'm going to teach you about the shop, we should stay here." She tugged at his tie once more.

"All right." He reached around and took the handcuffs from her. "But we won't use these."

She lowered her lashes, studying him through their lacy length. A half smile formed at her lips. "You're right. Handcuffs are a little too advanced for now. We'll start with something simple."

She slid off the desk and took his hand. "First, let's take a little tour." She led him back out into the store, which was deserted now, the doors locked and lights dimmed.

Old-fashioned Tiffany-style lamps made pools of light on the antique wardrobes and bookcases that housed store displays. The genteel furnishings made the racks of bondage straps and battery-operated vibrators that much more sensual, like Victorian postcards of naked women.

The only woman he wanted to see naked was the one who held his hand. He studied the way her bottom moved beneath the caressing leather of the skirt, and thought of cupping her in his hand, feeling the warmth and smoothness of her skin.

She paused in front of a tall bookcase filled with

various bottles and jars and pulled him close to her, so that their thighs touched. Her perfume mingled with the spice and floral scents surrounding the display. "Good sex is a feast for the senses," she said, her voice hushed. "Men respond most strongly to the visual, so we have a number of items to enhance that visual experience. Costumes." She indicated her leather outfit. "Videos." She nodded to the wall of tapes in the back corner. "Props." A wave of her hand took in a pegboard of body jewelry.

He slipped his hand from her grasp and caressed her back. "I'm beginning to understand the appeal of the costumes." He tried to pull her to him, but she resisted, and continued her lecture.

"As I was saying the other day, sex also involves the other senses. Smell. Taste. Touch."

Was this to be a continuation of the little demonstration she'd given when she'd handcuffed him to the bondage display? His heart pounded in anticipation. She collected several items from the display, standing on tiptoe to reach the top shelf. "Take off your clothes."

She was taking this dominatrix gig too far, giving him orders. He put his hands behind his back. "No."

She frowned. "Mitch, if you're not going to cooperate—"

"I want you to undress me."

Her eyes widened, the pupils expanding, and she opened her mouth and let out a long breath. "*Ohhhh.*" Smiling, she set aside her jars and bottles and reached once more for his tie.

He forced himself to stand still, to let her touch him without giving in to the urge to touch her in return. Instead he openly watched her, studying the curve of her jaw as she bent forward to loosen his tie, admiring the swell of her breasts above the leather corset, the slenderness of her fingers as she undid the buttons of his shirt.

Her fingernails grazed his skin and he sucked in his breath, and felt his stomach tighten as she brushed her hand across his pebbled nipples. She caressed his stomach, trailing her fingers along the dark V of hair disappearing into his waistband. His erection strained against his fly, demanding release. Instead she cupped him through the cloth and smiled up at him. ''I can tell we're both going to enjoy this.''

He wanted to tell her to hurry, but made himself wait. Her turn would come soon enough. She undid his belt, then slid down his zipper with agonizing slowness, her head bent over him, as if she needed to see what she was doing. When he sprang free at last she blew her hot breath across him and he jerked in her hand.

She laughed and helped him out of his shoes and socks and pants, then she reached for the fastening of her corset.

His hand stayed her. ''Now it's my turn.''

She pulled away. ''No, I'll do it.''

''But I insist.'' He took her wrists and pulled her hands away. She resisted a little, but finally relented. He fought a smile. She didn't like not being in charge, even in this small thing.

He made himself linger, though his first instinct was to rip away these barriers that kept him from seeing her fully. He started with the dog collar and studded wrist cuffs, then moved in and down, stripping her of the corset and skirt. When she was down to only the garter belt, stockings and ankle boots, he was tempted to stop, but continued, unfastening the garters and peeling the translucent silk from her thighs.

His efforts revealed a single butterfly tattooed at her hip, its wings an iridescent green and blue. He smoothed his hand over it. "If you hadn't noticed, I don't need any costumes or props to get turned on visually." Jill was enough all by herself. Not just her gorgeous body, but all of her, mind and spirit. She had an innate sensuality he hadn't encountered in a woman before.

She eyed his erection. "I noticed." She reached behind her for one of the jars. "But maybe some of our products would arouse you even more." She unscrewed the lid from the jar and scooped up a fingerful of some bright blue paste.

"What is that?" he asked.

"Body paint." She demonstrated by drawing a blue line from his navel down to his shaft. Two more strokes made this an arrow pointing downward. Gathering more paint, she continued the line down the length of his shaft, then circled the head. She considered her artwork. "I've always wondered what blue balls looked like. Now I'll know." She returned to her painting, caressing, stroking, all in the name of art.

She looked up at him and smiled. "Now you try."

He took the proffered jar and dipped in a finger. It was smooth and cool, and slightly slippery. Remembering pictures he'd seen in *National Geographic* as a kid, of some tribal brides, he began decorating her breasts with concentric circles of blue.

Her skin was hot, and satin smooth. By the time he reached her nipples, they were straining toward him. He caressed them with his thumb, eliciting a moan from her that sent a jolt of fierce desire through him. He shoved aside the jar of paint and pulled her to him, his head bent to suckle her.

The paint tasted of chocolate and mint, setting up a

tingling sensation in his mouth as he licked and sucked. She writhed and moaned, the force of her response arousing him all the more. He transferred his attention to her other breast, shifting her so that her legs straddled his thigh.

He pulled back enough to look at her. Her nipples were swollen and wet from his mouth, made all the more erotic by the circles of blue paint that focused his gaze on those tantalizing tips. She looked at him through half-closed eyes, hazy with desire. "Maybe we'd better go into the office," he said.

She took his hand and led him back through the store. Once again, he watched the seductive sway of her hips, his fingers itching to touch her. In the office, she stopped by the daybed, and he tried to guide her down onto it, but she pushed him back. "I still have a few more things to show you."

"I have everything I want to see right here." He bent his head to her breast once more, but she slipped away from him and out into the showroom once more.

He started to follow her, then changed his mind and lay back on the bed, hands behind his head, waiting to see what she would surprise him with next. Why had he been so resistant to this plan in the first place? A fling like this was just what he needed before he settled into the hard work of running his own restaurant. And Jill was the perfect woman to share it with.

She returned, her breasts swaying gently as she walked toward him, mesmerizing. She knelt on the bed beside him and uncapped a small black bottle. "I thought now would be a good time to explore the other senses. Smell." She wafted the bottle under his nose and he inhaled sweet strawberries. "Taste." She dotted the oil on his lips. It tasted like warm jam. "And touch."

She dribbled oil across his chest and spread it out with her fingers. "Have you ever had a massage?" she asked.

"Once or twice at the gym—"

She straddled him, her knees on either side of his torso, the wet heat of her desire against his stomach. He swallowed hard. "I've never had a massage like this."

She smiled, and began kneading him with her hands, her fingers stroking along his ribs, tracing languid circles around his nipples. She bent and blew across his chest, and heat blossomed along the path of her breath. The sensation of heat, then cold, dry, then moist, sent wave after wave of desire reverberating through him. He arched against her, impatient with need.

But she wouldn't be rushed. She teased him, licking at his nipples, then drawing away. She wriggled against him, holding him captive between her thighs. He could have thrown her off of him with one move, but forced himself to wait, willing to let her have her way with him. You couldn't call something torture when it felt so good.

He cupped her breast in one hand and flicked his thumb across her nipple, eliciting a moan. "You're very sensitive," he said.

She nodded and caught her lip between her teeth as he pinched her lightly. He put his arm around her and drew her down, until he could take her in his mouth once more. His other hand slipped between them to find her moist clit, and began to rub gently back and forth.

"No. Not yet—" But her words died as he suckled harder, and she leaned into him, urging him for more. He transferred his attention to her other breast, and plunged two fingers into her, the feel of her taking his breath away.

She rocked over him now, head back, little moans

escaping from her parted lips. He stroked her back with his free hand, caressing her, silently urging her on. "Yes, baby," he whispered, his own desire building to the point of pain. "Let me feel you come."

The force of her climax shook them both, her body tensing around him with a power that took his breath. His heart hammered in his chest as he pulled her down against him, and he grabbed at her in desperation when she pulled away.

"It's okay. I only had to get this." She opened her palm to reveal a selection of condoms. "Do you prefer ribbed or unribbed, lubricated, flavored or plain?"

She might have been asking if he wanted cream or sugar with his coffee. He laughed and selected a condom from the pile. "I assume we sell these?"

"Of course." She knelt beside him and deftly rolled the condom over him. Her touch sent a tremor through him and he gripped the sides of the daybed to steady himself. He moved over to let her lie beside him, but she moved back. "I thought I'd be on top."

Why did that not surprise him? He grinned. "I've got a better idea. Sit down facing me." He sat up and scooted back to make room. When she was sitting, one foot on either side of the narrow daybed, he slid forward again, until he was at the point of entering her. "How's this?"

Her eyes widened as he nudged at her opening. Then she grinned and draped her legs over his. "I see there are a few things I don't have to teach you," she said.

They moved together then, face-to-face, chest to breast, stomach to stomach, thigh to thigh. He felt her tighten around him as they rocked together, coaxing him into long, smooth strokes that sent his arousal spiraling upward. He put his arms around her, holding her as he withdrew and returned, unwilling yet to surrender to the storm of sensation overtaking him. He wanted to look into her eyes a moment longer, to watch her face transformed by her need for him, to feel this closeness to her.

A low moan escaped her and she tightened around him. She cried out when he thrust against her, but not in any kind of pain. Then his own release quaked through him, leaving him breathless, sightless, deaf to any sound but the staccato drumbeat of their hearts.

He didn't know how much time passed before he opened his eyes to look at her. Her face was flushed, her hair mussed, her eyes heavy-lidded and her lips curved in a smile of satisfaction. He smoothed her hair back from her face, wondering how it was possible to feel so close to someone he scarcely knew. The thought both thrilled and frightened him. "So what happens next?" he asked.

She gently withdrew from him, to the end of the bed, avoiding his gaze. Her sudden shyness puzzled him. Hadn't she felt the connection between them? Surely sex wasn't always like this for her.

"No need to rush things," she said. "We have four weeks." She wrapped a sheet around her and stood. "I'll let you know when we can get together again." With all the dignity of a princess, she swept past him, out into the showroom where they'd left their clothes.

JILL'S HAND SHOOK as she gathered her scattered clothing from the floor. She told herself it was just the aftermath of physical release, but she knew that wasn't the only reason she felt so weak and jittery. Sex with Mitch had been incredible...awesome...fabulous. But it had also been...different. More...real, if that was any way to describe an almost out-of-body experience.

Maybe it had to do with the way Mitch always took everything so seriously. Even when she'd been trying to get him to play with the body paints, he'd drawn a very deliberate design, refusing to give in to nonsense.

And when he made love to her, it was with the same dedication and purpose. As if it mattered for more than just that moment.

She was going to have her hands full, keeping things on an even keel with him. After all, the whole point of this was to convince him to keep the store open. She wanted the next few weeks to be fun. Adventurous. Even educational. But *not* serious.

He emerged from the office and came over to her, but made no move to put on his own clothes. She watched him out of the corner of her eye, admiring his flat stomach and muscular chest. He was gorgeous. Everything she could want in a sexual partner. Her gaze shifted to his face, to the frown always lurking at the corners of his mouth. *Damn it, Mitch, why don't you smile?* she wanted to shout.

"So you're saying you intend to call the shots here," he said.

So *that* was what was bugging him. She might have known. She looked up from fastening the garter belt. "Of course. This was my idea, so I get to set the rules."

He leaned back against an antique table, arms across his chest. "Is that how it always is with you and men— you make the rules?"

She did up the leather corset. "Do you find that threatening?"

"Not threatening. But it does tell me something interesting about you."

She froze in the act of reaching for her skirt and turned to him. "What's that?"

"It tells me the only one really afraid here is you. As long as you're always in charge, always calling the shots, then you don't take a chance of getting too carried away."

Now who was playing amateur psychologist? Of all the ridiculous notions.... She shook her head and picked up the skirt. "You don't know anything."

"Don't I?" He opened his hand to reveal the handcuffs she'd been playing with in the office. "Where did these come from? We don't sell them in the store."

"They're Grif's. They were in his desk."

"Grif's?" He stared down at the cuffs. They glinted silver in the lamplight. "Did you and he—?"

"No!" She jerked up the zipper to her skirt. How could he think she and his uncle—? "No," she said again, her face hot with embarrassment. "He was a reserve deputy at one time and they were part of his gear."

Mitch's shoulder's slumped. She hoped he was ashamed of himself. "No matter what you think of me, I don't go to bed with just anybody," she said stiffly.

"Hey, it's none of my business." He glanced at her. "But I'm curious. Have you ever let someone use handcuffs on you? Would you let someone tie you up and have their way with you?"

She tried to look unmoved, but a blush betrayed her. "That's none of your business, either."

A faint smile tugged at his mouth. "I didn't think so. You'd tie someone else up, but you'd never surrender that kind of control yourself."

"You don't know what you're talking about." She half turned away from him.

He tossed the cuffs onto the shelf in front of her. They landed with a clang and slid into a bottle of Kama Sutra oil. "I'm beginning to think I know you pretty well, Jill.

You like to have fun, but you don't want any consequences. I'm not so sure that's possible."

"Does that mean you don't want to continue with our little project?" Disappointment tasted bitter in the back of her throat.

He shook his head. "No, I'm interested in continuing. But don't be surprised if it doesn't turn out the way you think it will. I told you before that I'm not the type of man who changes his mind."

"And I told you I'm not the kind of woman who gives up."

He smiled then, surprising her with a grin. "Then we make an interesting pair, don't we?"

Interesting wasn't a word she'd have used. Aggravating. Impossible. Exciting. Maddening. No, interesting didn't begin to describe the emotions Mitch Landry made her feel. Emotions she had to admit she wasn't sure how to handle.

9

JILL MADE A POINT of ignoring Mitch when he came in the next morning. It never hurt to make a man wonder what you were up to—especially a man like Mitch, who had the ridiculous idea he knew her so well.

She kept busy helping one of the part-time employees, Mike, rearrange the dwindling merchandise. They were already out of some of the customer favorites, but Mitch refused to let them order anything more. Fortunately Sid had discovered some extra stock in boxes in the back of the storeroom. By spreading out the remaining merchandise and adding a few new items, the store still looked presentable.

After his shift, Mike went home, leaving Jill alone until Sid started his shift at four. About two-thirty, a timid-looking man came in and stood just inside the doorway, looking ready to bolt.

Jill assumed her most inviting smile and sashayed toward the new customer, a stocky, middle-aged man with the apprehensive look of a rabbit who'd just wandered into a wolf's lair. "May I help you, sir?" she asked.

He looked around the store, eyes wide, then turned back to Jill. "Do you have anything in here to help the most unromantic man you ever met?"

She blinked. What was with all this talk of romance all of a sudden? "Um, what exactly did you have in mind?" she asked.

He directed his answer to the floor. "My twentieth wedding anniversary was yesterday and I totally blew it. My wife says she's going to take the kids and move in with her sister if I don't make an effort to be more romantic."

"So you came here?" She wasn't sure if that was a good sign or not.

"I saw the sign that said you sold lingerie." His gaze searched the room once more and came to rest on a display of nipple rings. "Maybe I made a mistake."

He started backing toward the door, but Jill reached out and caught him. "No, we do sell lingerie. And candles and massage oil and lots of romantic things like that." She thought the guy was sweet, wanting so much to please his wife. The least she could do was help him. "Why don't you start by telling me what happened yesterday?"

He flushed. "Like I said, it was our anniversary, and I blew it."

"You mean you forgot?"

He shook his head. "Worse. I gave her a set of tires as a gift."

She stifled a laugh. "A set of tires!"

He winced. "She needed new tires. I was worried about the old ones. These were very nice." He bowed his head. "I thought she'd realize I wanted to keep her safe."

Oh, how sweet! It was all she could do not to say it. Still, she could see the wife's side. "New tires were a very practical gift. But women deal with practical things all day, from what to do about the kids' schedules to how to handle a boss's request to what to fix for dinner. So when it comes to special occasions, they want not-so-practical things. Things to remind them that they're more to you than a wife and mother. That they're special.''

He looked confused. ''But what?'' He nodded to the mannequin in the window, which today displayed the ever-popular French maid's costume. ''Peggy would never wear something like that.'' His face reddened.

She smiled and patted his arm. ''I understand. You want something...softer to show your wife how you feel. Come right over here.'' She led him to a rack filled with lacy gowns in ice-cream colors. ''This is our honeymoon collection.'' She held up a sky-blue gown of diaphanous silk, with a matching peignoir. Lace inserts at strategic locations kept the gown from being totally revealing, while still allowing for a very sexy outfit. ''I think any woman would love something like this.''

''What about this?'' He held up a red satin and wired bustier, with cutouts for the breasts and matching crotchless panties.

Jill managed to keep a straight face. ''That is very sexy,'' she said. ''But is that something your wife would normally wear?''

His face fell. ''No. But then, she usually wears my old football jersey and a pair of wool socks to bed.''

''Then I don't think it's a good idea to start with this.'' She took the red satin set from him. ''Maybe you could work up to it, though.''

He brightened. ''Maybe so.''

She selected two more gown and peignoir sets, black satin boxers and a matching robe and laid them across her arm, then led him to the massage oil cabinet. ''The thing to remember about women is that, while men are aroused by what they see, women respond better to the other senses—what they feel and smell and hear. So things like satin gowns appeal to them.'' She indicated the lingerie on her arm. "And sensuous smells like our massage oils." She uncapped a tester bottle and held it under his nose. "Sandalwood and sage," she said. "Very erotic."

"Umm, what do I do with it?" He held the bottle as if it contained volatile chemicals.

She smiled. "What I suggest is that you light some candles in the bathroom and bedroom." She pulled down a selection of lavender, vanilla and ylang-ylang scented candles. "Then run a bubble bath for your wife." She chose a sage and rosemary bubble bath. "I'm assuming you've already sent your children to stay with relatives or friends."

He nodded. "Then what?"

"You pour some wine and invite your wife to take a bubble bath. Leave the lingerie for her to put on when she's through. Tell her you'll be waiting when she's done. While she's bathing, you slip into something sexy." She held up the boxers and robe. "And you fold back the covers and warm the massage oil in a bowl of water. When she comes out of the bath, you lead her over to the bed and tell her you're going to give her the most wonderful massage she's ever had."

"But I don't know anything about giving massages." He looked doubtful.

"You can learn." She handed him *Massage for Lovers: An Illustrated Guide.* He flipped through the pages, pausing to look closer at one. "They do *that?*"

She looked over his shoulder. "That's one of the more advanced moves. I suggest you start off with her feet."

"Her feet?"

"Sure." She set aside the lingerie and poured a small amount of oil into her hands. Then she took his hand. "Pretend this is your wife's foot. You'd smooth your hands across the soles of her feet, then across the tops. Use your thumbs in a circular motion to rub along the arches. Massage the heel. Between the toes. Across the instep. Not too hard, mind you.''

"That feels good." His eyes had a glazed look.

She released him and stepped back. "Everything's in the book. It's much easier than you think."

"And this massage will make her forgive me?"

"Not just the massage, but the whole experience. The fact that you took the time and trouble to put together an evening that focuses on her and how much she means to you. First you pamper her—with the wine and bubble bath, the candles, the lingerie and the massage. Then you make love to her like you're newlyweds all over again."

His face reddened. "I'm forty-five years old, not twenty."

"Sex is in the mind as much as it is physical," she assured him. "Focus on giving your wife as much pleasure as you can and I promise you, you can't go wrong."

He cleared his throat and looked around. "Do you think I need any, uh, accessories?"

"Why don't you stick to the basics at first. Then you can bring your wife with you one day and see if there's anything that interests both of you."

He looked at her again. "Do you think I could ever convince her to dress up in one of those costumes?"

She hid her smile behind her hand. "Um, maybe. Now which one of these gowns do you think your wife would like best?"

He chose the sky-blue number, as well as the black boxers and robe for himself, along with the candles, bubble bath, massage oil and book. At the last minute he added another book. *Pleasuring a Woman.* "I think I might need to brush up on a few things," he said.

She smiled and added the book to his purchases. "I don't think you have anything to worry about." She handed him his receipt to sign. "And I think your wife is a very lucky woman."

He signed the slip and returned the store copy to her. "I guess I think I'm a lucky man to have her."

She sighed and looked after him as he left the store. What would it be like to have someone who cared that much about you after twenty years? She'd never dated a single man more than nine months. Had never seen the point, really. Life was too short not to do everything you could, and be with everyone you could. You never knew when your time would be up. If you married young and made a mistake, you might live whatever time you had left full of regrets.

But she was older now. Maybe she ought to think about finding someone for the long haul. If she could only find someone who didn't believe commitment was a synonym for settling down. She didn't ever intend to settle when every day offered so many things to enjoy if you'd only look for them.

MITCH FOUND THE HANDCUFFS hanging from his office doorknob when he left work that afternoon and slipped them into his jacket pocket. Jill was busy with a customer on the other side of the store and didn't glance up when he walked past. She had gone to great lengths to avoid him all day. He hadn't pushed her, though part of him had wanted nothing more than to drag her back into the office and try for a recreation of what they'd experienced last night.

He told himself maybe they'd both benefit from a little cooling off. They'd have time enough in the next few weeks to continue their little experiment.

He reached in his pocket for his car keys and found the handcuffs again. Shaking his head, he unlocked his car door and tossed the cuffs on the passenger seat. Wait until he told Meg about this one. Well, he wouldn't tell her everything. Just enough to surprise her.

He'd asked Meg to come with him this afternoon to run an errand. "What kind of errand?" she'd asked when he'd telephoned.

"A shopping errand." He didn't care to elaborate further until they were in person. He wasn't all that comfortable with what he was going to do, but he felt he had a responsibility to see it through. He hoped having Meg along would make it easier.

Fortunately, she hadn't asked any more questions. "I'll go shopping anytime," she said. "Especially if we get to spend your money."

She was waiting for him out in front of her building. "Sharon's trying to sleep," she said as she opened the car door. "She was at the E.R. late last night." Sharon was Meg's roommate. She worked nights as an aide at Boulder County Hospital.

Meg started to sit, then jumped up again and pulled out the handcuffs. "What in the world—?" She laughed. "I have a feeling the story behind these might be very interesting."

"They belonged to Uncle Grif." He waited for her to fasten her seat belt, then pulled out of the parking lot. "Did you know he used to be a reserve officer with the Jefferson County Sheriff's Department?"

"Really?" She looked at the cuffs. "And that's why he had these things?"

"I'm not saying that's the only reason he had them, but certainly one reason. He had a gun, too."

"*Ooooh.* And what did you do with it?"

"It's locked in the safe. I have to check into the legalities of keeping it or disposing of it."

"I guess it's yours now, along with these." She hooked one end of the cuffs over the rearview mirror. They dangled there, glinting in the sunlight.

"Take those off of there!"

She grinned and shook her head. "Oh, no. I think they're very appropriate for the man who owns Just 4 Play. Think of it as an advertisement."

He frowned at the cuffs, but let the subject drop. He had more important things to discuss. "I need you to help me pick out a grave marker for Grif."

"A grave marker? Is this your so-called shopping errand?"

"I want your opinion. He was your uncle, too."

"How about a concrete golf bag and a martini glass?"

"Even two weeks ago, I would have agreed, but now I'm not so sure. There was a lot more to Grif than I thought."

"He was Dad's big brother. It stands to reason they'd be something alike."

"Yeah, but even when Dad was alive, I don't remember Grif coming around much. When he did visit, he never stayed long."

"I guess he was too busy, or... I don't know."

"Or what?"

She shrugged. "Maybe he wasn't comfortable with the whole family scene. You know, before Mom got sick, she and Dad were happy together, and they had the two of us. We were your stereotypical middle-class American family and there was Grif, a bachelor with no kids. Maybe he felt left out."

"Maybe."

"What do you think?" She angled toward him. "You

have friends who are married with kids. Do you feel like a fifth wheel around them?"

He tried to remember the last time he'd visited with any of his married friends. It had been a while. "Once friends marry and have families, they have a whole different frame of reference than you do. You don't have that much in common anymore. So maybe that was what kept Uncle Grif from coming around as much, though you'd think family would be different."

She sat back in the seat and stared out the window. "Do you think about getting married one day and having children of your own?" she asked.

"Sure." The question sent an odd tremor through his chest. "One day."

She looked back at him. "I hope soon."

He forced a laugh. "It's not like I'm that old."

"No, but I'll be going away to medical school in another year and I hate to think about leaving you here, alone. I'd feel better if you had someone special to be with."

"I'm a big boy, sis. I think I can take care of myself."

The news didn't seem to cheer her. "How's Jill?"

He didn't miss the significance of the change in subject. "Jill is fine. She's my employee. She's not 'someone special.'" He managed to keep a straight face as he told the lie. Jill was certainly more than just an employee now. As for being special...

"I don't know. I thought she was pretty special. You acted...different when you were with her."

He tightened his grip on the steering wheel. "You're imagining things. I don't act any different with Jill than I do with any other woman." Unless you count alternating between having a hard-on that wouldn't quit and wanting to break dishes out of sheer frustration whenever she was around.

Meg reached over and patted his shoulder. "You're not a very good liar, bro, but I forgive you. I'm glad to see you a little more relaxed. Whether it's Jill or the store that's done it, I'm happy."

This was her idea of relaxed? This constant feeling of being on edge? "What makes you think I'm so relaxed?"

"Not relaxed exactly, but more, I don't know, going with the flow." She reached up and thumped the handcuffs, making them jangle and dance. "For instance, a month ago you wouldn't have let these hang up here for even a minute. You were way more concerned with your image then. Maybe it was hanging around with Lana."

"Maybe it was because at the time I thought I had an innocent little sister who shouldn't be exposed to such things."

She threw her head back and laughed. "And now I've destroyed your illusions by buying a vibrator. Which works very well, by the way."

He could only take one hand off the steering wheel to cover one ear. "I don't want to hear about it."

Still giggling, she shook her head. "You are so easy to get a rise out of. It's almost not fair."

"Then don't say things to provoke me."

"I said it was *almost* not fair. It's too much fun to stop."

He pulled into the parking lot of Rocky Mountain Mortuary and Monuments. "Try to control yourself while we're in here. This is a solemn occasion."

For the next hour, they looked at marble monuments, granite memorials and simple brass plaques. Mitch rejected out of hand the alabaster angels and a heart-shaped stone designed for a couple, but that left plenty of choices.

"What do you think?" he asked Meg.

"The brass plaques are the least expensive."

"Many people prefer the plaques for ease of maintenance," the solemn saleswoman said. "We can also include a stainless-lined vase for flowers."

Mitch shook his head. "The plaques seem a little conservative for Grif." He glanced at the saleswoman. "My uncle was a pretty flamboyant character."

"The rose granite is a very popular choice." She led them to a red stone obelisk.

"It's pink," Meg said. Her eyes met Mitch's and they shook their heads.

"White marble is a classical choice." They followed her to a square marker in gleaming white.

"It's beautiful," Meg breathed.

Mitch ran his hand along the smooth marble. It was cold. Refrigerator cold.

Cold as the grave.

He shivered. "It's still too plain." He looked at the saleswoman again, not sure how to make her understand what he was looking for, when he wasn't sure himself. "Grif was the type of man who liked to stand out."

She smiled and nodded. "I think I know just the thing." She led them toward the front of the showroom, past carved cherubs and pillars, to a glossy black stone. Mitch studied his reflection in the mirror-smooth surface. Did he really look so stern and solemn? "This is our Legacy model," the saleswoman said. "One of our more expensive offerings. Some people don't like it because they think it's too solemn. Others feel it conveys a certain dignity."

Dignity. Something he'd never associated with Uncle

Grif while the man was alive. But now, from the distance of death, he saw another side to his father's flamboyant older brother. He saw a man who had lived life on his own terms, and gone about quietly doing good, not expecting praise or accolades. That in itself was a rare kind of dignity. "I'll take it." He opened his wallet and took out a sheet of paper on which he'd scribbled a list of Grif's accomplishments. "And here's what I want on it."

He paid a deposit, not even wincing as he wrote out the check. As they walked back to the car, Meg reached over and took his hand. "I think Uncle Grif would approve," she said.

"I hope so." He slid into the car and stared up at the handcuffs hanging from the mirror and almost laughed. What a perfect symbol of the complicated man his uncle had been. And what a perfect way to symbolize his own tangled-up life. He felt caught by his uncle's legacy and his own dreams, and by one sexy, seductive saleswoman who promised heaven and in the meantime made his life hell.

SID PAUSED ON THE FRONT steps of the townhouse and nervously wiped his hands on his pants. He'd dressed conservatively, in a pair of khaki Dockers and a navy polo shirt, but the effect was offset by his pink Mohawk and the various hoops, silver balls and chains hanging about his body. He'd tried taking a few of them out, but decided the empty holes looked worse than all the jewelry. Besides, she'd seen him before and hadn't freaked out or anything.

Of course, you could say she'd been distracted by other matters at the time....

Oh hell! What was he even doing here? He was out of his freaking mind.

He started to turn around when the door opened and she stood there, blinking. "Sid, what are you doing here?"

He'd intended to act all serious and dignified, but the minute he saw her, he couldn't keep a goofy smile off his face. "Hi, Lana. I, um, I stopped by to see how you were doing. I mean, you were pretty upset last time I saw you."

She returned his smile and actually reached out and took his hand and pulled him into the apartment. "How sweet. Won't you come in?"

He hesitated. "Um, if you were on your way out, I could leave..."

"I was only going down to check the mail. That can wait." She pulled him inside and shut the door behind them.

He stood in the small entrance hall and tried not to stare—at her or her home. She was beautiful, of course, her dark hair hanging loose around her shoulders. It was longer than he'd thought. "I like your hair like that," he blurted, then immediately regretted it. Gee, she was going to think he was just full of class.

She fingered one of her dark locks and looked pleased. "Do you? I usually wear it up at work, but here at home I like to leave it down."

"It looks nice. Soft."

Soft? What kind of thing was that to say to a woman? It's not as if hair could be hard. Well, maybe, but not *her* hair.

"Won't you come in and sit down." She led him into a living room that was decorated all in white, from a soft ivory shade to the flat white of milk. The sofa was covered in a white brocade. He was almost afraid to sit on it. What if he had grease on him from his motorcycle? He settled for sort of perching on the edge. It wasn't comfortable, but then, nothing would be as long as he was in the same room with *her*.

She sat down across from him, in a white leather chair. "How did you know where I live?" she asked.

He squirmed. One look into her gorgeous green eyes and the story he'd made up to tell her flew right out of his head. "I picked the lock on Mitch's office one night and looked the address up in his planner." He cringed, waiting for her disapproval.

But she continued to smile at him. "Mitch would pitch a fit if he knew." She leaned forward and put her hand on his knee. "But don't worry. I won't tell."

He about stopped breathing when she touched him. She must like him a little bit to do that. Her hand looked small and pale against his thigh. Only when he started feeling dizzy did he remember to inhale again. She smelled like vanilla. His favorite. Or at least it was now.

She took her hand away and leaned back. "Do you often go around picking locks?" She didn't sound as if she disapproved. In fact, she looked interested.

"Um...not often. Back in high school I got into a little trouble."

"Were you a *bad* boy, Sid?"

The way she said the word "bad" made him break out in a sweat. Like it was something she liked. A lot. "I guess I was."

She twirled a lock of hair around her finger, a Mona Lisa smile on her face that made his heart pound. "Oh, I think you still are. A very bad boy."

He sat up straighter. "Yeah, well, I guess I can be."

Just 4 Play

He risked a grin. "I can still pick a lock or bypass an alarm system when I need to."

"Then maybe you can help me."

His smile faltered. Was she plotting some crime? He glanced around the room again, at the rich upholstery, the gleaming brass lamps, the oil paintings on the wall that looked like they belonged in an art museum. She didn't look like she was hurting for money, but you never knew about some people.... "Uh, what do you want me to do?"

Instead of answering the question, she leaned back in the chair and folded her arms across her chest, her expression transformed to a pout. "Mitch thinks I'm repressed."

His spirits sank to somewhere around his ankles. Mitch again. He should have known she wouldn't be over a guy like that so soon. After all, the two of them were a perfect pair: both rich, beautiful, dignified and solemn.

"I'm not repressed." She frowned. "Well, maybe a little. But he didn't help any by treating me like some fragile little virgin. I mean, I know I haven't had much experience, but I can learn." She leaned toward him again her eyes pleading. "A woman can learn these things, can't she?"

He stared into her eyes. They were the most gorgeous shade of green. Like verdigris on copper. Or new aspen leaves reflected in a pond. Or—

"Sid, I'm asking you to help me. Will you do it?"

He blinked, forcing himself to pull away from those green depths. "Help you with what?"

She reached out and took his hand. Her fingers were cool, her skin soft as lambskin. "Will you help me to come out of my shell? I know there's so much more to love and…and to sex…I'm tired of missing out. Teach me how to be a wild woman, Sid.''

He knew he ought to say no. That she was only using him to win back Mitch, the man she really belonged with. But when she squeezed his hand and gazed at him with that pleading expression in her eyes, he couldn't bring himself to say no. He swallowed, trying to find his voice. ''All right,'' he croaked. ''I'll teach you. To be a wild woman.'' He just hoped one day Mitch would appreciate the sacrifice Sid was making for him.

10

MITCH WAS IN HIS OFFICE the next morning when Sid knocked on the door, then stuck his head in. "Um, Mitch, there's a couple of dudes here to see you."

Mitch didn't look up from the file box he was going through. "If it's salesmen, tell them we don't want any." He pulled out a file folder labeled Thanksgiving 1985 and opened it. Apparently Grif had kept every receipt, letter and report he'd ever written or received, each meticulously sorted and filed. Most of the stuff was meaningless paper, but every once in a while Mitch found something interesting. For instance, here was a receipt for fifty frozen turkeys. *Fifty.* What would you do with fifty turkeys?

"I don't think they're salesmen. They say you know them. Somebody named Archie and an oriental dude— Ping or Ling or—"

Mitch shoved the file folder back in the box. "It's Ping. Chef Ping. He's the chef for my new restaurant. And Archie Patterson is the architect." *What the hell were they doing here?*

He followed Sid out of the office and found Archie, impeccable as always in a gray Armani suit, nose to nose with Blowup Betty, while Chef Ping, wearing a blue and red track suit, examined a cock ring as if it might be a fascinating new kitchen tool.

Mitch rushed over to them. "Gentlemen, what brings

you here?'' He put his hand on Archie's shoulder and steered him toward the door. ''If you'd wanted to meet, we could have arranged to have lunch. In fact, why don't we go somewhere now? My treat.''

''It's only eleven o'clock.'' Archie stopped and frowned at him. ''I never eat before noon. It upsets my digestion.''

''We came to see this place.'' Ping laid aside the cock ring and smiled at him. ''I want to find the best place for my kitchen.''

Fine. He supposed the only thing to do was to humor them. ''I thought back in this corner.'' He gestured toward the far right-hand side of the store. ''That's where the plumbing is located.''

Ping waved his hand in dismissal. ''No matter where the plumbing is located. Must consider the best feng shui. The best location for my kitchen is here, in this area.'' He indicated a space now occupied by the costume racks. ''We''ll have eating areas over here.'' He marched across the room and gestured toward the bondage display. ''And the cash register goes here.'' He strode to the far left side of the building. ''This is a very good site for money.'' He nodded, then turned and collided with Jill.

She was dressed as Nurse Betty today, in a short white skirt, a blue and white striped pinafore that barely covered her breasts, white fishnet hose, spike heels and a scrap of a nurse's hat. As a prop, she carried an oversize syringe with a long rubber needle. The effect was both alarming and erotic. Ping's mouth gaped open, then he snapped it shut and bowed low. ''Am honored to meet you, beautiful lady.''

Mitch groaned. Ping spoke English better than many

native-born speakers, but he liked to use his pidgin English to catch people off guard. Or to charm women.

Jill certainly seemed charmed. She giggled as he bent over her hand. "Nice to meet you, too. What brings you to Just 4 Play?"

"My friend here—" He nodded to Mitch. "Is to open grand restaurant, where I am master chef. I create masterpieces of Chinese cuisine." He squeezed her hand. "You come. Eat free."

Archie sidled over to Mitch. "Nice place you have here," he said. "You sure you want to close it?"

"Yes." He looked around. Sid was helping a customer choose from an array of spiked dog collars. Two coeds were giggling over by the greeting cards and an older man contemplated a display of rubber garments with the solemnity usually reserved for major investment decisions. He would have expected solemn, fastidious Archie to be offended by the tackiness of the products if not their sexual nature. "What's so great about it?" Mitch asked.

"It's so…unusual." Archie picked up a pink feather duster and fluttered it back and forth. "So…fun."

There was that word again. The nastiest three-letter word he knew. "About the restaurant," Mitch prompted.

Archie reluctantly laid aside the feather. "Yes, the restaurant. As soon as Ping decides where the best 'ambiance' is for everything, I'll get to work on the plans."

Jill had led Ping over to the costume rack and was showing him a gladiator's breastplate and short skirt. The chef was nodding and grinning as if she'd just suggested they run away for a wild weekend fling, though the short, round chef didn't really seem Jill's type. "He'll look ridiculous in that getup," Mitch said.

"Yes, I agree, he's much more the Roman Emperor type. Say, a short toga…"

Mitch glared at Archie, then stalked over to the chef and Jill. "Ping, I thought you came here to discuss plans for the restaurant."

"Yes." He looked up from adjusting the breastplate over his track suit. "I think this young lady would make a perfect hostess, don't you?"

Apparently Jill had noticed the slipping accent. She winked at Mitch, then turned her hundred-watt smile on the lecherous chef. "Thanks, but I don't think the restaurant business is for me."

"Why not? Wonderful late hours. You meet so many interesting people." He leered at her chest. "Perhaps not so interesting as here."

"Chef Ping, why don't you come into my office and we can go over the floor plan." Mitch took Ping's arm. "You can show me again where you want to put the kitchen."

"Yes, yes. But first, I will take this." He held up the gladiator costume.

"Great. It comes with its own sword." Jill held up the plastic prop.

"Oh, no, I don't need that. I have my own sword." He waggled his eyebrows suggestively.

Mitch curled his fingers into fists. One more word and he'd be forced to strangle the chef. If the man wasn't such a brilliant cook, he would have done away with him sooner.

Jill led the way to the front counter, Ping trailing at her heels like a cocker spaniel pup. Along the way, he snatched up a bottle of Kama Sutra oil and another of Motion Lotion.

"Oh, I'll take some of that." Archie stepped forward

and claimed his own bottle of lubricant. "And this." He added the pink feather duster.

Mitch stifled a groan and stepped back. One problem with owning a business like Just 4 Play was that you learned way more about people that you really wanted to know.

"Uh, boss, can I speak to you a minute?"

Mitch hadn't even noticed Sid standing beside him. Another measure of how distracted he was. "Sure, Sid. What's up?"

A good question, since the store manager didn't look quite himself today. Mitch couldn't put his finger on what was wrong. Maybe it was the long-sleeved white shirt Sid wore that covered most of his tattoos. Or maybe the ordinary tennis shoes replacing his usual motorcycle boots, rendering him two inches shorter.

Mitch's gaze traveled upward. No, it was the hair. There was a definite blond stubble on either side of the Mohawk, which didn't look as bright as usual. "You're growing in your hair," he said.

Sid self-consciously ran his hand over the stubble. "Yeah. I guess I ought to shave it all clean and start over, but I haven't got around to it."

"Just looking for a change?"

"Uh, yeah." He sidled toward Mitch's office. "Can we talk a minute? In private?"

"Sure." They moved into the office and Mitch shut the door and took his place behind Grif's massive desk. It was emptier now than when he'd first taken over the business, though he'd kept Grif's bowling trophy and police cuffs in sight to remind him of the many sides of his uncle. "What can I do for you? Is something wrong?"

Sid turned a straight-backed chair around and strad-dled it. "I sort of need some advice."

"Definitely shave your head."

Sid stroked the rooster-comb center tuft of hair. "You think so?"

He nodded. "I do."

"Okay, but that's not what I came in here to talk about."

Mitch sat back, hands folded on his stomach. "So spill."

Sid glanced toward the door, then leaned forward, voice lowered. "I want some advice on women."

Mitch laughed. "I'm not exactly an expert in that area."

Sid frowned. "I'm seeing a new woman. A very classy lady. I thought you might know what she would like."

"What she would like?" He picked up the cuffs and began playing with them. Snapping and unsnapping them. "Do you mean what she would like for dinner, or to do on a date, or as a gift? I suppose that depends on the lady."

"No, I meant what she would like in bed."

Mitch choked. "What? Why would I know that?"

Sid looked more unhappy than ever. "You know more about posh women than I do."

Mitch tossed aside the cuffs. "Posh" women? Did he know anyone who fit that description? He shifted in his chair. "Wouldn't she like what all women like?" What-ever that was.

Sid shook his head. "Women are different. Some like things real active. Others want them loud. Some want you to get a little rough with them. Or they want to get a little rough with you."

Mitch contemplated this wonderful array of women. Clearly he'd been missing out. He leaned forward, elbows on the desk. "I don't mean to disillusion you, but I haven't had your experience in this arena." He cleared his throat. "Most of the women I've been with are pretty conventional."

Sid scooted his chair forward. "Meaning?"

"You know… Lights out. Clothes off. Missionary position." He shook his head. In the current setting, all that seemed so dull.

Sid nodded, his face serious. "Okay, I can do that. So they don't want anything special?"

"Come to think of it, Sid, I think anything special would be appreciated." Until he'd come to Just 4 Play, he hadn't realized how much variety existed in the sexual world. Maybe Jill was right and he could benefit from a little more risk-taking and adventure in the bedroom.

Speaking of Jill, she was still out there with Chef Lecher and his flirty architect. He shoved out of his chair. "I'd better get back to Ping and Archie."

Sid rose also. "Thanks, Mitch. This has been really helpful."

He didn't see how, but he nodded. "Good luck with your new girlfriend."

"Yeah, I'm gonna need it."

Back in the showroom, he found Jill perched on the stool behind the counter, listening as Ping related the plot of a movie. "Is most popular film in China," he said. "The hero is samurai who sleeps with one hundred women. All beautiful." He leaned forward, showing all his teeth. "Almost as beautiful as you."

Jill looked up and caught Mitch's eye. She looked

heavenward and sighed. A clear signal for him to rescue her.

He clamped his hand on Ping's shoulder. "Now that you've finished shopping, let's go into my office." He steered the chef toward the door. "I think it's time for Jill to go change clothes." If she insisted on dressing in costumes at work, he'd have to find her something more suitable. Like a nun's habit.

AS SOON AS THE DOOR to Mitch's office closed, Jill's smile faded. "I can't believe he's going to let those two turn this place into a restaurant," she said.

Sid looked up from a magazine he was paging through. "It could be worse, you know. He could be opening some chain franchise." He looked around. "One of those theme restaurants where all the waiters wear costumes and the food has cute names."

She straightened her pinafore. "Now there's an idea. We could open a sandwich shop at one end of the store and call it the bondage café. The counter staff and cooks could dress in whips and chains."

"Yeah. And if you complained about the food, a man in a G-string and mask would come out and whip you."

Jill giggled at the thought, but immediately sobered. Apparently their one scorching sexual encounter hadn't been enough to convince Mitch to change his mind about closing Just 4 Play. "Sid, you have to help me," she said. "What can we do to convince Mitch to keep this place open?"

Sid turned a page in the magazine and shrugged. "I don't know. Maybe he's right. Maybe this isn't the kind of place a gentleman should be associated with."

She stared at him. "A gentleman? Since when do you

give a flying fig about that?'' She leaned closer, scrutinizing him. ''What's gotten into you anyway?''

He gave her a blank look. ''Nothing's gotten into me. I just think this is Mitch's business and he's entitled to do whatever he wants with it.''

She snatched the magazine out of his hand and turned it over to the front. ''*Esquire*? Since when do you read *Esquire*?'' She looked from Sid to the magazine and back again. ''And what's with the long-sleeved shirt and the hair and…'' Her gaze dropped to the floor. ''Tennis shoes?'' She put her hand to his forehead. ''Are you feverish?''

He swatted her hand away. ''I'm not feverish.'' He grabbed the magazine and stuffed it under the counter, his face flushed. ''A man has a right to change his image, doesn't he?''

''Yeah, but why?''

He shrugged and looked away. ''Maybe I think it's time for a change.''

She sat back, stunned. Sid, of the tattoos and earrings and outrageous hair was trying to be *ordinary*? Not even his mother, to whom he was devoted in every other way, had been able to convince him to tone down his image. What had happened to him?

''It has to be a woman,'' she said.

His face grew redder. ''Why would you say that?''

''Only an attempt to impress a woman would make a man change everything about himself.''

He made a grunting noise and turned his back to her. She shook her head. ''Sid, it won't work.''

''You don't know what you're talking about.''

''It won't work because if you want someone to love you, they have to love you for yourself. If they don't, it's all a sham.''

"Maybe my real self is more conservative than you realize." He turned around again. "I wasn't born with pink hair and a dozen tattoos, you know."

She folded her arms across her chest. "Has this woman actually objected to your hair and tattoos?"

"Well...no. But she's very conservative herself. And I'm sure her family—"

"We're not talking about her family, Sid. What does *she* think of you?"

His mouth turned down and he shook his head. "I don't know. She says she wants to hang out with me, but...I don't know."

She slid off the stool and put her arm around him. "I'll let you in on a secret, but only if you promise not to tell any other men."

"What's that?"

She leaned closer and lowered her voice. "Women love bad boys."

He frowned. "What are you talking about?"

She grinned. "Women love guys who are rebels. Unconventional. Dangerous. Men with a wild side, whether it's hidden or right out there. We think they're exciting, and they also allow us to indulge in the fantasy of taming them."

He glanced at her. "So you want wild men who aren't really all that wild?"

"In a manner of speaking." She squeezed his shoulder. "My guess is that this conservative woman is really longing to ride off in the darkness with you on your motorcycle, to have all the adventures she could never have with the ordinary, conservative men she meets every day."

Sid made a face. "I don't know..."

"Trust me on this, Sid. Women...especially conservative women…like wild men. Be yourself and this woman will be thrilled."

He scratched his ear. "Maybe." He frowned at her. "Does this mean that wild women like conservative men?"

"I'm not sure it works quite that way, but it's an interesting theory."

"I was just thinking of you and Mitch."

"Me and—" She laughed. "He does present a challenge, but that's as far as it goes." She glanced toward his closed office door. "Mitch and I are playing a game. But that's all we're doing."

Sid shook his head. "Whatever you say. I don't think you give the man enough credit. He's the type who takes even games seriously."

"Tell me something I don't know." She straightened her pinafore. "But I'm still calling the shots. That's all that matters to me."

"Maybe so." He shrugged. "Or maybe he only wants you to think that. Mitch might have you right where he wants you and you don't even realize it yet."

She glanced toward the office door. She would admit Mitch had been keeping her hot and bothered lately, but that was as much her doing as it was his. After all, one stuffed-shirt businessman was no match for a wild woman like her. Maybe it was time to turn up the heat another notch.

11

THAT AFTERNOON, JILL LEFT a message on Mitch's voice mail, telling him she thought it was time for another "lesson." "Meet me at the shop after work," she said. "I have a surprise for you."

As soon as the store closed, she gathered up her "props" for the evening. Thank goodness for her employee discount. She lit candles around the office, then changed into a pale blue silk negligée. Last time she'd aimed for tough and sexy. Tonight she wanted Mitch to see a softer side of her.

While there was something to be said for spontaneity and sex, she had to admit planning a seduction and waiting for Mitch to arrive added a delicious edge to desire. As she walked around the room arranging items to set the stage, her body tingled with awareness. The silk caressed her skin and sent tremors of arousal through her. She hoped Mitch would be here soon. Had she ever anticipated the arrival of a lover so much?

The bells on the front door chimed, announcing his approach. Her pulse beat faster as she turned to greet him. The look on his face when he saw her made her throat tighten. He stopped, one hand on the office door, and his gaze swept over her like a long, languid caress. "You look beautiful," he said at last, softly shutting the door behind him. "Silk suits you."

"It's from our Bridal Nights collection." She held out

her arms to better model the short peignoir and matching panties. "Not everything we have here is sleazy."

"I never said that."

"No, but you thought it."

He was dressed more casually tonight, in a pale blue golf shirt, khaki shorts and leather sandals. She hugged him, slipping her hands under his shirt to caress his bare back. "I thought we'd try something a little different tonight," she said.

He shaped his hand to her hip. "Everything with you is different."

"I wanted to show you some more of the merchandise we carry." She helped him slip the shirt over his head, then led him over to the bed. "Why don't you sit right here, like this...." Before he could protest or resist, she snapped the fur cuffs to his wrists and fastened them behind his back. Then she propped pillows around him. "There. Are you comfortable?"

He arched one eyebrow. "Around you? Never." His voice was a low growl, his expression guaranteed to send a jolt of heat straight to her groin. He settled back against the pillows. "But this will do for now."

"Good. I promise I won't hurt you." She leaned over the desk and switched on the stereo. Soft music filled the room. "The CD is called 'Sensual Nature,'" she explained.

She sat back and looked at him. Though his expression was relaxed, his shoulders remained rigid, as though he was ready to burst from the cuffs at any moment. She smoothed her hand down his arm. "Relax. Just let yourself go with the flow. Part of the appeal of being tied up is the idea that you can really let yourself go because nothing that happens is your fault. It's a way for people to lose their inhibitions."

"What would you know about inhibitions?" But his tone was teasing.

"You might be surprised. Now sit back and be prepared to enjoy yourself."

"Are you going to blindfold me, too?"

"No. Tonight I want you to see everything and pay attention."

"Will there be a pop quiz later?"

"You never can tell." She unfastened the single pearl button at the neckline of the peignoir and let it slip from her shoulders. She was left wearing bikini underpants and a strand of pearls connected to her nipples by elastic loops. The pearls swayed with each movement, tugging gently at her nipples.

Mitch's eyes widened. "Doesn't that hurt?"

"No, it's very comfortable. It's from our body jewelry collection."

She gently massaged her breasts, smiling as he began to breathe faster. "Do you like to watch?"

He wet his lips. "I like to watch you."

"I like watching you watch me." She moistened her fingertips and rolled her nipples between thumb and forefinger, tugging them into stiff, aching points. Mitch licked his lips and swallowed, his jaw tight.

"I want to watch you, too." She rocked forward onto her knees and helped him out of his shorts. He wore blue bikini briefs beneath his shorts, the fabric stretched taut by his erection. She smiled. "What do you think? Should we let him out to play?"

He leaned toward her, as far as the cuffs would allow. "If you do, I promise I won't hurt you."

Laughing, she slipped the underwear down his hips, across his perfect cheeks and down his thighs. She took her time, letting her fingernails graze his skin, admiring the way his erection strained toward her. He was hot and heavy in her hand. She cradled him for a moment, letting the tension build between them.

"Is this my surprise, because I have to tell you, I was expecting more."

"Your smart comments are destroying the mood I'm trying to create here. What can I do to shut you up?"

He gaze flickered to her breasts. "I can think of a few things."

"Hmm. How about this?" She guided one breast to his mouth.

Needing no more encouragement, he began to lick and suckle, first one breast and then the other as she knelt in front of him. His tongue traced circles around each nipple, flicking at the thin elastic holding the pearls in place. Heat built within her with each caress of his mouth.

She felt on the verge of climaxing, and she'd barely started with her plans for the evening. She sat back again, moving out of his reach, and took a deep breath, collecting herself. The air conditioner came on, sending cool air across her damp nipples, and she bit back a moan.

She picked up a bottle she'd laid out on the table beside the daybed. "We have a number of different lubricants for sale," she said, surprised at the tremor in her voice. She squeezed a drop onto her finger then spread it on his erection. He was incredibly hot and hard, the skin over his balls stretched tight. He pulsed in her hand, silently communicating how much he wanted her.

She caressed and stroked him, bringing him to the edge. When he was trembling in her hands, she drew away. "You're torturing me," he rasped.

"I am." She smiled. "I have lots more planned for our evening."

She moved away from him again, and slipped off her panties, then sat at the end of the bed, legs apart so that he could see her. She applied another drop of lubricant, and touched herself. The lubricant was hardly necessary, she was so wet and ready for him.

He groaned, his body straining for her, his gaze raking over her like a heated touch. She stilled her trembling hand, pulling back, her gaze locked to his. The air between them seemed to hum with unfulfilled desire.

"Don't stop," he said in a rough whisper.

"I thought it might be fun to show you one of our vibrators." She selected a small red cylinder from the items on the table. "This one is called a Pocket Rocket." She twisted the barrel and the vibrator began to buzz. She held it against his leg. "It's actually great for massage."

"And I'll bet everybody who buys one uses it for that."

She laughed. "Well, some probably do."

"Show me what *you* use it for."

She cradled the vibrator in her hand and studied him through veiled lashes. Was she ready to reveal this much of herself to him? It was one thing to surrender to desire in his arms, quite another to let him watch. "Go on," he urged. "I want to see you come."

She rocked back on her heels, legs apart, the pearls tugging at her aching nipples. With her hands, she spread apart her folds and found the sensitive nub at the heart of her desire and held the vibrator alongside it. Fierce arousal jolted through her. Mitch stroked her leg with his foot, silently encouraging her. She forced her eyes open to look at him as wave after wave of sensation flooded her, and the tenderness in his expression sent her over the edge.

She closed her eyes, giving herself up to the sensations, shaking with her release, a keening cry rising above the music. When at last she shut off the vibe and lay back, he was still watching her, his eyes dark, demanding. "Do you know what you want, Mitch?"

"I want you. Now."

With shaking hands, she unrolled a condom and sheathed him, then slid over him and began to move, riding him. His hands still bound behind him, he arched against her, driving himself into her, each collision sending new shock waves through her, building her arousal once more.

She came quickly, catching her lip between her teeth and moaning. He joined her, his own moans deep echoes of her cries. As soon as she collapsed against him, she reached around and unfastened the cuffs. His arms came around to pull her tighter against him, rocking her as if he would never let her go.

They didn't talk, merely held each other. Words seemed inadequate after what had just happened. She lay with her head cradled against his shoulder, his arms still around her tightly. She felt as if they were still joined somehow, even after he had withdrawn himself from her.

The candles flickered, sending shadows dancing across the walls. The CD stopped playing and silence enveloped them. She thought he'd fallen asleep and closed her own eyes, but opened them again when he spoke. "I liked watching," he said.

"It's very erotic," she agreed.

"It is." He caressed her shoulder. "But it's not just the act, it's the idea that you would be so open. Sharing all your secrets."

She frowned. She hadn't meant it that way. "I have plenty of secrets left."

He turned and propped himself on his elbow, so that he was looking at her. "So I'm right. Underneath that fun-seeking exterior, you have things to hide, just like the rest of us."

She looked away. "I don't have anything to hide. But that doesn't mean I have to tell you everything."

"Of course you don't. But if you want to, I'm ready to listen."

Why did he have to do this to her? She sat up, pushing away from him. "You're getting too serious. You're supposed to be focusing on physical pleasure, not all this emotional stuff."

"I guess I can't separate the two."

"Well, that's your problem." She climbed over him, out of bed, and headed for the dressing room, where she'd stashed her clothes.

What was it with Mitch, anyway? she thought. *Why did he always have to read so much into things?* She tugged her jeans over her hips. Just because they had great, mind-blowing sex didn't mean they had any deep emotional connection. Sure, maybe they clicked on a deeper physical level, but he ought to be enjoying that, instead of analyzing it to death.

She found her bra and fastened it around her. Why did she waste her time with him? Was saving the store really worth being subjected to this…this analysis? Just because he made her feel like no man had ever made her feel didn't mean what they had was so special. She pulled her shirt over her head and shoved her feet into her shoes. There were lots of men out there and plenty of them would be interested in a good time with her.

But some small voice inside of her whispered that none of those other men would ever get to her the way Mitch had in the short time they'd been together.

JILL DIDN'T VISIT THE cemetery often. She avoided places like this, that made her feel so sad and lonely. But two days after she and Mitch made love, she found herself drawn to Rocky Mountain Perpetual Care. Not that it wasn't a beautiful place. The flat expanse of ground on the edge of town was bisected with low stone walls and clumps of pine and aspen. Visitors had a good view of the Flatirons in the distance, their gray and red rock faces reflecting the bright summer sun. Here and there, flowers bloomed in jars and vases beside the stones.

She knelt and shoved the bunch of supermarket daisies she'd brought into the vase at Jenny's grave. The cemetery was beautiful, but in a still, sterile way. Jill preferred livelier surroundings, places with noise and busyness to drown out the grief that tended to sneak up on her when she was alone and quiet like this.

She pulled up a grass runner that was encroaching on the brass plaque and brushed her hand across the engraving. Jennifer Sheldon Davenport 1970—2000. "Surprised to see me here, sis?" she said. "Maybe not, if you've been paying attention to what's going on in my life. Can you believe I'm letting a man mess with my head this way?"

She sat back and drew her knees up, wrapping her arms around them. When she was in college, she'd come home on weekends and pour out her boyfriend troubles to her sister. Jenny was married with her own problems then, but Jill had been too caught up in her little world to notice.

Jenny would smile and shake her head and say the same thing she'd probably say now if she were here: "Jilly, you had better start thinking with your head instead of your hormones or some man is going to knock you for a loop. You'll be saying 'I do' and 'I will' and you'll never know what hit you."

Only later had Jill thought to ask her sister if that was what had happened to her. "Do you wish you'd thought more before you married Greg?"

"I wish I'd waited a while." Jenny turned onto her side, trying to get comfortable in the hospital bed. Even with the morphine drip, everything hurt by then. "Oh, Jilly, there was so much I wanted to do with my life. So many fun things I never got to try."

Jill hadn't cried then, but she had wept oceans of tears later, mourning all the good times Jenny had missed. Her big sister had married at nineteen and spent the next ten years working to put her husband through medical school, then caring for his ailing mother. She had postponed having children, given up vacations and classes, put off learning to ski or to paint or any of the things she once talked about doing. Then in the space of a year, her husband had left her and she'd developed pancreatic cancer.

"I've been having enough fun for both of us," Jill said, pulling more grass from around the grave marker. "But Mitch—he's a hard man to figure out. I mean, it's obvious we're total opposites as far as the way we think and feel about things. But get us in bed and suddenly we're in perfect synch. At least physically."

She yanked at a stubborn weed. "The whole point of this little seduction is to show him how much *fun* sex can be, but he always ends up taking things way too seriously. How am I supposed to convince him to keep the store open if he can't just relax and enjoy the moment instead of getting all philosophical on me?"

And that's the only reason you're interested in him? Because you want to save the store and keep your job?

She winced. She didn't believe in ghosts or people reaching out from beyond the grave, but she knew her sister well enough to know this was something Jenny would have said. Jenny was big on telling the truth and taking responsibility for your actions.

She brushed dirt away from the marker. "Okay, so maybe I have the hots for him, too. And you know me—I love a challenge. I'd love to help Ice Man thaw out a little."

A ground squirrel poked its head up from a nearby clump of grass and chattered at her. Jill laughed. "Don't mind me. I'm just sitting here talking to myself." She rose and brushed the dirt from her denim skirt. "I guess I have to figure my own way out of this one, huh, sis?" She smiled down at the brass marker. "I think if you were here, you'd tell me to go with the flow myself. I mean, it's not as if I'm not enjoying myself."

She turned and walked back toward her car, through the neat rows of markers, past the occasional more ornate memorial carved in stone. With only two weeks left until her deadline, she really needed to get busy. There must be some way to get Mitch to reveal his inner wild man—that part of him that had to appreciate the appeal of a store like Just 4 Play.

Maybe the store was the wrong place to act. To Mitch that was a place of business, where he was reluctant to shed his businessman's demeanor. "I need to get him away from the office," she mumbled. "But how? I could ask him out, but what if he says no? Maybe Meg—"

"Do you always talk to yourself like this?"

She jerked her head up and stared, wide-eyed, at Mitch Landry in the flesh. He was standing one row over, beside a large black tombstone. The sun behind him spotlighted his broad shoulders and glinted on the gold flecks in his hair. A breeze pushed back the sides of his coat, revealing a crisp white collarless shirt beneath. He looked like a model for a men's clothing catalog, or the kind of man who starred in her best fantasies—all lean muscle, fabulous hair and brooding good looks. *Oh man, do I have it bad,* she thought as she walked toward him.

12

MITCH WAS STARTLED TO LOOK up and see Jill moving between the rows of grave markers. She'd walked past without even seeing him before he finally found his voice and called out to her.

"Hi, Mitch," she said as she walked toward him. "Um, what brings you here?"

She was wearing some silky, summery top and a long jean skirt, slit up the side. She looked young and vibrant and every part of him wanted her in a way he couldn't remember ever wanting a woman. "I was about to ask you the same thing," he said, surprised at how calm he sounded.

She glanced behind her. "I was visiting someone."

Who? he wondered. *A relative? A former lover?* "So am I." He nodded to the stone. "What do you think?"

She stepped back and bent to read the inscription on the stone. "Griffeth Landry. 1945—2003. Businessman, sportsman, philanthropist. His generosity benefited many." She smiled up at Mitch. "Grif would have loved it."

He shoved his hands in his pockets and regarded the stone. The masons had done a good job with it, shaping a simple tablet, outlining the letters in gold leaf. The results were bold and dignified. A big statement for a big man. "I hope so. I wanted to do something...he did so much for everybody else, but never really made a big deal of it.''

She nodded. "That was Grif. He said he liked to work behind the scenes.''

Her voice held a note of fondness. Mitch envied her whatever memories made her smile that way. "Did he spend much time at the store?" he asked. "I mean, did you get to know him very well?"

"He spent quite a bit of time there." She laughed. "He liked to flirt. And he told bad jokes. He came across as a guy who really knew how to have fun.''

"Unlike some people you're too polite to mention.''

She looked away, biting her lip. "I didn't say anything.''

"You didn't have to. I know what you think of me." He sighed. "And you're right.''

She whirled to face him again. "I am?"

He nodded, feeling grim. "I know I'm not the most exciting guy to be around. I do tend to take things too seriously sometimes." He shrugged. "What can I say? I haven't had a lot of time for fun these past few years.''

He started walking away. She caught up with him and slipped her arm through his. She was warm and smelled like jasmine. "Don't be so hard on yourself. You can always learn how to have fun.''

He looked down at her. "You seem to be making every effort to teach me.''

She squeezed his arm. "Don't tell me you haven't enjoyed our lessons.''

"I never said I didn't enjoy them." Truth was, he'd enjoyed them entirely too much. When he was with Jill, he forgot about all his responsibilities and obligations. Every sense focused on the moment as the past receded and the future disappeared.

"Oh, it's obvious you enjoy certain aspects of our time together." She stopped and faced him, looking into his eyes, as if searching for something. "But I never get the impression you've really let yourself go. Abandoned yourself to the moment."

"Just let it all hang out. Have a good time with no strings attached, is that what you mean?"

"I didn't say no strings." She wagged her finger at him.

"Oh, yes. The store." He shook his head. "You won't change my mind about that."

"Because it isn't respectable?"

"That's part of it." And maybe because he felt out of his league there, like an alien on another planet. Better to go with a restaurant, something more conventional and familiar.

"Fun and respectable don't always go together." She smoothed his lapels. Her fingers were long and slender, the nails coated in pale pink.

"They do in my case."

She trailed one finger down the center of his chest, sending lightning bolts of sensation radiating outward. "I'm still determined to change your mind."

He captured her hands in his and looked around them. "This seems like a strange place to be having this conversation." He looked at her again. "I know it's none of my business, but what *were* you doing here?"

"Visiting my sister." On impulse, she tugged him back the way they'd come. "I'll show you."

He released her and she raced between the rows of graves. He followed at a slower pace, striding over the grass with heavy steps. He joined her beside the marker and read the inscription. "Older sister?" he asked.

She nodded. "Two years older."

Play the *Lucky Hearts* Game

and get...

2 FREE BOOKS
and a FREE MYSTERY GIFT...

yes! YOURS to KEEP!

I have scratched off the silver card. Please send me my *2 FREE BOOKS* and *FREE Mystery GIFT*. I understand that I am under no obligation to purchase any books as explained on the back of this card.

Scratch Here!
then look below to see what your cards get you... 2 Free Books & a Free Mystery Gift!

350 HDL DU2A

150 HDL DU2R

FIRST NAME | LAST NAME

ADDRESS

APT.# | CITY

STATE/PROV. | ZIP/POSTAL CODE

(H-B-04/03)

Twenty-one gets you
2 FREE BOOKS
and a **FREE MYSTERY GIFT!**

Twenty gets you
2 FREE BOOKS!

Nineteen gets you
1 FREE BOOK!

TRY AGAIN!

The Harlequin Reader Service® — Here's how it works:

Accepting your 2 free books and mystery gift places you under no obligation to buy anything. You may keep the books and gift and return the shipping statement marked "cancel." If you do not cancel, about a month later we'll send you 4 additional books and bill you just $3.80 each in the U.S., or $4.21 each in Canada, plus 25¢ shipping and handling per book and applicable taxes if any.* That's the complete price and — compared to cover prices of $4.50 in the U.S. and $5.25 in Canada — it's quite a bargain! You may cancel at any time, but if you choose to continue, every month we'll send you 4 more books, which you may either purchase at the discount price or return to us and cancel your subscription.

*Terms and prices subject to change without notice. Sales tax applicable in N.Y. Canadian residents will be charged applicable provincial taxes and GST. Credit or debit balances in a customer's account(s) may be offset by any other outstanding balance owed by or to the customer.

"Were you a lot alike?" He tried to imagine a slightly older Jill. Surely there couldn't be two women like her in this world.

"We used to be. When she was in high school, she won a glee club award for 'Most Enthusiastic.' When she was in college, her freshman class voted her 'Girl Most Likely To.'"

"Most likely to what?"

She grinned. "You fill in the blank. Jenny would do almost anything."

"What happened?"

"She married young, spent a lot of years taking care of other people, being responsible and dependable and all those things." She looked at him, her eyes bleak. "She was thirty years old when she died of cancer. She never got to do all the things she used to talk about doing with her life."

"So you're determined not to make the same mistake?"

She shrugged and turned away, hugging herself. "Let's just say Jenny taught me an important lesson. 'Life's too short' isn't a cliché, it's the truth."

"So your philosophy is, if a person wants to do something, they should do it, and worry about the consequences later?"

"Not if it's robbing a bank or jumping off a cliff, but most things, yeah." She stretched her arms over her head. "People don't take enough chances in life."

She whirled to face him. "If you could do anything you wanted right now—anything—what would you do?"

He looked into her eyes, the color of a mountain lake, dancing with life and light. "If I could do anything, what would I do?" he murmured. He put his hands on her

shoulder and drew her close. "This." Then he bent and
kissed her, a soft meeting of their lips that deepened as
he felt her melt against him.

She tasted of peppermint, warm and sweet and meant
to be savored. Her lips were satin-soft, her tongue agile
and teasing. He nipped the side of her mouth and she
laughed, a sound that rose between them like champagne
bubbles, light and celebratory. He pulled her closer and
felt the hard points of her breasts against his chest, his
erection straining at his fly. She ground against him, letting him know she wouldn't object if he tried to take
things further.

Damn! Why did he get into these situations in public?
Reluctantly, he released her. She stepped back, eyes
glazed. But she was smiling. "What was that all about?"

He shrugged. "You could say I'm learning to act on
impulse."

"I like your impulses." She wound her arms around
his neck and pulled him close once more. "Why don't
we try that again?"

Hands at her waist, he pushed her gently away. "I
don't think so."

Her face clouded. "Why not?"

"For one thing, those two old women over there look
likely to have a stroke any moment now if we keep this
up."

She followed his gaze to a pair of matrons standing
some distance away. The two women stared, open-
mouthed, brows furrowed in disapproval.

Jill smiled and waved. "It's all right," she called.
"We're just rehearsing." She leaned closer to Mitch and
whispered, "It's one play you won't want to miss."

Choking back laughter, he dragged her toward the

parking lot. "You are incorrigible," he scolded as he unlocked his car door.

"Guilty as charged. Who wants to be corrigible anyway?" She put her hand over his and stopped him from opening the car door. "So now what?"

He pretended not to know what she meant. "Now I'm going back to work."

"After that kiss?" She put her hands on her hips and scowled at him. "I can think of a few other activities that would be more appropriate. Most of which involve both of us getting naked.

He chuckled. "I assure you I'm tempted."

"So why not give in to temptation?" She tugged at his arm. "Didn't you say you were going to try to change your super serious ways?"

"I did. But I prefer to take things at my own pace."

"Neither of us is getting any younger here, Mitch. What's the big attraction of going slow?"

If she only knew how much he wanted to drag her into the car right now and get after it. He studied her face, looking for some clue as to her true motives here. "I already told you nothing you can do will change my mind."

"That's what you said. I'm not so sure I believe that." She reached up and undid the top button of his shirt. "That's enough for me to keep trying." She moved to the second button. "Or are you afraid I'll succeed?"

He put his hand over hers to stop her from going further. "Maybe you haven't noticed, but it's broad daylight out and we're in the parking lot of a cemetery."

"So?" She glanced around them. The two matrons were making their way across the parking lot. Jill smiled and waved and they hurried away. Then she looked back at Mitch, her expression serious. "Tell me the truth—do you want me, right now?"

He glanced down at the obvious bulge in the front of his trousers. "I don't think there are any doubts about that."

"Then what are you waiting for?" She walked around the car and opened the passenger door.

"What are you doing?"

She smiled and slid into the passenger seat and faced forward, ignoring him.

He got in the car. "What are you doing?" he asked again.

"You said you wanted me now. I want you, too." She reached over and squeezed his thigh, then slid her hand over to cover his crotch. "I'm teaching you to be more spontaneous."

"Jill, we can't—" But she was already unzipping his pants, pulling down his underwear to caress him. He uttered a noise between a gasp and a groan.

"I think we are." She dragged her fingers up the underside of his penis, her fingernails lightly raking the sensitive head.

He glanced around him, but the images he saw were filtered by a haze of desire.

"Don't worry. No one will see us. Haven't you noticed how few people come to cemeteries in the middle of the day in the middle of the week?" She kissed his ear, her teeth nipping at his earlobe, sending an electric shiver through him. "The car windows are tinted and you're parked at the far end of the lot. There are plenty of spaces closer, so no one is likely to park beside us."

"What if they do?"

"If they do, we'll simply explain we were comforting

each other in our grief.'' She opened her purse and took out a small gold-capped bottle.

''What's that?'' he asked.

''A little something to make things go smoother.'' She poured lotion from the bottle into her hand and the exotic aroma of jasmine and spices filled the car. *Her* scent.

She smoothed the lotion across her hand, then took hold of him once more. He jerked in surprise, but her hand on his thigh steadied him. Her caress was firm, but light, skillful. She traced the length of his shaft, then slipped farther down to cup his balls, squeezing gently. His breath caught, and again she kissed his ear. ''Do you like that?''

''Uh.'' It was the only sound he could utter, she had him so mesmerized, her fingers encircling him with a steady pressure. She began drawing circles around the base of the head, her tongue echoing the movement against his neck.

She was leaning over the stick shift, her upper body pressed alongside him. The thought passed through his mind that this probably wasn't very comfortable, but then that bit of common sense was banished by another surge of desire as she rapidly slid her hand up and down his straining erection.

He slipped his arm around her, enjoying the sensation of her breast soft against his side, her hair tickling his neck. She increased the pressure on his penis and he let out a long, low groan. Who would have thought an old-fashioned hand-job could have him on fire this way? He was like a teenager again, at the mercy of some girl he'd brought out in his car. Except Jill wasn't ''some girl.'' She was a woman capable of confusing and delighting him in the same breath.

''Relax,'' she whispered. ''Enjoy the moment.'' She

bent and sucked at his nipple through his shirt. He caught sight of himself in the rearview mirror, his eyes glazed, jaw slack. Anyone looking in the car at this moment would have no doubt what was going on.

He struggled to assume a composed expression, but Jill's insistent hand and teasing mouth made the effort futile. He was literally shaking, close to losing control. He put his hand on her back, thinking to tell her to stop now, he'd finish this himself, but then it was too late. He shuddered with release, pressed back against the seat, eyes closed. He didn't give a damn who saw him now, only please, don't stop.

He felt her draw away, and somehow got it together enough to dig his handkerchief from his pocket and hand it to her. After a moment, she returned it, and he cleaned himself off and zipped up his pants. Only then did he look at her. "That was pretty incredible."

She smiled. "See, the world didn't come to an end or anything. There are rewards for living in the moment."

He nodded. "I can see that." He shifted in his seat and leaned toward her, pressing her back against the seat with one hand. "Now it's your turn."

Her smile vanished. "That isn't necessary."

"But I insist." He let his gaze drift over her, from the sexy pout of her mouth, over her erect nipples, barely discernable against the fabric of her dress. His eyes came to rest on her crotch. "Take your underwear off."

"Mitch, really."

"Take them off." The words weren't a request, but an order. Her eyes widened and for half a second he thought she might slap him and storm out of the car, but instead, she stayed, and shimmied out of her underwear.

The pair of white silk bikinis she handed him was warm and slightly damp, scented with her musk. He felt himself growing hard again as he reached over and flipped up the front of her skirt to reveal the nest of light brown curls between her legs. "Let me see," he said, coaxing her thighs apart.

A sly smile on her face, she complied, playing the wanton. But her hands, curled into fists at her side, betrayed her uneasiness. She wanted to be the one to give orders, not to take them. He reached his hand between her legs. She was hot and wet. "So jerking me off turned you on," he said.

She nodded and ran her tongue along her lips. "Yeah."

"But maybe I can do better." He slid one finger into her and felt her tighten around him. He buried his thumb between her folds until he found the erect nub, the "magic button" that would start the fireworks. Her eyes fluttered closed and her lips parted. His erection twitched in response.

He tried to move closer, but the stick shift was in the way. He looked around them, wishing they were someplace less public. He had half a mind to start the car and drive to his apartment, where there was privacy and a bed and room to do this properly.

She squirmed beneath him, arching toward him, silently pleading for release. No, there was no time for relocating now. He wouldn't make her wait any longer.

He stroked her gently, then with more firmness. Fast, then slow, the scent of sex and jasmine and the sight of her writhing beneath him making him hard all over again. He watched her face as she lay back and surrendered herself to the experience, the moment, just as she was always preaching at him to do.

He felt the growing tension in her, saw her arch against his hand, her head thrown back. She moaned softly, a sound that rose in pitch, eery and erotic. As her body tensed with her final release, he pulled her close, burying his face in her neck, the tremors of her climax vibrating through him.

They sat for a long while, her head crushed against his shoulder, his hand still on her, until she gently moved out of his embrace. "For a man who was reluctant at first, you catch on quick."

"I always aim to please, ma'am."

She made a face. "Well, *sir,* you know what would please me most."

So they were back to that, were they? Did she never give up? "I'm not going to keep the store open," he said.

"Then I guess I'll have to keep trying to change your mind." Her eyes sparkled, as if she was in on some secret joke.

He shook his head. "What am I going to do with you?"

"I'd say you seem to be doing a good job of figuring that out." Her laughter floated back to him as she slipped out of the car. He watched her walk away and wondered at the elation rising in his own throat. He and Jill were playing an odd game here, one he was sure he would win. But who was to say if he let her win, he'd really be a loser?

13

IT WAS JILL'S TURN TO OPEN the store the next morning. She arrived feeling worse for wear after a restless night. Thoughts of Mitch kept her awake. When she'd finally fallen to sleep, she'd dreamed of Mitch, his sweat-slicked, naked body tied to her bed while she tortured him with her tongue.

She'd awakened horny and irritable. Men! Despite her best efforts, he'd once again ended up with the last word yesterday. Honestly, why did they have to make sex into this whole power struggle thing?

She'd fix him. On her way to work, she'd come up with a plan. Soon she'd have him so hot and bothered he'd be begging to come over to her place and let her show him how it's done. She smiled to herself as she went around the store, gathering up various items and attaching sticky notes to them. When Mitch found these "gifts" on his desk, he'd have a good idea of what she had in mind for him.

She was still chuckling to herself when Sid came in the back door. At least, she thought it was Sid. He'd shaved off the Mohawk and removed most of his jewelry except for a single, discreet diamond stud in his left ear. In place of his usual T-shirt and jeans or leather he wore an actual suit, charcoal-gray wool complete with pin-striped shirt and a red and navy tie. He carried a brief-case, which he placed under the counter.

He turned and caught Jill watching him. "What are you staring at?"

"Sid—what have you done?"

He smoothed his hand over his naked scalp and tugged at his tie. "How do you like my new look?"

"I...I don't know." She walked around him, marveling that he had put together such a completely white-bread conservative ensemble. He looked like he could run for office. And win. "It's so different."

"The clerk at Joseph A. Bank said it was the perfect suit for a young businessman on his way up."

"I'm sure it is, but..." She bit her lip. "I take it you're still seeing this woman—the conservative one?"

He sorted through the morning mail. "We've had dinner once. We're going out again tonight."

"So she hasn't seen the 'new you' yet?"

"No, it's a surprise." He looked up from the mail, his expression anxious. "Do you think she'll like it?"

"Sid, I think she probably liked you before. Didn't you listen to anything I said, about women liking bad boys?"

He shook his head. "She isn't like that."

"How do you know if you don't give her a chance to see the real you?"

His shoulders sagged. "She wants me to help her get her old boyfriend back. I'm trying to change her mind."

She fingered the edge of his suit coat. "Is this how her old boyfriend dresses?"

He nodded. "Except he's not bald." He touched his naked head again. "And he has money." His brow furrowed. "I haven't figured out how to overcome that yet."

"You shouldn't have to overcome anything," she said. "She should like you for yourself."

"Women say that, but I don't believe it."

She put her hands on her hips. "Are you saying we're liars?"

He dropped a pile of junk mail into the trash can beside the counter. "Let's just say you have a distorted view of reality."

"*I* certainly don't."

He laughed. "You're one of the worst. Look at you. From the minute you met Mitch, you've been ragging on him about having more fun, taking more risks. You're like every other woman I ever met. You meet a man and the first thing you do is try to remake him."

"Don't tell me you don't agree that Mitch needs to loosen up." She grabbed a cloth and began furiously polishing the glass of a display cabinet. "And don't forget, I'm doing this to save your job."

"I never asked for your help, did I? Maybe this is my chance to move on to something else."

"Something your new girlfriend would approve of?"

"Why not? Maybe that's a point in my favor. If women want to improve men, they should appreciate the cooperative ones."

"There's no such thing as a cooperative man." She grabbed up the bottle of glass cleaner and stormed off to the opposite side of the store. Of all the ridiculous, infuriating attitudes. You go out of your way to help a man, and he doesn't even appreciate it. As if she didn't have enough problems in her life right now, she had to deal with not one, but *two* impossible men.

WHEN MITCH WALKED IN the front door of Just 4 Play, he wondered if someone had turned the air-conditioning down too low. The air definitely held a chill, though he soon realized it had nothing to do with the thermostat.

"Here's your mail," Sid said, handing him a stack of envelopes.

Mitch tried to avoid staring at his manager's newly shaved head. To think he'd grown used to a pink Mohawk. "Has Archie Patterson called to say the new plans are ready yet?" he asked.

"He hasn't called since I've come in." Sid's voice was frosty. "Jill opened this morning. You could ask her."

Mitch looked at Jill, who was busying herself taking books off a shelf and putting them back in the exact same spot. She hadn't said a word when he walked in. Was she embarrassed about yesterday? "Jill, did Archie Patterson call this morning?"

She didn't look up. "No. Maybe he's forgotten all about your plans. Maybe *he* thinks you should keep this place the way it is."

"Maybe some people know how to embrace change and move on," Sid said. "*Some* people aren't stuck in the past."

Now what was that all about? He looked from Sid to Jill and started to say something, but she looked as if she'd gladly bite his head off. He turned to Sid. "Uh, nice suit."

Sid smoothed his lapels. "Do you think so? Thanks."

Shaking his head, Mitch retreated to his office. After a restless night, he'd hoped for a peaceful morning, but apparently he wasn't going to be so lucky.

Considering that the cause of his restlessness was out there now rearranging books and ignoring him, he supposed peace had been a little much to expect. He'd stayed up half the night alternately cursing and congratulating himself on letting her seduce him at the cemetery yesterday. No man in his right mind would have turned down an opportunity like that.

But that didn't mean Jill had any kind of hold over him. She couldn't manipulate him into doing what she wanted just because she knew how to manipulate him sexually.

But knowing that was cold comfort at three in the morning when he woke from episode six and counting from what might be the world's longest running wet dream. This particular version had involved a naked Jill wielding a cat-o'-nine-tails and a can of whipped topping. He got hard again thinking about it.

As soon as she'd left yesterday, he'd realized he still had her panties. He'd stuffed the scrap of white silk into his pocket and found his hand straying there for the rest of the afternoon. They were still there, keeping him balanced on the sharp edge of desire.

Yeah, a peaceful life, much less a peaceful morning, was really reaching for it.

He walked over to the desk and the first thing he noticed was the objects grouped in the center of the blotter. He picked up a bottle of green lotion. *Go the distance!* it proclaimed. *Increase your endurance.* A yellow sticky note on the front bore a message in Jill's handwriting. *You're going to need this.*

He examined a black satin blindfold. *What you don't see can drive you wild.*

Nipple nibblers. *Your bod or mine?*

He laughed. "Cute. Very cute. And definitely your bod." He could think of several ways to put all of this "merchandise" to good use.

He sat behind the desk and flipped through the mail. "Now this is interesting." He studied an envelope stamped with the Boulder Chamber of Commerce's seal.

He slit open one end and shook out a heavy embossed invitation.

The pleasure of your presence is requested at our Annual Awards Banquet. Now why would the Chamber of Commerce invite the owner of Just 4 Play to their banquet, when they'd previously turned down Uncle Grif's application? He tossed the invitation in the trash. If they wouldn't accept Grif, he didn't want anything to do with them.

An hour later, he was reviewing cost estimates for the remodeling work when the phone rang. "Mitch, it's Mort." As usual, Lana's dad sounded loud and chummy, more like a used car salesman than a banker. "Did you get your invitation to the Chamber Banquet yet?"

"It came this morning. But I'm not a member. Why do they want me at their banquet?" He picked up the blindfold and turned it end over end. The satin was cool and slick beneath his fingers. It might be fun to try this on Jill and...

"They want you there because I told them they want you there," Mort boomed.

Mitch laid aside the blindfold. "Do they know I'm the new owner of Just 4 Play?"

"They know you're the future owner of Ping's Peking Palace, the first five-star oriental restaurant in Boulder county."

"Except that the restaurant isn't open yet."

"It will be, boy. Archie Patterson came by this morning to show me the plans."

Mitch frowned. "I haven't even seen the plans yet. What's he doing showing them to you?"

"Oh, Archie and I go way back. Besides, he knows I'm the money man here."

"Sure." Mitch fought a sour feeling in his stomach.

"When you see Archie again, tell him the man whose name is going on this would appreciate seeing those plans sometime."

"Now don't you worry about a thing. This is going to be big. I have a sense about these things and I'm never wrong. A year from now, we could be talking about a whole chain of Ping's Peking Palaces throughout the southwest. In five years, we could go national."

Except that's not what Mitch wanted. He wanted one good restaurant that he could watch over and control. Already, he could feel that slipping away from him.

Mort must have taken his silence for agreement. "Good, I'll look forward to seeing you at the banquet."

"Uh, will Lana be there?" Not that it mattered, but he wanted to be prepared, so it wouldn't be awkward.

"No, I asked her to accompany me, but she has other plans that evening." He lowered his voice. "Just between you and me, she's seeing someone new. This time it might be serious."

Was Lana ever anything but serious? "Why do you say that?"

"I've never seen her like this. She's dressing differently. Acting differently. She even forgot our Tuesday night dinner date. She never misses that."

Mitch smiled at Mort's peeved tone. "That sounds serious, all right."

"I don't know what's going on. She's either ill or in love."

"I'm happy for her."

"You could have had her if you'd played your cards right. But I won't hold it against you. I like the way you think and I believe we've got a real future together. See you Saturday evening."

Just what he wanted, a future of loudmouthed Mort

Montgomery telling him what to do. He hung up the phone and tried to imagine Lana in love. The thought made him smile. Good for her. He was glad she was happy.

He fished the banquet invitation out of the trash and read it again. Mr. Mitchell Landry *and guest.* Who could he invite to go with him? He could go stag, but then there'd be that awkward empty chair at his table, and perhaps pointed remarks from Mort Montgomery about what a fool he was for letting Lana get away.

His gaze wandered to the collection of playthings on his desk. He smiled. Yes, he'd ask Jill. This would be the perfect chance for them to get to know each other better, away from the sex-charged atmosphere at work. He'd have a chance to explain all the reasons closing the store was the right thing to do for all of them.

WHEN SID ARRIVED AT LANA'S condo that evening, he was surprised to find her dressed in a miniskirt and silky blouse instead of her usual suit. His confusion must have registered on his face. "Don't you like it?" she asked.

"Yeah… Yes. It looks nice. Real nice." The blouse was a soft pink shade, almost the color of her skin. She'd left the top button undone, so he could see the deep valley between her breasts.

He waited for her to say something about his suit, but she didn't. Instead she stared at his head. "You shaved your head."

He smoothed his bald pate, still self-conscious about all that naked flesh. "Yeah, uh, I was getting a little tired of the Mohawk."

"Oh. Well, I like the bald look. I mean, it looks good on you." She shut and locked her door, then slipped her arm through his and walked with him to the curb.

"I thought we'd go to the Boulderado, if that's all right," he said.

"Oh." She looked disappointed. "I eat there all the time." She squeezed his arm. "Let's go someplace different."

"Okay. Like where?"

"There's this new Indian restaurant over by the mall. I hear you sit on the floor to eat."

A trendy place. He should have known she'd like something like that. "Sure. That's cool."

They reached his bike. He hadn't been too sure about the Harley, but it was the only transportation he had. "I hope you don't mind riding my bike. Or we could take your car...."

"No, the bike is great." She ran her hand along the leather seat. "I've always wanted to ride one."

He gave her a helmet, then strapped on his own. He'd had to get a smaller size when he shaved his head. She climbed on behind him and hugged him close. Her skirt rode up high on her thighs. He was aware of her breasts pressed against his back. She had nice breasts. Full and round. He shifted in his seat, hoping she wouldn't notice his arousal. She'd probably think he was some kind of pervert.

He started the bike and she squealed. He grinned as he guided the bike onto the street. He'd heard some women really got off on the bike's vibration between their legs. Lana snuggled closer, her arms tight around his ribs. Maybe she was scared she'd fall off.

He found the restaurant without too much trouble, a low-slung building decorated inside with lots of red and gold draperies, low mahogany tables and lots of floor pillows. The waitress led them to a table in a shallow alcove. Instead of sitting across from him, Lana scooted around the table to sit beside him. "Isn't this cozy?" she said.

"Yeah." He wished he had the nerve to put his arm around her, but he didn't want her to take things wrong. A sophisticated guy would no doubt take things slower.

They ordered wine and tandoori chicken. When the food arrived, Lana plucked a morsel of chicken from the skewer and offered it to him. "Tell me if it's any good."

Her fingers grazed his mouth as he accepted the chicken and her eyes seemed to sparkle with delight in the lamplight. Feeling bolder, he chose a piece of chicken to feed her. "What do you think?"

"Mmm." She suckled his fingertips and all the breath rushed out of him. His appetite for food fled, replaced by another, stronger appetite.

He looked away, not sure what to do. Did she have any idea how crazy she was making him?

"Why are you being so quiet?" she asked. "I thought you were going to teach me to be a wild woman."

Yeah, so she could get Mitch back. But Mitch didn't want her back. And Sid did. Want her, that is. "Uh, yeah." He picked at his food, not even seeing it. "So what do you want to know?"

She leaned close and licks her lips. "I want to know how to drive a man wild."

She was doing a pretty good job with him already. "Well, yeah. There are a lot of things you could do." For instance, just sitting there beside him eating dinner was doing a pretty good number on him.

She leaned closer still, her breast resting against his arm. "Kiss me, Sid. That's a good place to start, isn't it?"

He looked around at the other diners. Despite the alcove, their table felt exposed. "Uh, I don't think this is the place.'' He struggled up onto his knees, thankful for the long suit jacket to hide his obvious erection, and signaled for the check. ''Why don't we go somewhere quieter?''

Outside once more, she clung to his arm as they walked to the bike. ''Will you take me to the store?'' she asked.

''The store? You mean like the grocery store?'' They were out on a date and she wanted to go shopping?

''No, I mean the store where you work. Just 4 Play.'' She giggled. ''What a name.''

He stopped and looked at her, surprised. ''But... you've already seen it.'' And from what he remembered, she hadn't liked the place much.

She made a face. ''I was upset then. I didn't really look around.'' She stroked her hand down his arm. ''I want you to give me a private tour.''

14

THE STREETS AROUND Just 4 Play were quiet, most of the businesses closed and deserted. Sid steered the bike through the alley around back and parked beside the Dumpster. He let them in with his key, then reached into the alarm panel and unhooked a wire.

"What are you doing?" Lana whispered.

"Bypassing the alarm." He pulled her inside behind him and shut the door.

"Why not just turn it off?"

"It registers with the alarm company when it's turned off. I'd rather not have to explain what I'm doing here with you."

Small lamps on tables through the store allowed them to see most of the merchandise. He showed her the costumes first. That was about the tamest thing he could think of to start with. She admired the belly dancer's costume, then held out the ever-popular Nurse Betty. "I think the dancer is cute, but what's so sexy about a nurse?"

"Uh, well, guys get off on things that don't always make sense to women." Good thing he hadn't shown her the schoolgirl outfit. Or the baby doll pajamas. He shrugged. "Our brains are wired differently, I guess."

"That's why I'm here. To learn about things like that." She pulled out a carpenter's tool belt and held it against him. "You'd look nice in this."

"Really?" He'd never been much for costumes, himself, but if she liked it…

She'd already moved on to the lingerie. "How do you think I'd look in this?" She held up a red lace thong.

He swallowed hard. "I think you'd look good in anything, Lana."

"Oh, Sid, you're so sweet."

That's me. A regular patsy.

She took his hand and led him to a display of body jewelry. "Why aren't you wearing *your* jewelry tonight?" she asked.

He patted his eyebrow, which felt naked without its customary ring, not to mention the barbell he'd removed from his tongue, and half a dozen other studs and loops he'd left lying on the dresser. "I thought maybe it was a little much," he said. "That you didn't like that sort of thing."

She looked startled. "Where did you get an idea like that?"

He flushed. "Well, you know… You're kind of conservative and all…"

She frowned. "Do you think that's a bad thing?"

"No! Of course not. I just thought…" He swallowed hard. He didn't know what to think. Why hadn't he kept his mouth shut?

"It's okay. I guess to someone like you, I do seem like a real stick in the mud."

"Someone like me?"

"You know, someone…unconventional." She looked him up and down. "Someone…extraordinary. Not someone ordinary like me."

He started to reach for her, but hesitated. "Lana, I don't think you're ordinary at all."

She raised her chin. "I'm trying not to be. That's why

I had you bring me here." She studied the display again and selected a set of nipple rings. "How do these work?"

"Uh, you know, they uh, they clamp on to…on to your nipples." He was grateful for the darkness to hide his blush. Honestly, he usually had no problem talking about anything and everything to do with sex. He spent his days explaining the finer points of dildos and the best ways to heighten sexual arousal to total strangers and never even blinked. But with Lana, it was different…

She looked puzzled. "And that feels good?"

"Well, it makes them more sensitive."

She handed them to him. "Maybe you could try them on me."

"N…now?" He glanced around them. "Here?"

"Don't you want to help me be a wild woman?" She started unbuttoning her blouse. Underneath, she wore a lacy black bra that fastened in front.

He couldn't believe she was doing this. Maybe he'd fallen asleep and this was some wild dream. This was *Lana.* Miss High Society. And she was taking her clothes off. For *him.*

Her bra drifted to the floor beside her shirt. He forced himself to breathe deeply. *Just stay cool,* he reminded himself. *Don't let her think you can't handle this.*

Her breasts were just as he'd imagined, full and heavy, the nipples dark and thick. Her skin looked like ivory in the dim light. "Go ahead," she said. "Put them on."

His hands trembled, so that he had to make several tries to attach the rings to her nipples. His fingers brushed against her and she let out a breathy gasp. He stifled a groan and wondered if he'd embarrass himself by coming in his pants. He finally got the rings on her and stepped back to try to regain his composure.

The chain that connected the rings hung down into her cleavage, tantalizing. She looked down at herself, then smiled at him. "You're right. It feels good...sexy."

It looked sexy as hell. He didn't know how much longer he could keep up this charade of pretending not to want her.

"Now you look overdressed." The next thing he knew, she was taking his jacket off. She started unbuttoning his shirt. He stood there like a statue, afraid to move. If he so much as touched her, he wouldn't be able to stop.

He sucked in his breath as her fingernails grazed his chest. "Lana, I really don't think..."

"That's much better." She undid the last button and pushed the shirt back onto his arms. Her eyes widened when she saw the rings in his own pierced nipples. "*Oooh,* we match." She hooked her pinky in one of the rings and tugged lightly. Just enough to send a jolt of electricity through him.

He clamped his hand over her wrist and gently pushed her away. "I wouldn't do that if I were you."

Her smile vanished. "Did I hurt you? I'm sorry. Let me kiss it and make it better."

The first swipe of her tongue over his sensitive nipple almost brought him to his knees. A low groan escaped him and he put his arms around her, thinking he ought to push her away, but unable to do anything but cling to her.

She laved first one nipple, then the other, her own naked breasts brushing against his stomach. His cock strained against his fly, painfully erect. He was so close to the edge now the slightest breath might set him off.

Finally she raised her head and smiled at him. "Is that better?"

He managed to nod and grunt something unintelligible. How long before he could get away from her, into the bathroom where he could give himself some relief?

But his torture wasn't over yet. As he watched, dazed, she unzipped her skirt and let it slide to the floor. She wore black lace bikini panties, and thigh-high stockings held in place by a garter belt.

Shut your mouth, Sid, he warned himself. *You're starting to drool.*

"Is this okay?" she asked, adjusting one of the stockings. "I used to think garter belts were for old ladies, but I understand men really like them."

"Uh, yeah." Men like him. Something about that few inches of naked skin above the top of the stocking....

He shook his head, trying to clear it.

"What's the matter, Sid? Don't you find me attractive?"

"Attractive?" Where did that squeaking in his voice come from? He cleared his throat and tried again. "Believe me, Lana, any man who saw you now wouldn't ever be able to think of another woman again."

The answer didn't erase her look of disappointment. "We're not talking about any man, Sid. We're talking about you." She took a step toward him.

He backed up. No sense going there again. "Of course I think you're attractive," he said. "You're gorgeous."

"Then why are you avoiding me?" She had him backed against the wall now. He closed his eyes and tried to think of something non-erotic. Algebra equations. Motorcycle maintenance.

"Look at me, Sid. Please."

He opened his eyes, and found himself lost in two of

the most beautiful green eyes he'd ever seen. "Why do you think I wanted to come here with you tonight?" she asked.

"Because...because you wanted to find a way to get Mitch back." The words cut him, like broken glass.

Her eyes widened. "Is that what you thought?"

"You said Mitch thought you were repressed. That you didn't want to be that way."

"So you agreed to help me so I could get Mitch back?"

He nodded. Right now, the whole idea sounded pretty stupid.

She reached for his hand and held it. "This doesn't have anything to do with Mitch." She placed his palm flat against her belly. It was warm and soft, and oh, so female. "I asked you to help me because I wanted to be with you." She guided his hand down, beneath the elastic of her panties, toward her heated center. "Feel how wet I am for you?" she whispered.

He slid his finger into her. She closed around him, hot and slick. With his other arm, he gathered her close, burying his face in her neck, breathing in the sweet scent of her. He couldn't believe how he was shaking. But she was shaking too, tremors moving through her as he stroked her with his finger, moving slowly back and forth, forcing himself not to hurry.

After what could have been a minute or twenty minutes, she gently pushed away, forcing him to withdraw his hand. Smiling, she reached for the zipper on his trousers. "Let me see you," she said.

He might possibly have set a new record for stripping down. Shoes, socks, belt and trousers went sailing across the room, until he was standing before her, naked except for his nipple rings and half a dozen tattoos.

She looked away, and he was pretty sure she blushed. "What should I do next?" she whispered.

Her shyness touched him. He gathered her close once more. "You don't have to do anything," he said. "Just follow my lead."

Scooping her into his arms, he carried her to Mitch's office, to Grif's daybed. He swept a stack of papers from the spread and deposited her there, then leaned over and switched on the desk lamp. Candlelight would be better, but that would come some other time. He hoped there would be many other times for them.

He hooked his thumb under her panties and slid them down her hips. She got the idea and helped him finish taking them off. She reached down to unsnap the garters, but he stopped her. "No, leave them. I like them like that. Sort of a frame." He smiled down on her, savoring the sight, then backed toward the door.

"Where are you going?" She sat up, alarmed.

"I'll be right back."

He grabbed a pack of ribbed condoms from the display by the front counter, then on impulse snagged a feather duster and dusting powder from a shelf. When he returned to the office, she was still sitting up, looking worried.

"Hey, you didn't think I'd leave, did you?" He sat beside her and laid the condoms and dust on the corner of the desk.

"What's that?" She looked at the feather duster.

"Something I thought you'd like." He flicked the tip of the feathers across her nipple and she gasped. He reached for the jar of dust. "Lie back now. Enjoy."

The dust shimmered in the lamplight, like powdered gold. He laid a trail across her breasts, down her torso, between her thighs, then followed with the duster, tickling, teasing. She gasped and writhed, her eyes dark pools, her lips parted.

He trailed the duster to her crotch, and parted the folds, revealing the swollen bud hidden there. As he stroked, she moaned and arched toward him. "Sid!" she cried, anxious.

"Shhh." He lowered his mouth to her breasts, suckling first one, then the other, the nipple rings clicking against his teeth. He substituted his finger for the feathers, rubbing, stroking...

He could sense her reaching, nearing the edge. He lowered his mouth and began to lave and suckle in earnest, tasting her juices as she cried out in release.

He fumbled with the condom packet, ripping the cellophane and throwing it to the floor. She sat up and helped him roll it on, though the first touch of her fingers almost sent him over the edge. For once, he was grateful for the slight dulling of sensation the condom provided, to help him last a little longer.

He knelt between her legs and entered her, groaning as he filled her. Slowly...so slowly...he began to move, long sure strokes, then faster, more forceful ones.

She wrapped her legs around him and dug her nails into his buttocks. He stroked her with his thumb, feeling her tighten around him as she neared a second climax. Closing his eyes, he increased his pace, giving himself up to the heat and pressure and driving sensations.

With a final powerful thrust, he cried her name as the shuddering climax tore through him.

He lay atop her, not wanting to crush her, but craving this closeness. She pulled the covers up over them and smoothed her hand down his arm, idly tracing the outline of his dragon tattoo. "Sid, do you think I'm too repressed?" she whispered.

He tried to choke back his laughter and ended up coughing. She sat up and watching his spasms, her brow furrowed. "What's so funny?"

"You." He reached down and tweaked her nipple ring. "You are definitely not repressed."

"Oh good." She smiled and reached for the feather duster. "I've been thinking…maybe now it's my turn to use this on you."

SPILL, GIRLFRIEND. YOU ARE going to tell all before this car goes anywhere."

Jill frowned at her best friend, Cassie Walters. "What makes you think I have anything to tell? I just felt like going shopping."

Cassie tapped the steering wheel of her new Saab. "That's not what you said on the phone. You told me we had to make an emergency shopping trip, and that you needed me to help you pick out a killer outfit. What I want to know is why? Who is this outfit supposed to slay?"

Jill worried her lower lip between her teeth. Okay, so maybe she'd been a little panicked on the phone. When Mitch had asked her to be his date to the Chamber of Commerce banquet, she'd had a sudden picture of herself and Mitch, seated at a long table surrounded by Lana Montgomery look-alikes in designer gowns and real diamonds. "I have to find an outfit for a fancy dinner," she said.

"What kind of dinner? A wedding reception? A date with a playboy millionaire?"

"Um…a Chamber of Commerce banquet."

Cassie turned toward her. "The Boulder County Chamber of Commerce Awards Banquet this Saturday night?"

Jill nodded glumly. "Totally not my scene."

Cassie laughed. "Not exactly my scene either, but Guy and I will be there."

"You will?"

She nodded. "He's up for 'Young Entrepreneur of the Year.'"

"Congratulations. His store must be doing really well." Guy Walters owned a large outdoor equipment store in Boulder. He'd fallen for Cassie when she and Jill worked at his favorite coffee shop. He'd pursued her relentlessly until she admitted she was in love with him. The man who'd been Boulder's most eligible bachelor was now a besotted newlywed.

"Stores. He just opened another one at Flatirons Mall."

Make that newlywed millionaire. "That's great. Tell him I said so."

Cassie lowered her sunglasses and looked Jill in the eye. "You're changing the subject here. *Who* asked you to the Chamber banquet?"

"Oh…my boss." *My handsome, aggravating, too-sexy-for-his-own-good boss.*

Cassie made a face. "I thought your boss was some middle-aged playboy."

"Yeah, he was. But he died. This is his nephew, who inherited the store."

"Does this nephew have a name?"

"Mitch. Mitch Landry."

"Ah. Now we're getting somewhere. So tell me about Mitch."

She shrugged. "What's to tell?" *That I can't stop thinking about him? That every time he walks by my nipples salute? That he's obviously trying to drive me crazy?*

"Well...how old is he? What's he look like?"

"He's in his early thirties, I guess. He has brown hair and brown eyes, and he's tall. Of course, everybody's tall to me."

"Brown hair and brown eyes." Cassie shook her head. "That doesn't tell me anything. Is he George Clooney or Groucho Marx? Has he got a butt you'd follow anywhere or a face that would stop a truck? Does he get your motor running or make you run the other way?"

Jill started giggling. "Stop! Stop! Where do you come up with this stuff?"

Cassie had to wait for her own laughter to subside. "Sometimes I'm just inspired. Now come on, confess! Is Mitch Landry a hunk or not?"

Jill blotted her eyes with her fingers. "Definitely a hunk," she said. "And yeah...he gets my motor running all right."

"So have you slept with him yet?"

"Cassie!"

"Well, have you?"

She nodded. "We have." Although there hadn't been any sleeping involved at all.

"Then what's the problem?"

Wasn't that what she'd been trying to figure out? "Mitch and I are good in bed, but otherwise, we're total opposites. He's so conservative and serious." She shook her head. "Mostly I think he doesn't like it when I try to call the shots."

"So stop calling the shots."

She made a face. "Where's the fun in that? Besides, if I wait around on slowpoke Mitch, nothing will ever happen. The man's conscience and his overblown sense of responsibility keep getting in the way."

"So what you need is a dress that will make him forget all about responsibilities?"

"Yeah. But I can't look like a slut or anything. I don't want to embarrass him in front of all those business people."

Cassie started the car and put it in gear. "I'm sure we can find something suitable. By the time we're through, Mitch won't know what hit him."

They headed for Pearl Street and the stores along the pedestrian mall. Jill remembered the shopping expeditions they'd made when Cassie and Guy were first dating—when Jill first discovered Just 4 Play. Back then, Cassie had been the reluctant one, not wanting to get involved with Guy. But he'd persisted, and look how well things had worked out.

Now she was not only working as a massage therapist in Guy's store, she was ski racing in the winters. She'd gained the kind of confidence Jill had always hoped she'd find.

Not that Jill wanted that kind of success with Mitch. She wasn't looking for flowers and lace and happy ever after. Those things were fine for Cassie, but not for someone like her. That kind of life was too ordinary. Too boring.

They headed for the evening gown section of Jessica McClintock. As they flipped through the racks of gowns, Jill rejected one after the other. "Too dowdy."

"Too slutty."

"Makes me look fat."

They trooped to the next store and started over again. "This Mitch guy must be really special, huh?" Cassie said as she rifled through a rack of designer knockoffs. "Are you in love?"

Jill almost dropped the dress she was holding. "Of

course not. How ridiculous. What makes you think I'm in love?" She shoved the silk sheath she'd been holding back onto the rack. "I'm only doing this to try to keep my job."

Cassie frowned. "You have to sleep with him to keep your job?" She leaned forward, her voice urgent. "Jill, he sounds like he ought to be reported!"

"No, it's not like that. Mitch would never... It's just..." How could she explain? In the cold light of day this whole scheme of hers sounded preposterous, even a little silly. "Mitch wants to close the store and open a Chinese restaurant," she said.

"Oh, no!" Cassie touched her fingers to her lips. "But it's such a nice store. And doesn't it make money?"

"It makes tons of money, but that doesn't matter to Mitch." She pulled out a gold lamé one-shoulder gown and frowned at it. "He thinks a restaurant would be more respectable."

"I suppose it would be." Cassie went back to looking at dresses. "But it wouldn't be nearly as much fun. I still don't see what this has to do with your relationship with him."

Jill shoved the dress back onto the rack and pulled out a green velvet number. "Mitch doesn't see the fun side of Just 4 Play. I think he thinks we just sell a bunch of tacky, sleazy stuff. I thought if I could actually show him some of the merchandise...in action, so to speak... he'd rethink shutting us down."

"Uh-huh. Are you sure this is just about keeping your job?"

She avoided looking at her friend. "What else would it be about?"

"I don't know. When you talk about Mitch, he sounds like a nice guy. Really decent."

She made a face. "I'd like it if he were a little more *indecent.*"

Cassie smiled. "You know what I mean. He sounds like the kind of man a woman could settle down with."

"I'm not interested in settling down. You know that."

"But why not? I mean, with the right man…"

Jill shook her head. "I don't want to look back in ten years and see all the things I didn't get to do because I tied myself down too young."

Cassie's smile faded. "This is about Jenny, isn't it?"

Jill looked away. "She told me not to make the same mistake she did."

"Jill, you're ten years older than Jenny was when she got married." Cassie's voice was soft, but every word was an arrow to a bull's-eye. "You don't have to worry about putting your life on hold the way she did. You've already done so many things she didn't get to do— you've finished your education, traveled, learned new things."

"Who says I'm ready to stop doing those things?"

"Making a commitment to another person doesn't mean you have to give up any of that. It can mean you have someone to share all those things with."

"Easy for you to say. You married an outdoor adventurer. Mitch is Mr. Conservative. Mr. Responsible." Not that she'd consider marrying him. The attraction she felt for him was purely physical. Nothing more.

"I'm only saying you ought to give Mitch a chance. Has he given you any reason to think he'd stifle you?"

"Only that he's conservative, responsible, worried about what people think…." And he had the ability to make her forget about everything and everyone when he was around. Is that what being in love did to people? Made them lose track of themselves?

Cassie laughed. "Okay. Okay. I get the idea. But it wouldn't hurt you to think about finding *someone* to settle down with. And Mitch seems like as good a candidate as any."

She rolled her eyes. "Don't do this to me, Cassie."

"Do what?"

"Try to 'convert' me. I swear, happily married people are as bad as ex-smokers or recovering alcoholics. They want everyone to see things their way."

Cassie smiled. "Okay, so maybe I am guilty of a little of that. But you're my best friend. I want you to be as happy as I am."

"I'm happy. And I'll be happier when Mitch finally admits that sex can be fun and a store devoted to sexual fun is a great idea."

"Okay. Do you think this dress will do the trick?"

Midnight-blue chiffon fell in tiny pleats from a banded collar, with a keyhole neckline that would show a lot of cleavage, without looking trashy. The soft fabric would drape every curve, and a slit up the side would give a glimpse of leg when she moved.

"Sexy, but classy." She nodded. "It has definite possibilities." With the right accessories, she'd give Mitch an evening he'd never forget.

15

MITCH COULDN'T BELIEVE he was actually *nervous* about this date with Jill. First of all, it wasn't really a date. It was a social obligation. A business function. A chance for him to explain his reasoning about the store and make her understand that, while he was definitely attracted to her, she wasn't going to change his mind about what he should do with his future.

So why was he nervous? He glanced in the rearview mirror and smoothed his hair. Maybe he should have worn the gray silk tie instead of the navy…

Oh, hell. He sounded like an old woman. *Get out of the car and get on with this,* he ordered himself.

Jill's apartment was in a converted house near the university. A Bohemian kind of place where students, professors, artists, musicians and various free spirits congregated. A sign beneath the apartment number read No Whining!

Mitch rang the bell and waited. The door across the hall opened and a white-haired man in a pink paisley shirt peered out. "If you're one of those evangelist fellows, you don't want to mess with Jill," he said. "The last one quit the ministry after a half hour with her. Last I heard, he was working as one of those Chippendale dancers."

"Um, I'm not an evangelist." He straightened his

jacket and wondered again if he should have gone for the gray tie.

"She's pretty rough with salesmen, too. Keeps 'em talkin' for hours, never buys anything."

"It's all right, Professor Simon. Mitch is my date."

Relieved, Mitch turned to smile at her, but the expression faltered before it reached his lips. Dazed, he had an impression of soft curves draped in some sort of shimmery blue fabric. Her hair was up, revealing the long creamy column of her neck and the soft curve of her bare shoulders. She looked beautiful. Elegant. And sexy enough to make a man forget his own name.

"Date, huh?" Professor Simon grunted. "Not your usual type. Thought he was one of them evangelist fellows."

"Everything's fine, Professor. I promise." She put her hand on Mitch's arm. "Why don't you come inside while I get my wrap."

He followed her inside, eyes focusing on the subtle sway of her hips. The fabric of her dress shifted over her bottom with each step. He fought the urge to reach out and cup her backside. Would it feel as smooth and satiny as it looked?

"Don't mind Professor Simon. He takes a sort of fatherly interest in me—thinks he has to look out for me." She handed him a fringed silk shawl and turned her back to him.

He draped the shawl around her shoulders. From this vantage point, he was looking almost straight down on the oval cutout in the front of her dress, into the deep cleft between her breasts. The hard points of her nipples were just visible beneath the folds of fabric, teasing him with their nearness. He felt himself grow harder, and forced his gaze away.

"What happened with the evangelist?" he asked when she'd turned to face him again.

She laughed. "Oh, that. Well, he was really a very handsome young man. I told him good looks were as much a gift from God as a beautiful voice or a talent for teaching. And that since it was sinful to waste a talent, he really ought to be taking advantage of that great body of his instead of hiding it under an ill-fitting suit."

Mitch could imagine an innocent young man falling under the spell of Jill's unabashed sex appeal. The poor boy probably forgot all about religion as soon as she opened the door. "So he really became a Chippendale's dancer?"

"A very good one, from what I hear."

She locked the door behind them, then walked beside him to the car. The fabric of her dress rustled when she walked, making him think of the sound it would make sliding to the floor.

He opened the passenger door and she slid inside, the dress falling open at midthigh to reveal her smooth, lightly tanned skin. So she wasn't wearing panty hose. What else wasn't she wearing?

He reminded himself he had no intention of finding out as he walked around to the driver's side. The whole point of this evening was to convince her how wrong it would be for them to continue this pretense that anything she could do would change his mind.

"I found out some friends of mine will be attending the banquet tonight."

"Oh, who is that?"

"Cassie and Guy Walters. He owns Mountain Outfitters. He's up for an award."

"You'll have to be sure to introduce me."

"I will. You'll like them both." She smiled. "Actually you could say it's because of them that I got the job at Just 4 Play."

"How is that?"

"I took Cassie shopping one day not long after she'd started seeing Guy. I'd been in a couple times before, but I guess that was the first day I really saw the possibilities of a place like that to help someone in a relationship. I went back a couple of times by myself to shop and one day I saw the Help Wanted sign in the window and knew that was the job for me."

"What did you do before that?"

"I was a barrista in a coffee shop." She laughed. "Don't look at me like that."

Too late, he realized he had been frowning at her.

"I know exactly what you're thinking, and I've heard it before." She adjusted the shawl across her shoulders. "Why is a woman with a college education content to work at so-called menial jobs?"

"I wouldn't have used the words 'menial' but you do seem overqualified for the work you've chosen."

"That's just it—it's work I've *chosen.* I like working with the public. And I like working an unconventional schedule, and not being forced into some corporate mold." She tied the ends of the shawl in a knot under her breasts. "This way, if I suddenly decide to take off on a six-month trip to the Amazon, it's easy for me to pick up and go."

Had he ever been that free in his life? He shook his head. Never. He couldn't even imagine. "What about your family, other obligations?"

"My mom and dad are in the Galápagos this year, studying turtles or something. Jenny was my only sibling. I don't even have a cat."

"No commitments," he murmured. "Don't you get lonely sometimes?"

She turned slightly toward him, the dress falling open at the knees. "Why should I be lonely? I have friends all over the world."

But there was a difference between having friends and having someone special to share your life with, wasn't there?

"I'm glad Cassie and Guy will be there tonight. I was afraid I wouldn't know anyone and you'd know everyone."

"Actually I don't know very many people who will be here." Mort, of course. Maybe Archie. A few others, familiar to him from various small business seminars or open houses held in the area.

"But I thought these were your friends."

He shook his head. "No. Acquaintances. Not friends." Strange, a few weeks ago he wouldn't have made the distinction. He would have seen the people at tonight's banquet as important contacts, people who could help him get ahead. People he wanted to have as friends.

Now the harsh words in the Chamber of Commerce's rejection letter to Uncle Grif left a bitter taste in his mouth. He no longer saw those business and society people as so important.

Jill reached out and squeezed his arm. "I'm sure we'll have a wonderful time tonight," she said. "In fact, I'm making it my personal mission to see that you enjoy yourself. After all, who knows when we'll have a night like this again?"

"I CAN'T BELIEVE I LET YOU talk me into doing this again." Sid bypassed the alarm, then shut and locked the door behind him and Lana.

She smiled and squeezed his arm. "Don't tell me you didn't enjoy last time."

Heat spread up the back of his neck as he remembered the last time. "You know better than that. But what's wrong with my apartment?"

"You have a roommate, remember?"

"We could always ask him to leave. He'd be cool about it. Or what's wrong with your place?"

"My place is so boring." She smiled and looked around them. "It's a shame Mitch is going to shut this place down."

"You didn't think that the first time you were here."

"I guess I changed my mind." She gave him a smoldering look. "About a lot of things."

He reached for her, but she moved away. "I was thinking tonight we might try on a couple of the costumes."

Frowning, he followed her over to the costume rack. It's not that he didn't enjoy being here with Lana, or being anywhere with her, for that matter. But how much of their sudden relationship had to do with him, and how much with the shop?

She selected the French maid costume and held it against her. "How do you think I'd look in this?"

"You know I think you'd look great in anything. In fact, I think what you've got on right now is pretty hot." He moved closer and pulled her into his arms. What she had on was a conservative black suit with a tight, straight skirt, a long jacket and a starched white shirt underneath. Ever since he'd picked her up this evening, he'd been thinking about peeling off that prim and proper outer layer to reveal the wild woman hidden underneath.

"Mmm. I'm glad you're wearing your leathers tonight." She nuzzled against the lapel of his jacket. "I think they're very sexy."

"Uh-huh." He kissed the top of her head, inhaling the vanilla scent of her perfume. "I still think we ought to get out of here and go someplace more private. What if someone comes in and we get caught?"

"The store's closed, isn't it? And Mitch isn't likely to show up. He's at the Chamber of Commerce banquet."

Sid frowned. He was sure he hadn't mentioned Mitch's plans to Lana. "How do you know that?"

"My father told me." She began kissing his throat. "I think he wants me and Mitch to get back together."

Sid stiffened. "Have you told him about me?"

"No. It's none of his business." She grinned up at him. "You're my little secret. Or maybe I should say, my big secret."

She tried to cuddle closer, but he gently pushed her away. "Lana, don't you think you're going to have to tell your family about me if we keep seeing each other?"

"One day, sure. But not right now. I'm tired of them interfering in my life."

He frowned. "Are you sure you're not just ashamed of me?"

Her eyes widened. "No! Sid, why would you say that?"

He crossed his arms over his chest and looked at her. "I'm not stupid. I know I'm not exactly the kind of guy a woman takes home to Mr. and Mrs. Establishment."

"I'm a grown woman. If I want to date someone, I will. And it won't matter to me what my parents or anyone else thinks."

He shook his head. "I think you mean that, but I'm not so sure you can."

She put the costume back on the rack and came over to him. "Sid, what is this about?"

He studied the toes of his boots. "I think…I care a lot more about you than any woman in a long time. Maybe more than I should. I just want to know what I'm getting into here."

He was startled to hear a sound like laughter. When she looked up, she was smiling and shaking her head. "Poor Sid. Don't you know you can't be practical or plan ahead when it comes to matters of the heart?" She stood on tiptoe and slipped her arms around his neck. "I felt something special the first time I saw you. It wasn't logical or reasonable. It scared me, but I couldn't ignore it. I didn't dare."

"But was it me that made you feel that way, or…or the leather and jewelry and wild hair…and the fact that I work at a place like Just 4 Play?"

She looked into his eyes. "As crazy as it sounds, I really think it was you. Something in you stirred up something in me." She pulled his head down to hers and kissed him, a long, slow, sweet kiss that made his heart pound and his head spin.

When they parted again, he smoothed his hands down her back. "So, you think we could make it in spite of our differences?"

"I don't know anything for sure. Except that you worry too much." She smiled. "Let's take it one day at a time and see where things lead." She pressed close against him. "Now do you want to be the carpenter tonight, or my Roman slave?"

SHORTLY AFTER THEY ARRIVED at the banquet hall, Jill retreated to the ladies' room to touch up her makeup. Mostly she wanted a chance to collect herself. She would need all her wits about her if this evening was going to turn out the way she wanted it to.

Just when she thought she knew Mitch, he surprised her again. Take tonight, for instance. She figured he'd be raring to go out there and mix and mingle, to make a good impression on all the movers and shakers in the Boulder business world. Instead, he'd seemed nervous, reluctant to even be here. As if he was afraid they wouldn't like him.

Or maybe that he wouldn't like them.

She pulled out her lipstick and touched it up. Ravishing Red. She'd read a study once that said that men instinctively saw red lips as a sign of sexual arousal. As if she wasn't already sending out half a dozen other unconscious signals. The truth was, she'd been hot and bothered all afternoon, thinking about tonight.

She could tell by the way Mitch looked at her when he thought she wasn't paying attention that he liked the dress. That he liked her in it. Now if she could only convince him that he'd like her more out of it.

The door swung open and Cassie walked in. "There you are. I've been looking all over. What are you doing hiding in here?"

"I'm not hiding. I needed to freshen up."

Cassie took a step back and let out a wolf whistle. "You do look hot in that dress, girlfriend."

She smiled. "I feel hot. Did you see Mitch?"

"I did indeed. He's the one who told me you were in here."

She watched Cassie's face in the mirror. "And, what do you think?"

"I think you need your head examined if you let this one get away."

She straightened and smoothed the dress over her

hips. "I think I'm using the right bait to reel him in tonight." She dropped the lipstick back into her purse. "Are you and Guy sitting at our table?"

"We weren't, but I switched place cards with some old man. I don't think he was too happy about it. Mitch seemed pleased, though."

"He probably took one look at you and forgot all about me." She shook her finger at her friend. "You'd better watch out, or I'll tell Guy."

"I'm sure Guy is worried." Cassie leaned toward the mirror and smoothed her hair. "I might as well be invisible, seated at a table with you and that dress. We'll be lucky if we're not mobbed by your many admirers."

"Better have some more wine. It's going to your head."

Still laughing together, the two friends joined Guy and Mitch at a table for six near the back of the room. The third couple introduced themselves as Barbara and Ben Berman. "Berman plumbing and hardware," Ben said, offering a card. "My specialty is low-flow toilets that really work."

"I guess that's pretty important." Jill managed to keep a straight face and slipped the card into her evening bag.

When she sat down next to him, Mitch leaned over to whisper in her ear. "Only three more hours of this. Aren't you glad you came?"

She choked off a giggle. "I'll do my best to keep you awake."

A troop of waiters dispensed salads to each table. Maggie Berman prodded hers with a fork. "What is this supposed to be?" she asked, holding up a dark green frill.

"It's arugula," Cassie said.

"Hmmph." Mrs. Berman dropped the offending morsel. "Looks like ditch weeds to me."

Halfway through this first course, Mr. Berman began a long story about installing plumbing at the state penitentiary. Jill slipped off her shoes and nudged Mitch's ankle with her toe.

His fork stilled halfway between his plate and his mouth. She watched him out of the corner of her eye, a faint smile on her lips. She began to stroke his calf, up and down, slowly. Sensuously.

He leaned over and whispered in her ear, "What do you think you're doing?"

"You looked a little uptight. I thought I'd help you relax."

"I don't need your help, thank you." He moved his chair over, just out of her reach.

Dinner arrived under a metal cover—chicken breast on a bed of rice, covered by a sunshine-yellow sauce, with a side of zucchini and carrots. "Hope you're hungry," Mitch said.

"Not for food." But she spoke only loud enough for him to hear.

She knew he had heard because he looked at her more closely. She picked up her fork and pretended great interest in her dinner.

Halfway through this second course, she noticed an older man at another table staring at them. "Mitch, who is that?" she asked, nodding toward the man.

He ducked his head, frowning. "That's Mort Montgomery. President of Guarantee National Bank."

"Is he related to Lana Montgomery?"

"He's her father."

She regarded the old man again. She supposed there was a faint resemblance around the nose and eyes, though Lana must get most of her good looks from her mother. "Is that why he keeps staring over here? Is he mad at you because you and Lana split up?"

"I don't think so. I think he's pissed off because he was supposed to be sitting here and Cassie switched the place cards."

She laughed. "Maybe you can speak to him later and apologize."

He shrugged. "I'm just as glad he's not sitting here. He gets on my nerves."

"Oh? Why is that?"

He glanced toward Mort, who had turned back around and was eating. Then he moved his chair closer to hers again. "He seems to think that because his bank is loaning me the money for the restaurant remodel, he can tell me what to do."

"One more reason not to remodel." She leaned back to allow the waiter to take her plate.

Mitch shook his head. "You never give up, do you?"

"Never." She met his gaze and held it. "I always get what I want…eventually."

"That's something we need to talk about—"

"Ladies and gentlemen. If I may have your attention, we'll get started with tonight's program."

The others at the table turned their chairs to face the dais at the front of the room. Waiters delivered dessert: chocolate-dipped strawberries.

Jill soon lost interest in the speakers and focused her attention on the strawberries, her absolute favorite dessert. They made the whole boring dinner worthwhile.

MITCH TRIED TO PAY attention to the banquet speaker, who was outlining plans for economic development for the coming year. Certainly this would have some bearing on Mitch's own success. He'd be wise to pay attention.

Except that Jill was sitting beside him, infinitely more interesting than the speaker. He glanced at her during a lull while the speaker shuffled through his notes and watched, mesmerized, as she selected a strawberry from the plate in front of her and began to lick off the chocolate coating.

Her tongue darted out to encircle the narrow end of the berry, then flattened to smooth over the sides. She worked quickly, daintily, finally sucking off the last bit of chocolate before popping the naked berry into her mouth.

He let out the breath he'd been holding and grabbed for his glass of water. "Mitch, are you okay?" She leaned toward him, concerned. Unfortunately this provided him with a stunning view of her cleavage. "I'm fine," he croaked, and drank more water.

"Here. Have a strawberry." She selected a berry from the dish and held it out to him. He tried to take it from her fingers, but she pressed it against his mouth. "Go ahead. Take a bite."

He bit, sweet juice spurting out and running down his mouth. She captured the drips with her fingers, and licked them off, sliding the full length of each finger into her mouth and withdrawing it slowly. "Good, isn't it?" she murmured.

Mitch looked longingly at his now empty water glass. Not that that had been doing much to cool him off anyway.

"Here. Finish your berry." She held the half-eaten fruit to his mouth again and he accepted it. But along with the berry, he captured the tips of her fingers. She giggled as his tongue brushed against her and her eyes darkened with arousal.

The speaker finished and announced the time had come to hand out awards. The Bermans declared that they were leaving. Mr. Berman solemnly shook hands all around and passed out more business cards.

Jill scooted her chair closer to Mitch, until her thigh was almost touching his under the table. "I want to see the podium when Guy goes up to get his award," she explained.

He nodded, aware of the warm length of her so close to him. She reached past him for creamer for her coffee and her breast brushed his arm. He was pretty sure she wasn't wearing a bra.

Guy was announced as Young Entrepreneur of the Year. He went up to accept the award, taking Cassie with him and leaving them alone.

Jill reached over and began stroking his thigh, her finger tracing the seam of his pants up the outside, then around to the inside. Up…up.

He grabbed her hand before she reached his crotch. Already his erection strained against his zipper. No telling what would happen if she touched him there.

She smiled, and obligingly moved their now-entwined hands away, this time to her own thigh, guiding him along the path of her slit skirt, up, up, to her hip, to her waist. Her skin was cool and silky against his fingertips.

She leaned over to whisper in his ear, "I'm not wearing any underwear."

He swallowed. "I noticed."

"Panty lines would ruin this dress, don't you think?"

He tried to pull away, but she held him fast, this time bringing his hand down, around her thigh to her crotch.

She was warm and wet and naked. Very naked. Shaved. The image this conjured raised his temperature another notch.

"Jill, you've got to stop this!" he hissed.

She looked at him with a challenge in her eyes. "Why?"

"Because it's crazy!" She was driving him crazy. If she kept this up, he'd be tempted to dive under the table with her, business community be damned.

She smiled. "You exaggerate. But to my way of thinking, even one reason why it's a good idea is enough to make it worthwhile."

He looked her in the eye and lowered his voice. "I don't intend for anything…physical to happen tonight. I invited you here so that we could talk and get to know each other better without sex getting in the way."

She released his hand and rearranged her shawl over her arms. "I know you're not really against sex, Mitch. You're just afraid to let yourself go. Afraid of what might happen if you put your own thoughts and feelings and desires first for a change."

Her words startled him. Was she right? Was all his talk of propriety and common sense merely a smoke screen to hide his fear? But what was he afraid of?

He looked around them, at the tables full of bored businessmen and women in their fancy clothes. Once upon a time his goal in life had been to impress people like them. To make them accept him into their ranks. To earn their respect for himself and Meg.

But now he realized that respect was worthless. Whatever they said to his face, it wouldn't change how they felt about him in their hearts. He would always be "that Landry boy" from the wrong side of town. Grif Landry's nephew who inherited the sex toy shop. For years after his restaurant opened, the old guard would probably still refer to it as "the Chinese place where the sex shop used to be."

He glanced at Jill. She was sipping her coffee and listening to Guy thank half a dozen people who had helped him to win this award. She looked like royalty, sitting there. Above them all. Maybe because she didn't care what anyone thought of her. He envied her that courage. Had her sister taught her that, or did she come by it naturally?

He shoved back his chair and stood. She looked up at him. "Where are you going?"

"I need to get out of here. Get some fresh air."

"All right." She stood and gathered up her purse."

"No, you stay." He lowered his voice, aware of the censorious looks from those around them. "Stay with Cassie and Guy."

"No, I'm coming with you."

16

SHE STOPPED HIM IN THE HALL outside the ladies' room. "Do you mind waiting while I go in here?"

He cocked one eyebrow. "Afraid I'll run away?"

"You might try." She trailed her finger along his lapel. "But I'd catch you."

He chuckled and shook his head. "I'll wait for you."

He leaned against the wall and thought about Jill. When had a woman ever made him laugh so much? Or made him want her so much? What was really happening between them? She said she didn't want commitments and he couldn't afford to give her any.

But she was lying. What woman—what person—didn't want a lasting connection to another person? Without that connection there was always a void to fill. Look at his mother. Though there had been subtle signs of her illness for years, it wasn't until after his father's death that she became unable to cope. She'd lost her connection to the man she loved, and eventually to the world.

Not everyone reacted so drastically, but still, it proved how much people needed to belong. He needed it. Jill needed it. They'd both find it one day, with someone else.

The thought hurt deep in his chest. Jill had shown him so much passion and given herself so generously, but knowing it couldn't last made him feel empty inside. If only his life weren't so complicated right now…

"Mitch! I've been looking all over for you. We need to talk."

He looked up and saw Mort Montgomery striding toward him.

He straightened, forcing a smile he didn't feel. "Mort. How are the awards going?"

"Long as usual." Mort pulled out a handkerchief and blew his nose. "Why some people think they have to thank everyone from their mother to the janitor, I'll never know." He shoved the handkerchief back in his pocket. "Listen, we were supposed to sit together tonight and then some woman had the nerve to change the seating cards. Not a friend of yours, I hope?"

He looked down at his shoes and made a noncommittal noise.

"She was probably a friend of that plumber, Berman," Mort continued. "Annoying man. Very lower-class. I can't believe they let someone like that in, but apparently someone on the board owed him a favor."

Mitch glanced toward the ladies' room door. What was taking Jill so long?

"I've been thinking about the grand opening for Ping's Peking Palace," Mort continued. "What would you think of hiring Chinese acrobats from the circus to perform in the center of the restaurant? We could bill it as a real cultural activity. It would get us a lot of attention."

Mitch shoved his hands into his pants pockets. "I haven't thought much about the opening yet. Remodeling hasn't even started."

"You've got to think ahead, boy. The key to success is making a grand statement. Don't settle for what the other guys are doing. I'm also thinking Chinese dancers. Pretty girls. You know what they say, sex sells.'' He elbowed Mitch sharply in the ribs. "And you'd know about that, wouldn't you?''

"Look, Mort, I appreciate your…your enthusiasm. But I want a more…a more *dignified* image for the restaurant. Something elegant. Not circus acrobats and exotic dancers.''

"No, no, no. If people want elegant, they'll go eat French food. Or steak. With Chinese food, they want fun. Entertainment. Eighty choices on the menu, chopsticks, food they can't recognize or pronounce.'' Mort tapped his chest. "You leave it to me. I know about these things.''

"And I know what I want in my restaurant.'' He straightened and folded his arms across his chest. "I didn't ask for your input, Mort, and I don't want it.''

"Well.'' Mort took a step back. "Are you forgetting where the money is coming from to pay for this pipe dream of yours?''

"It's coming from the bank. A legitimate business loan.''

"I got you that loan. They wouldn't have looked twice at somebody with no real background, no family name, no Ivy League education. I did it as a favor to Lana. I can see now she was smart in dumping you.''

"Goodbye, Mort.'' Jill or no Jill, he had to leave. If he stood here one minute longer, he was going to say something, or do something he knew he'd regret.

At that moment, she emerged from the ladies' room, her eyes glowing with some private mirth. She nodded to Mort, who stared at her, mouth opened, then slipped her arm into the crook of Mitch's elbow. "Come on,

darling,'' she said. "Let's leave this boring place with
all these boring people.''

She waited until they were in the parking lot before
she burst out laughing. He joined her, tension draining
from him. "I'll bet he's still standing back there with
his mouth hanging open,'' Mitch said. He squeezed her
hands. "You showed up at exactly the right time. I was
on the verge of decking him.''

"I was standing in the foyer, listening, trying to decide if I should interrupt or not.'' She made a face.
"He's not a very nice person, is he?''

He shook his head and unlocked the car door. "I think
he saw me as a puppet he could manipulate. And I guess
for a while at least, I let him get away with it.'' He
frowned and looked back toward the banquet hall. "I
thought he and others like him could get me to where I
wanted to be, so it didn't matter if I didn't particularly
like them or their methods.''

She came around the car and took his arm. "Let's not
go yet,'' she said. "You wanted fresh air. Let's go for
a walk.''

"All right.'' A walk might be just what he needed.
Fresh air and a chance to put some physical distance
between himself and Jill. If he stayed with her in close
quarters much longer, no telling what he might do.

THE PARK WAS ONE OF MANY such green spaces dotted
throughout the city. A shaded cinder path wound alongside Boulder Creek, interspersed with marble benches
and picnic tables. They passed a ball field, the vapor
lights casting a pink glow over the empty base paths and
pitcher's mound. They came to a bridge over a waterfall
and crossed over to a small island.

The night air was cool, but not uncomfortably so. Jill

drew her shawl more tightly about her shoulders and reached for Mitch's hand. He hadn't said a word since they'd left the parking lot. She knew his mind was still back at the banquet, perhaps rehearsing things he wished he'd said. Or things he wished he hadn't said.

"What will happen now?" she asked. "Will you lose the money for the restaurant?"

He shook his head. "It's a legitimate loan and it's been approved. I don't think they can pull it."

She heard the doubt in his voice.

"It's going to be a struggle to do things the way I want now. Mort's going to be after me every step of the way."

"But it will be worth it to have things the way you want," she said.

He glanced at her. "I'm surprised you're not telling me to give up on the restaurant."

They came to a bench by the side of the path. By silent agreement, they sat down. "You already know what I think," she said. "I'm just trying to be agreeable."

He laughed. "When were you ever agreeable?"

"Oh, I can be." She slid her arm around his neck and kissed him. Tenderly. A kiss meant to comfort as much as to arouse.

He responded, his arms encircling her, his mouth opening to taste her more fully. She slid into his lap, her breasts flattened against his chest, the sensitive tips aching with need. His erection strained between them. "You want me, Mitch. Why not admit it?"

"I never said I didn't want you." He looked at her, his eyes dark, and so serious. "But where exactly are we going with this…relationship?"

"Why do we have to go anywhere? We're two people

interested in pleasing each other and having a good time.''

''I'm not sure looking at it that way is such a good idea.''

''I think it's a very good idea.'' She tried to kiss him again, but he pushed her away.

''No, Jill. I mean it. There's no sense continuing what we both know won't lead to anything.''

Why does it have to lead to anything? She stood. All right. If he was going to be stubborn about it, she had a plan B. ''You're right,'' she said. ''Why should we do this to ourselves?'' She handed him her purse. ''Would you hold this a minute?''

He accepted the purse and she reached down and slipped off one shoe.

''What are you doing?'' he asked.

She handed him the shoe, then the other. ''I don't intend to be frustrated one minute longer.'' Then she started walking down the path, toward a grove of trees in the center of the island. ''Catch me if you can, Mitch,'' she called over her shoulder. ''I promise I'll make it worth your while.''

MITCH STARED AFTER HER, still cradling her shoes and purse. Was she going off the deep end? Crazy even?

He thought of his mother's first breakdown after his father's death. She'd taken off all her clothes and run screaming into the street. A terrified Mitch, only seventeen at the time, had run after her. It had taken him and two paramedics to subdue her.

But no, there was nothing manic about Jill's behavior. In fact, she was almost too casual. Deliberate.

He followed her down the path. A dozen yards farther

on, he came upon the shawl, in a heap in the middle of the path.

He picked it up. Some distance ahead in the darkness, he thought he heard her laugh. He set off again, faster now. He almost wasn't surprised when he spotted the dress, a dark blue puddle on the gravel. He added it to his collection and hurried on.

The path disappeared into the trees. When he emerged on the other side, he found her, seated on a marble bench in front of a cluster of bushes. She was naked except for a single strand of pearls between her breasts.

His steps slowed, then stopped.

The moon shown like a spotlight on her ivory skin, shadowing the valley between her full breasts, highlighting the dusky nipples. His gaze dropped and he saw that he'd been right before—she was shaved completely naked, her every secret exposed.

She stood and started toward him, the pearls swaying gently. He dropped the armful of clothing and stood still, waiting.

When she reached him, he gathered her into his arms. "Mitch, your heart is pounding."

"You frightened me, running away like that." He buried his nose in her hair, savoring her sweetness, fighting for composure. "I thought…" He shook his head. "It doesn't matter what I thought." He raised his head and smiled down at her. "You won't stop at anything to get what you want, will you?"

"Only because I want you."

What man could hear those words and not be undone? She loosened the knot on his tie and he helped her remove it, and the rest of his clothes, until he was standing naked before her.

She stroked his erection, sending a tremor through

him. Some part of him whispered that he could still stop her, but he was through lying to himself. "I want you, too," he whispered, and kissed the tender skin beneath her jaw.

She led him to the bench and pushed him down, then she straddled him. She was wet, and hot, and smelled of jasmine and sex. "What is that perfume you always wear?" he asked.

"Oriental Love Potion."

He fingered the pearls. "Do we sell it at the store?"

"Oh, yes. And lots of other wonderful things." She shifted in his lap, each movement bringing them closer together, closer to the edge.

She bent her head and began to kiss his nipples, first one, then the other, her tongue licking and teasing, first sucking, then bathing them with her hot breath. He tried to move away, to slow things down a little, but she clamped her thighs tightly around him, trapping him.

The pearls hung down, tickling him, and her hair, coming loose from its pins, trailed across his neck. He closed his eyes, telling himself he would sit back and enjoy. Everything would be fine.

A faint noise in the stillness startled him. He opened his eyes again and straightened. "Do you think it's safe here? Maybe we ought to go back to my car, to my apartment."

"It's a public place. Someone could come along any minute." She smiled at him. "That adds to the excitement, don't you think?"

"Then we'd better hurry." He smiled weakly. "I don't know how much more excitement I can stand."

She shifted, so that she was sitting sideways in his lap. "First, I want to show you something useful. Do you know what the G-spot is?"

"I've heard of it. I thought it was a myth."

She smiled. "Oh, no. It's very real. If you stimulate a woman's G-spot, you can give her the most incredible orgasm."

She leaned back, then took his fingers and guided them inside her. "It's a concentration of nerve endings two to three inches inside, toward the front. Stroke it gently."

He knew he'd found the right spot when she gasped. "Y…yes. That's it. *Ohhhhh.*"

He bent and suckled her nipples, raising his head from time to time to watch her. A warm flush spread up from her breasts. Her lips were swollen, parted, her eyes closed. She trembled and he sensed she was very close to her release. A wave of incredible tenderness swept over him. He loved that he could make her feel this way.

The crunch of gravel sent his whole body on alert. Then voices drifted to them, just on the other side of the path.

He grabbed Jill by the shoulders and shook her. "Someone's here," he hissed.

She looked at him, dazed. He shoved her toward the bushes behind them, then hurried to gather up their clothes and dove in after her.

On his knees, he peered through the bushes and watched a couple take their place on the bench. Jill knelt beside him. "My shoes!" she whispered.

She pointed toward one end of the bench. Her shoes lay there on their sides. "Maybe they won't see them," he said.

"Maybe not."

The couple began to kiss, the man's hand sliding under the woman's shirt to cup her breast. Mitch felt his cock jerk in response. Jill eased him back. "We might as well make ourselves comfortable,'' she said. Her tongue grazed the edge of his earlobe, sending a shiver through him that had nothing to do with the cold.

He lay down on the shawl and she nestled alongside him. It wasn't as close as he wanted to be to her, but it was as close as they could get.

On the bench, the woman began unbuttoning the man's shirt. ''I feel like a voyeur,'' he whispered.

''Then close your eyes and don't look.'' She kissed each eyelid shut, then skirted his mouth and began kissing her way down his throat, to his chest.

''What are you doing?''

He tried to stop her, but she shook him off. ''I'm distracting you.''

She kissed his nipples, then trailed a path to his navel, across his stomach, down to his cock. She licked the head, teasing it, then smoothed her tongue along the shaft. He thought of the strawberry, so expertly denuded by her tongue. He clamped his teeth together, strangling a groan. On the other side of the bushes, the woman giggled, then her laughter became a low sigh.

Jill leaned away from him, reaching for her purse.

''What are you doing?''

''I brought some condoms.'' She pulled out a packet and tore it open with her teeth. The condom looked like a bright red balloon.

''It's red.''

''Part of our Neon Nights collection.'' She began unrolling it over him.

''That looks ridiculous.''

She giggled. ''Yes, well, the male anatomy certainly proves the creator had a sense of humor.''

He bit his tongue to keep from laughing out loud. He couldn't remember ever laughing during sex. Sex was serious business. But not to Jill. With her it was…dare he say it? Fun.

His laughter faded as she slid over him. She tightened around him, then withdrew. Her strokes were long and sure, building in intensity. He closed his eyes and surrendered to the sensations. He brought his hands up to caress her buttocks, her breasts. The pearls swung between them, swaying with their rhythm.

Jill rode him hard, never letting up. He dug his heels into the ground, and groaned as spiraling waves of release washed over him. He told himself to stay in control, to wait for her, but he'd been to the edge already too many times tonight. As he finally went over, in his mind he screamed her name, though in reality it emerged a whisper. "Jill." He drew her close, savoring the sensation of her body beside his. "You are amazing," he gasped after a while.

He felt her smile against his chest. "I could say the same about you."

"Are Romeo and Juliet still out there?"

She raised up on one elbow to look out. "Still there. Looks like they could be there a while."

He closed his eyes. "Then I guess we're stuck here for a while."

"Then we might as well make good use of the time." She slid down his body once more, her skin warm and satiny against him.

He opened his eyes wide when he felt her tongue on him once more. "What do you think you're doing?" he growled.

Her laughter was muffled. "What does it feel like I'm doing?"

"No, Jill, I don't think—" But his body obviously had a different opinion. When he raised up on his elbows to look at her, he realized he was hard all over again. "I don't believe this," he said, looking down at himself.

She smiled and reached for her purse. "I have another condom."

"Another red one?"

"Green this time."

"Great. I'll look like an alien."

"I've always wanted to make love to an alien."

"You'll have to settle for me."

"Even better."

"Wait." He stopped her as she started to unroll the green condom. "Come up here for a minute." He patted the ground beside him.

She lay beside him with her head on his shoulder. He smoothed his hand along her shoulder, down the dip of her waist, across the curve of her hip. He wanted to fix this moment in his mind, this sensation of being so close to her.

They kissed, the long slow caress of lovers who have all the time in the world. The frantic urgency of their earlier lovemaking was gone, replaced by this sweet languor. He traced the bow of her mouth with his tongue, then trailed a path down her throat, pausing to feel her pulse throbbing against his mouth in a rhythm that matched his own heartbeat.

Behind him, he could hear the other couple, the rustling of their clothing, the low muffled moans that spoke of their own lovemaking. The sounds fueled his own desire. "Lie back," he urged Jill, pressing his palm against her stomach. "Let me enjoy all of you."

She lay back, eyes open, watching him. He stroked her breasts, first with his fingers, then with his tongue. He started slowly, intending only to tease a little, but her response urged him for more. As he licked and suckled, she squirmed beneath him, and bit her knuckle to keep from crying out. He'd never known a woman who was so incredibly responsive, or one so aware of her own body.

He moved down, trailing his tongue across her belly, to the juncture of her thighs. She was smooth and soft, totally naked, the sensation kicking his arousal up another notch. He traced his tongue along her sex, tasting the saltiness of their previous coupling.

He flicked his tongue across her, smiling at the way she arched toward him, offering herself. Then he began to lave her in earnest, caressing the tender flesh, his head turned to watch her reaction.

She was beautiful, in this as in everything else. Head back, eyes closed, hair in a wild tangle around her shoulders, she gave herself up to the moment, her body poised, anticipating ecstasy. He slid two fingers into her, wanting to feel the moment she came.

She let out a muffled cry as her climax rocked through her. He buried his face against her thigh, his arms around her, holding her as she shook. Then she was tugging at his hair, her voice a harsh whisper. "Hurry," she said. "I want you in me."

He fumbled with the condom, cursing the person who had designed the packaging. Finally he ripped the plastic with his teeth and rolled on the bright green bit of latex. "I do look like an alien," he muttered.

"No. The Jolly Green Giant." Jill's eyes sparkled with laughter and more than a little appreciation for his green-clad member.

"Fee, fie, foe, fum. Look out, Jilly, here I come."

She was laughing when he slid into her wet heat, but her laughter soon changed to low cries as they moved

in rhythm. He reached down to stroke her, coaxing her
to move with him to another climax.

Again, he kept his eyes open, watching her. He could
never get enough of watching her. He'd never known a
woman who was so open, so willing to share of herself,
to let him really see her in these moments of lovemaking. Jill didn't hide behind soft lights and dark rooms,
or turn her face away from him. She was willing for him
to see everything as passion overtook her.

His vision blurred as his climax surged through him,
stealing breath and thought. Jill followed him, arching
beneath him, her fingers digging into his back.

They lay together afterward, their bodies entwined,
unmoving, unspeaking. Her uninhibitedness moved him.
He didn't delude himself that he was the first. She'd
made no secret of her experience with men. And he had
had his share of women. But none like Jill. None so
reckless and open. None who made him feel more of a
man, more of a person, apart from family situation or
business prowess or social standing. When Jill looked at
him, he felt she really saw *him*. She had stripped him
naked physically and emotionally. Being with her filled
him with elation and scared him to death.

17

JILL WOKE THE NEXT MORNING, wondering if the previous night had been a dream. Had Mr. Conservative Mitch Landry really made her scream like that? Had they really gone through not two, but *three* condoms, including the Super Stud, which she'd only brought to show him the wide variety the store had to offer?

She closed her eyes and fell back on her pillow again. And had he really been so sweet and tender afterwards, helping her dress and then later, kissing her so sweetly at her door, refusing her suggestion that he come inside and never leave?

She felt like crying, just remembering. He had been such a *gentleman*. Sweet and caring as if…as if he really loved her.

She sat up again, heart pounding. What was happening to her? Of course Mitch Landry wasn't in love with her. In lust…but not in love. And why was she making such a big deal out of it? It wasn't as if she hadn't had great sex before. She smiled. Maybe not that great. With Mitch, it was always…different. Less about her own pleasure and more about pleasing him. He was always so busy worrying about other people—his sister, Grif, even her and Sid. She'd wanted to give him some moments solely for himself.

But then he always turned the tables and did so much for *her*. She glanced at her bedside clock. Less than eight hours since she'd seen him last and already she missed him. Not only the sex, but *him*. She missed his great smile, and the way he talked so formally when he was nervous, the way his mouth said he didn't approve of something she was doing, while his eyes told her he did.

She buried her face in her hands. "What have I gotten myself into now?" She was *not* going to fall in love with Mitch Landry. The idea of spending the rest of her life tied to one man was ridiculous. Especially a man like Mitch, who could be so infuriating.

She threw back the covers and headed for the bathroom. "Some women are the marrying type, but I'm not one of them," she said. "I don't mind hanging out with Mitch for a while, but he has got to understand that I'm not interested in anything permanent."

She stripped off her nightgown and turned on the shower. As she reached for a clean towel, she caught a glimpse of herself in the mirror, a dreamy expression in her eyes, her lips still swollen from Mitch's kisses. *Liar* the image said to her. She closed her eyes and stifled a sob. *Oh, girl, you have messed things up this time. What are you going to do?*

"JILL, WHAT AM I GOING TO do about you...about *us?*" Mitch was confident no one could hear him in the empty store. Just 4 Play was closed on Sundays and he'd come here with the excuse that he needed to work.

Really, he'd come here because it was the closest he could get to being near Jill without actually going to her apartment. He didn't dare do that. If he went there, he'd have to stay. And then he'd never want to leave.

But coming here hadn't been such a great idea, either. Everywhere he looked, something reminded him of her, or of their wild lovemaking here, at the cemetery and last night in the park. The belly dancer's costume she'd worn the day they met shimmered on a mannequin in the front window. The Neon Nights condoms were on a special sale rack by the front counter.

He stopped in the "notions and lotions" department and searched the shelves, then pulled down a bottle of Oriental Love Potion body oil. Closing his eyes, he inhaled deeply the jasmine-and-sex scent that was Jill.

"Get a grip, Mitch," he said out loud, and shoved the bottle of oil back onto the shelf. Last night especially had been awesome—the stuff of fantasy. But that was the whole point. Passion like that couldn't last in the practical, everyday world. Jill had said as much herself when she'd made it plain she wasn't interested in long-term commitment.

Even if it were possible for them to stay together—and that was a big *if*—he wasn't in any position to offer a woman permanence. If and when the restaurant got off the ground, he couldn't guarantee it would be a success. And he still had Meg's medical school tuition to pay for. It might be years before he could afford to get married and settle down.

He shook his head. No, he might as well stop thinking about Jill and get to work. The future depended on work, and it was something he was good at. Something he could control, unlike his mixed-up feelings for Jill.

He collected the Saturday mail from the basket under the counter and went into his office. Uncle Grif's smiley-faced daybed cover was crooked again, some of the smiles twisted into grimaces. He thought of the times he had lain there with Jill. She was a woman who could make even smiley faces seem erotic.

He pushed the thought away and tried to focus on work. He sat at his desk and opened the first envelope, the monthly bill from the security company. He supposed he'd have to let them know about the upcoming remodeling. They'd probably want to move some of the security sensors, or set them differently.

He scanned the bill, then turned to the attached report. It was a record of things like false alarms, number of times the system had reset itself, power outages and things like that. Mostly it was rows of zeroes. Which made the five in the column labeled "silent intruder" stand out. On five different evenings in the past two weeks, a "silent intruder" was recorded.

He picked up the phone and dialed the alarm company. "This is Mitch Landry at Just 4 Play. I'm looking at my monthly report and don't understand what a 'silent intruder' is."

"A silent intruder is when the motion sensors detect movement, but the alarm itself never goes off."

"You mean, the alarm is disarmed."

"No, it's still armed, but the movement detected never triggers an actual alarm."

He glanced up at the light box in the far corner of the room. Every room had a similar sensor, which glowed red with the alarm was armed, and green during the day when the alarm was shut off. "What would cause a silent intruder warning?"

"Have you noticed anything missing, sir? Any merchandise or money?"

He wasn't sure. He'd have to ask Sid, but the manager certainly hadn't said anything about any thefts or losses. "I don't think there's anything missing."

"Then it's either a malfunction or an animal."

"An animal?"

"A mouse. Or a squirrel. Sometimes they get into places looking for food. But they're not large enough to set off the alarm. If I were you, I'd put out a few traps, see what shows up.''

He hung up the phone, still puzzled. He hadn't noticed any signs of mice or marauding squirrels. And would an animal only show up a couple of times a week?

He made a mental note to ask Sid, and picked up the next envelope. A note on official county stationery informed him that his permits for Ping's Peking Palace had been approved. He could start work right away.

He laid the letter aside on the blotter and waited for the feeling of accomplishment or excitement or anticipation that should follow such good news. Instead a sense of disappointment filled him. The dream he'd held for so long didn't really seem like his anymore.

Archie still hadn't dropped by with the new plans, though he'd been quick enough to share them with Mort Montgomery. Mort was likely pissed at him and would spend the next few months, or years, making his life hell, interfering at every turn, as if the restaurant was his own.

He'd apply for Chamber membership and they'd probably accept him, and then talk about him behind his back the way they did the plumber, Ben Berman.

And Jill would leave, and take a job somewhere else, or take that trip to the Amazon she'd talked about. He'd have stuck to his guns and proven his point, but he'd have nothing to show for it.

He pressed the heels of his hands to his eyes and grimaced. Jill again. It all came back to her. Ever since they'd first made love, she'd turned his life upside down, and now he couldn't imagine not having her in his life forever, no matter how impossible that was.

And it *was* impossible. He couldn't be in love with Jill. It made no sense. It would never work. If he kept telling himself that, maybe he'd even come to believe it.

MONDAY MORNING WHEN SHE came into work, Jill decided Sid looked as awful as she felt. His hair was growing back in little spikes all over his head, and he had circles under his eyes a zombie would be proud of. When she had to ask him three times to hand her the price gun so she could finish marking down a group of clearance items, she couldn't hide her irritation.

"You know, you shouldn't party so hardy when you have to come to work the next morning," she said. "You're just about useless."

He gave her a vacant stare. "What? Did you say something?"

"Actually I've been talking for the last ten minutes and you haven't heard a word I've said."

"I'm sorry. I'm a little distracted, I guess."

"More than a little." She shoved aside the items to be priced and leaned on the counter across from him. "What's up?"

He sighed, and plucked at the ring in his right ear. At least he was wearing his jewelry again. Without it, he'd looked naked. "I think I'm in love."

"Uh-huh. Haven't I heard this before?"

"No, I mean *really* in love. As in forsaking all others and all that."

She studied him more closely. It was true she'd never seen Sid this...*moony*...before. "Who's the lucky woman?" she asked. "Anyone I know?"

"It's the one I told you about."

"The classy lady?"

He nodded. "I found out she doesn't want her old boyfriend at all. She wants *me*."

She grinned and shoved his shoulder. "Didn't I tell you? I'd say she sounds like a pretty smart lady."

He sighed again. "Yeah."

"So why don't you look happier?"

"Jill, what am I going to do? This woman is rich and beautiful and sexy and she wants *me*."

"I still don't see the problem."

"It's just…"

They fell silent as Mitch came in. "Good morning," he said, pausing by the counter.

My, didn't he look chipper? And good enough to eat. She kept her expression neutral. "Good morning, Mitch."

"Morning," Sid said glumly.

Mitch looked at the two of them. "Is something wrong?"

"Sid's upset because he's in love with a rich, beautiful woman who is also crazy about him."

Mitch frowned. "And why is this upsetting?"

Sid glared at her. "I've been trying to explain to Jill that me and…and this woman…are from such different backgrounds, I don't see how it can ever work out between us."

Mitch nodded. "I can see how that could be a problem." He tugged at the knot of his tie. "But maybe your differences are precisely what draw you together. Maybe this woman has spent years dating men just like her and she's bored."

Why did he look at her when he said that? None of the men she'd dated had bored her. Though none of them had excited her the way Mitch did, either. "Maybe Sid is exactly the kind of man she's been looking for for years," she said. She met Mitch's gaze and held it. And maybe it didn't matter what you thought you wanted or what you ought to have—when the chemistry was right, you couldn't help yourself.

The thought scared her, but she forced herself to face

it. She didn't know what was happening between her and Mitch, why he made her feel the way he did, but she wasn't going to run away from it. And she wasn't going to let him run away, either.

"I guess I'll just hope for the best and see what happens." Sid slid off the stool and stretched. "Did you have a good weekend, Mitch?" He glanced at Jill. "I forgot to ask you, how did the Chamber of Commerce banquet turn out?"

"Oh, it was fine." He pulled a packet of condoms off the display, examined it and put it back. "Yes. It was, uh, very nice."

Very nice? One of the most mind-blowing experiences of her life and all he could say was very nice?

She glared at him, but he didn't seem to notice. Why wouldn't he look at her? Was he embarrassed? Or worse, did he regret what had happened between them? *Why* were men so hard to figure out?

"Sid, have we ever had a problem with mice?" Mitch asked.

Mice? She blinked. What did mice have to do with anything?

Sid shook his head. "No, I don't think so. Why?"

"Oh, just curious." He started away from them, then turned back. "Do we have a video camera?"

"Uh, yeah. I think there's one in the closet in Grif's— I mean your office."

He nodded. "Thanks."

She stared after him, anger building, as he walked into his office and shut the door.

"So the banquet went okay?" Sid asked.

"I thought so. Now I'm not so sure." She shoved the price gun at him. "Will you finish marking these? I have something I have to do."

When she stepped into Mitch's office, he was halfway in the closet. "Mitch, what's going on?" she asked.

He emerged from the closet, a video camera in his hand. "The security alarm's been showing an intruder some nights. The security company thinks it might be a mouse or some other small animal. So I thought I'd set up a camera to see if I can find out what it is."

"I'm not talking about that. I'm talking about us." She moved over to stand in front of him. "I mean, what's going on with us?"

"You mean besides fantastic sex?" His mouth twitched, as if he was trying not to smile.

How could she stay angry when he looked at her that way? "So you admit it was fantastic?"

He nodded. "I've got scratches on my back to prove it."

She couldn't hold back the laughter anymore. "What have you done with the serious man who used to work in this office?"

"A better question might be what have *you* done with him?" He set aside the camera and gathered her into his arms. "And what am I going to do with you?"

"You could start by kissing me."

He did so, a long slow kiss that led to his hand cupping her breast. "You know, there's this nice daybed right here."

She pulled back. "I'll admit it's tempting, but it wouldn't be very nice to leave Sid with all the work."

He gave a mock sigh. "I suppose you're right. And I have to call the architect. I need to talk to him before Mort Montgomery does."

The elation she'd been feeling vanished. "You mean, you're still going through with the remodel?"

He looked puzzled. "Why wouldn't I?"

"I thought after the other night, what you said about Mort, and the Chamber of Commerce people...after what happened between us..."

He frowned. "You didn't really think I'd change my plans just because of what happened in the park, did you?"

"Yes, I did. I thought I'd finally made you see how good sex could be...how the products we sell here are fun and...and even helpful—I thought you'd feel differently about the store."

He took a step back. "When I was making love to you last night, I wasn't thinking about the store, or about merchandise, or any of those things. I didn't realize to you it was just a form of propaganda."

"Mitch, that's not what I meant—"

He turned away. "I think you'd better leave now. The sooner I can get started on the remodeling, the better for all of us."

She stared at his back, fury growing within her. "I thought that night I was finally getting through to you—making you see that you could live life on your own terms instead of selling out to somebody else's vision of what you ought to do and be."

He whirled back around. "No, what you were really doing was trying to make me fit into *your* vision of what I ought to do and be. You want a man you can fit into your mold and that man isn't me."

She stepped back, stunned by this outburst. "That... that's not what I meant at all," she stammered. But was it? Had she been trying to make Mitch into a different type of man to justify her attraction to him?

"Just...go," he said.

"It could have been so good between us," she whispered. "If you'd have taken the moment for what it was, and not tried to read more into it."

He stood still, his head bowed, not answering. After a moment, she turned and fled, swallowing tears. She'd been right all along. She and Mitch had no future together. They looked at life too differently.

Then why did it hurt so badly to lose him, if she'd never really had him in the first place?

18

Mitch waited until Jill and Sid were gone for the night before he took the video camera out and set it up. He'd spent the day talking to the architect and the construction superintendent, discussing permits and blueprints, reviewing estimates and data sheets. He'd filled every moment with facts and figures, details and numbers, not giving himself a moment to think about Jill and what had happened between them.

But now, alone in the darkened store, the hurt came rushing back. Hurt that he'd been naive enough to believe she really felt something for him, instead of realizing she'd been using him, playing with him to get what she wanted.

She'd warned him, hadn't she, that she was out for fun? "You always take things too seriously," she'd said, and she'd been right.

Fine. That's the kind of man he was. Life was full of serious matters. Obligations. Responsibilities. Maybe Jill couldn't see that, but he knew. And now that she was out of his life, he'd get back to those responsibilities. Forget emotion and passion.

Right now, he concentrated on setting up the video camera. He'd purchased a simple motion detector that would start the tape running when triggered. Of course, if it was something as small as a mouse, he might not get lucky enough to spot it. But if it was something bigger...

He opened the back of the camera to insert a blank tape and was surprised to see a tape already in it. He popped it out and read the hand-written label. "Bachelorette Party." Had somebody been making their own naughty video? Sid...or even Jill?

He walked over to the TV cabinet and inserted the tape into the VCR. While it rewound, he found the remote control and turned on the TV. This was either going to be very interesting...or very dull. But it wasn't as if he had anything better to do tonight.

Jill's face appeared on the screen, her hair done up in two little-girl pigtails. As the camera moved back, he could see she was wearing baby-doll pajamas and fuzzy pink slippers. She had a bottle of champagne in one hand, a pint of ice cream in the other. "Welcome to Cassie Carmichael's bachelorette party," she said.

Cheers went up from the half a dozen other women in the room. They were dressed similarly, in pajamas and slippers, more ice cream, bottles of wine and boxes of chocolate scattered around them. "As you can see, we have everything we need for a great party." Jill gestured at the various refreshments. "And we're ready to give Cassie a last blast with her gal-pals before she becomes an old married woman."

More laughter and applause. "Everybody knows all the best parties involve presents," Jill continued to narrate as the camera focused on a large pile of gaily wrapped packages. "So we've gotten together to present Cassie with a few things we know she'll be needing in her married life."

The camera shifted to Cassie as she tore into the first of her gifts. Hoots of laughter greeted the unveiling of a voluminous flannel nightgown and one of the largest pairs of panties Mitch had ever seen. "Those are for the nights when you don't want him near you," a woman in red, footed pajamas said.

"And for the *other* nights—" A black woman in an oversize football jersey handed over a silver gift bag. Mitch recognized Just 4 Play's logo on the bag.

Cassie pulled out a leopard-print bustier and thong and made a face. "They don't look very comfortable."

"Honey, you won't be wearing them that long," someone said.

Jill stepped forward and took the lingerie. "Allow me to demonstrate." She mugged for the camera. "When choosing sexy lingerie, you want to give it the drop test." She released the leopard-print ensemble and watched the pieces drift to the floor. "You want to know how good they look lying on the floor, because that's where they'll be spending most of their time."

Gales of laughter greeted this announcement and Jill curtsied for the camera.

The next box revealed an extra-large bottle of aspirin and a positively giant purple vibrator. "For times when he's too much...or not enough!"

Other gifts included body paints, penis-shaped soap, an assortment of colorful condoms and a blindfold and feather duster "to keep him in line."

Mitch found himself chuckling along with the women. They were having such a good time, and Jill was directing it all. "All right, all right," she said, clapping her hands to get their attention. "Now it's time for party games. And the first one is...True Confessions!"

"Uh-oh, what kind of game is this?"

"Do we really have to tell the truth?"

"I'm only going to tell false confessions. They're much more interesting."

Jill sat on the floor amid a pile of pillows. "The idea is for each of us to tell our favorite sexual fantasy," she said. "I'm talking your deepest, darkest desire. The thing that gets you excited just thinking about it."

"All right, but then I'm going to need to borrow that vibrator, Cassie."

"No. It's all mine." Cassie grabbed the toy the women had already dubbed "the purple monster."

"No fair! You already have Guy Walters. He ought to be stud enough to keep you busy."

Jill shushed them. "All right everybody. Who wants to go first?"

The black woman—Mitch finally figured out her name was Geneva—stuck up her hand. "I'll do it. And it's not gonna surprise any of y'all to know that my fantasy involves food."

A new wave of laughter. Geneva sat back and closed her eyes, a smile on her face. "All right. Here goes. My fantasy involves being blindfolded while some *handsome* man has his way with me."

"If you're blindfolded, how do you know he's handsome?" Jill asked, giggling.

"I just know he is. Now this is my fantasy. You hush."

"All right, all right. Go on."

"Okay. So this *handsome* man—did I mention he smells really good too? Anyway, he puts this blindfold on me that's made out of this soft, satiny stuff, and he takes off all my clothes…real slow. Then he takes a feather and starts stroking me with it. Tickling, then just barely trailing across my nipples." She covered her breasts with her hands. "Then he has something soft and

Just 4 Play

furry, like rabbit fur, and he's doing the same thing, stroking me with it, all over. And all the time he's doing this, he's telling me how beautiful I am, and how hot he's getting just watching me.

"Then he takes a piece of ice and starts doing the same thing, trailing it all across my body, until he gets to right down between my legs, and I can feel it all melting there."

The other women were silent, focused on Geneva as she described her fantasy. Mitch could feel the tension between them, and his own growing arousal.

"Already, I'm so turned on I can't hardly stand it," Geneva continued. "But instead of doing anything about it, this man goes away and leaves me alone."

"The bastard!" someone said.

Geneva chuckled. "No, because he comes back. Now, he starts feeding me things." Her smile broadened. "Good things."

"Like what?"

"Like plump, ripe strawberries. And a peach that's so juicy the juice runs down my chin and drips onto my breasts and he has to lick the juice off. And rich, dark chocolate, with raspberry liqueur in it, that spurts out when you bite into it."

"I'm getting hungry just listening to this fantasy," Cassie said. "Somebody pass me that box of chocolates."

"He brings champagne and gives me a sip, then dribbles it down my body, across my breasts and my stomach, across my thighs and between my thighs. It's cold and the bubbles tickle, and then his mouth is on me, very hot."

"Speaking of hot..." One of the women fanned herself.

"By this time it feels like every nerve in my body is on fire for this man. I'm aching for him, begging for release. He kisses me, and says he has something else for me to taste. Then I feel his weight shift and something touches my lips, and I realize it's him."

"*Ohhhh.*"

"Now there's something you won't find in your refrigerator."

"At least, I hope not!"

Geneva's laugh was low and throaty. "At first, I take just the head in my mouth. I run my tongue around it and I hear him moan. And I know he wants me as much as I want him. So I go a little deeper. But he's really big, so I can't get him all."

"Of course he's really big."

"This *is* a fantasy."

"After a little bit, I can tell he's really close to coming, so I push him down, and he enters me. We start moving together, in this perfect rhythm. He knows just what to do to take me to the edge, then back off, so that each time, I climb a little higher. And he holds himself back, until finally, I can't stand it anymore, and I just...shatter around him. And then he comes too and it's...it's incredible." She sighed, and opened her eyes. "And that's my fantasy. And as soon as I find that handsome man, I intend to make it come true."

Jill fanned herself with a magazine. "Whoo, Geneva. Can I borrow that fantasy some time?"

Geneva curled her legs beneath her. "Now I want to hear *your* fantasy."

"Yeah, you started this." Cassie nudged her. "What's your true confession?"

Jill laughed. "After Geneva's 'gourmet' experience, mine is going to seem pretty silly."

"Does it involve midgets or circus clowns?" a woman asked.

"No."

"Then it can't be that silly."

"All right. Here goes, then. My fantasy is to be kidnapped by a marauding pirate."

"A pirate? As in a wooden leg and eye patch?"

She giggled. "No! As in a gorgeous man in tights and jack boots, and one of those flowing shirts unbuttoned to his navel. With a sword and everything."

"He'd better have a sword or this fantasy's going to be awfully disappointing!"

Jill shook her head. "In my fantasy, this swashbuckling pirate comes to my bedroom one night and kidnaps me and takes me back to his ship, where he makes me his prisoner."

"I've always heard rape fantasies were popular, but they've never done much for me," one woman said.

Jill turned to her. "Oh, no, he doesn't rape me. In fact, he's a perfect gentleman."

"Where's the fun in that?"

Jill smiled. "His goal is to *win* me. After all, I'm an innocent virgin."

More loud laughter. Jill assumed an expression of mock offense. "I said this was a fantasy. Anyway, my pirate is determined to teach me the joys of sex. So, for the first day, he only talks to me. He tells me how beautiful I am, and how he's going to make me feel even more beautiful.

"The second day, he brings me a new silk gown that is so soft and almost transparent. It's cut low over the tops of my breasts, but just sort of flows over the rest of my body. And he rubs perfumed oil on my wrists and my neck and between my breasts.

"The third day, he kisses me. On the cheek and on the throat and finally on the lips. He teases me with his tongue, mimicking what he's going to do to me later.''

"You have to watch those tongues," someone commented.

"On the fourth day, he finally touches me. He strokes my back and my bottom and fondles my breasts. He teases my nipples with his fingers until they tingle and ache. He caresses my thighs but never goes any further.''

"This man has some self-control. I'll say that.''

"The fifth day, he kisses my breasts, and licks my nipples, sucking and teasing until I'm practically screaming with need. I'm hot and aching and begging him to give me relief, but he tells me I'm not ready yet.''

"Now that's cruel!'' someone protested.

"The sixth day, he comes to me naked. I can see how much he wants me. How much he needs me. He strips the dress off of me and begins kissing me again—my mouth and then my breasts. But this time, he holds me closer, letting me feel his body against mine. He trails kisses down my stomach, down to my crotch, to where I'm aching for him.

"I want him so badly I think I'll come right away, but he doesn't let me. 'Not yet' he whispers. Then he kneels between my legs and enters me. I'm so ready for him and he fills me completely. He starts moving in and out, and at the same time, he's stroking me with his thumb. We're moving together and waves of sensation rock through me. And when I finally come it's like a jolt of current through me. And then he climaxes right after me. And it's the most awesome experience.''

"I wouldn't care if a guy *did* have a wooden leg if he could do that for me," Geneva said. "Whoo, girl, that was *hot*. Too bad there aren't any real pirates anymore.''

"Yeah." Jill sighed, a dreamy expression on her face. "Too bad."

Mitch leaned forward and switched off the tape. He was shaken, moved beyond arousal to a kind of empathy. Who would have thought a take-charge woman like Jill craved being swept away like that? Beneath her no-nonsense exterior was someone vulnerable and…and romantic.

So why then did she insist on taking the lead in sex? Was she afraid of what would happen if a man came along who *could* sweep her away?

He put the videotape in his desk drawer and sat staring into the darkness. Maybe all of Jill's talk of no commitments and keeping things casual was a lie. He knew damn well *he* felt something special when he was with her. Was it so far-fetched to believe she'd felt it, too?

He got up and finished setting up the camera. He didn't know why Jill was afraid, but he knew one thing about fear: the more you tried to ignore it, the stronger it became. Maybe he and Jill needed to look their fears in the eye and shrink them to a manageable size. Together, they could figure out where to go from there.

19

ORDINARILY, JILL WAS NOT the sort of person who minded being alone. Sure, she enjoyed going out with friends and having a good time, but she could get just as much satisfaction at home alone curled up with a good book or a movie.

But tonight, nothing satisfied her. Every book she picked up was boring; everything on television seemed silly. She paced her apartment, irritated at everything she saw. Damn Mitch Landry! *He'd* done this to her. He'd taken something wonderful and fun and made it complicated. All his talk of responsibility and duty and…and commitment had worn off on her.

She caught sight of her reflection in the darkened kitchen window and shook her head at her woeful expression. "The next thing you know, I'll be mooning over babies or…or buying *sensible* shoes!" Who would have thought Jill Sheldon—the original "Wild Woman" —would sink so low?

The doorbell rang and she went to answer it, hoping it was a psychic pizza deliverer bringing her a free pizza, or a salesman she could torture.

Her stomach did a somersault when she looked out the peephole and saw it was Mitch. He had a big bunch of flowers and a shopping bag. With trembling fingers she unfastened the locks. "Mitch! Hi." Honestly, why was she so happy to see him? She tried to frown. "I thought we didn't have anything to say to each other,'' she said.

He walked past her into the apartment, and turned and handed her the flowers. ''I'm man enough to admit I was wrong. I want to make it up to you.'' He reached into the shopping bag and pulled out a bottle of champagne and a deluxe assortment of chocolates.

She accepted these gifts, fighting a smile. ''You really know your way to a woman's heart.''

He followed her into the kitchen. ''Why don't I open the champagne while you find some glasses,'' he said.

''All right.'' She avoided looking at him while she hunted in the cupboards for two champagne flutes and a vase for the flowers. What exactly was going on here? Was Mitch really willing to agree to a relationship on her terms?

He poured the champagne and held up his glass. ''To us.''

She stared at the bubbles gathering on the rim of her glass. ''Um, what about us?''

''I guess that's what I'm here to figure out.'' He leaned back against the counter. ''I'm hoping you'll cooperate with me in a little experiment.''

''Experiment?'' The skin along her arms tingled. Something about the look in his eye…

''Oh, I think it's something you'll like.'' He loosened his tie.

She set aside her glass and moved closer. ''Then maybe I'll cooperate.''

''Good.'' He whipped off the tie and pulled her closer in a long, slow kiss.

Now this was more like it. If they could concentrate on their physical attraction…

Something tightened around her wrists. She realized

it was the tie. Laughing, she tried to pull away, but Mitch drew her back to him. "It's okay," he said. "Trust me."

He picked up the shopping bag and tucked the champagne bottle under one arm. "Which is your bedroom?"

"First door on the left." She nodded in the right direction.

He headed toward the bedroom, pulling her along behind him. A nervous giggle bubbled in her throat, along with a slow smoldering heat that started between her legs and curled through the rest of her body. What was Mitch going to do?

In the bedroom, he set the shopping bag and champagne on the bed, then went around lighting candles, until the room was bathed in a soft, golden glow. He folded back the duvet on the bed, then turned to her. "I'm going to undress you."

He seemed to be asking permission, so she nodded. After all, he'd seen her naked before. And it was what she wanted too, though she'd prefer to undress herself.

That was impossible with her hands tied behind her, however, so she stood still while he unbuttoned her blouse and peeled it back across her shoulders.

He worked slowly, deliberately exposing her a bit at a time. His breath was warm across her stomach as he bent to unsnap her jeans, and goose bumps rose on her flesh as he moved away and the cooler air of the room rushed over her.

He steadied her and helped her step out of her jeans and then she stood there, clad in bra and panties, her blouse wrapped around her wrists. He smiled and snapped the waistband of her panties. "Cute."

She looked down at the white cotton underpants decorated with little pink hearts. "If I'd known you were coming, I'd have worn something more erotic."

"I happen to think pink hearts are very erotic." He unfastened one wrist, then slid the blouse off of her, followed by the bra. He tossed the clothing aside, then bound her again. She thought of protesting, but didn't, telling herself she could do this. She could trust him.

He gathered her breasts in his hands, holding them. Her nipples rose against his palms, demanding attention, but he only squeezed her gently and moved away.

He untied one wrist and helped her into bed, then raised her hands over her head and bound them loosely to the bedpost. "Comfy?" he asked.

"I'm not *un*comfortable." At least not physically. What was he going to do? She wasn't worried he'd hurt her, but she didn't like not knowing what was going on. Not being in charge...

He moved to the side of the bed and began undressing. She turned her head to watch. He removed his clothes slowly, but she didn't have a sense that he was putting on a show for her, only that he was not a man in a hurry. Which was too bad, because she was already feeling impatient for something...anything...to happen.

He turned to face her, candlelight flickering on his bronzed skin, sharply etching every muscle and plane. She couldn't deny this man stirred her in a way no other had.

He sat on the edge of the bed. "I've been thinking more about what you said, about the products we sell being fun and even useful. So I thought it would be a good idea for me to get better acquainted with some of them."

She smiled. "That's what I've been saying all along."

"See, I *have* been listening." He picked up the shopping bag. "So I did a little shopping this evening." He pulled out a satin blindfold.

"Is that for you?" she asked.

"No, it's for you." He leaned over her, lifting her head from the pillow and fastening the blindfold. It was soft, completely obscuring her vision. She shivered and licked her lips. "I'm not sure I like this."

"Oh, you'll like it. I promise." She heard the rustling of the bag. "Another thing I found was this." Something tickled her jaw.

She smiled. "It's a feather."

"A Fantasy Feather Duster, to be exact." He trailed it along her throat, around her breasts. She gasped when it touched her sensitive nipples.

"How does that feel?" he asked.

"It...it tickles a little." She giggled as he brushed the feather across her abdomen. "But it also feels...nice." The feather trailed across her thighs, down her legs, to her feet. Back up again, to pause over her sex, barely touching her.

She arched toward it, craving more, but it retreated.

She sagged against the bed again, but a new sensation claimed her attention. Something soft and furry cuddled against her neck. "That's not an animal, is it?" she asked, alarmed.

He laughed. "No. It's actually those fur-lined hand-cuffs you 'demonstrated' to me a couple of weeks ago." He dragged the fur across her breasts. "I remembered how soft the fur felt."

"Yes. It is soft." And very erotic. Blindfolded, it seemed every other sense was on alert. The slightest touch set her to tingling. As he stroked her with the fur, she felt every movement keenly. She imagined she felt his gaze on her, too, watching her. The thought excited her even more.

The bag rustled again and suddenly the scent of strawberries surrounded her. "I found this at the store, too." His finger brushed her lips and she tasted strawberries. "Strawberry Nipple Nibblers."

"I see you really do know the stock." He kissed her and the heat of his mouth made her lips tingle.

Then he massaged some of the cream into her nipples and they began to tingle also. He kissed her breasts, first one and then the other, and took the nipples into his mouth. "Tastes good," he mumbled.

The cream made her more sensitive than ever. As he flicked his tongue across her, then suckled harder, she writhed beneath him, her impatience building.

He smoothed his hand across her belly, then slid lower until he was parting her folds to find her pearled center. He stroked her gently, and she felt a corresponding tingle. "Mitch!" she cried.

He licked her, gently at first, then with more pressure. She told herself to relax, to surrender to the pleasant urgency, but she was too on edge. She didn't like feeling trapped this way, or not being able to see...or...oh sweet mercy, she'd never felt so out of control before, hurtling toward climax without having any say in the matter.

When she was sure she couldn't hold out any longer, he raised his head, leaving her trembling. He laid his hand on her thigh, soothing her. "It's all right," he said, his voice ragged. "We're only getting started."

More rustling, then the smell of peaches. "Taste this." She obediently opened her mouth and he fed her a bite of peach. The fruit tasted sweet, the flesh velvety against her tongue. Juice ran down her chin and he hastened to lick it up. She smiled. "That's good," she said. "Let me have some more."

He fed her another bite, only this time, it was strawberry, the seeds crunching between her teeth. "I remember watching you eat strawberries at dinner the other night,'' he said. ''I never got a hard-on watching somebody eat before.''

''Untie me and I'll show you more.'' She hoped he didn't hear the pleading in her voice.

He chuckled. ''Oh, no. I'm not ready to untie you yet. Tonight, I'm in charge.''

The words sent a shiver through her.

He fed her more strawberries, and chocolate filled with sweet caramel. Something about all this was vaguely familiar, but she didn't have time to figure it out. Every moment, new sensations swept over her.

She heard the clink of a glass, and he stretched alongside her, his body warm, his arousal prodding her in the hip. ''Do you trust me?'' he asked.

''No.'' She didn't trust anyone.

He covered her breast with his hand, thumbing her nipple, sending jolts of sensation through her. ''Come on now. Do you trust me? You know I won't hurt you.''

''I know you won't hurt me.'' She was sure of that. But she didn't like lying here so passive, only receiving and not giving.

''All right then. Tell me what you feel.''

Something cool and liquid trickled across her chest, pooling in the valley between her breast. She smelled the tang of wine, then felt Mitch lapping at her. ''Champagne.''

He trickled some of the wine between her lips, then across her breasts. He chased each drop with his tongue, capturing it all before it could dampen the sheets. He moved down, filling her navel, tracing a path to her heated center, where he licked up every drop, and stayed to bring her to the edge once more.

She arched toward him, moaning with need. ''You're

very close, aren't you?'' he murmured. ''Almost there.
I promise, it'll be good.''

His fingers slipped inside her, stroking. ''What was
that about the G-spot? Was it right…here?''

''Mitch! Oh…oh!'' She bucked beneath him as he
stroked faster. He began licking her again, banishing her
last bit of control. Light and heat filled her, and she
screamed his name.

He lay alongside her, holding her as aftershocks raced
through her. Then he undid the blindfold and looked
down on her, his face so serious. ''Are you all right?''

She wasn't sure she'd ever be the same again. She
smiled weakly. ''That was incredible.''

He smoothed his hand up her arms. ''See? It can be
good, even if you aren't calling the shots.''

She nodded. ''I guess it can be with you.''

He reached for the binding at her wrists. ''Do you
want me to untie you?''

She started to answer yes, but something in his eyes
asked her to trust him still. She swallowed her fear and
shook her head. ''No, it's all right. I…I trust you.''

He crushed her to him, his kiss fierce. His hands still
on her, caressing, he knelt between her knees and entered her. Desire swelled anew within her, and she
closed her eyes and gave herself up to the wonderful
friction of his thrusts.

She arched toward him and he slipped his hands under
her buttocks, holding her up off the bed as he drove
deeply into her, each stroke stronger and faster. She felt
herself climbing again to that wonderful height. But this
time, she wasn't afraid. She gladly surrendered control
and fell freely, even as she felt the power of his own
release.

Afterward, they lay together, not speaking. Her arms

freed, she wrapped them around him, and savored his solid warmth. The candles burned low, and some of them went out. "What are you thinking?" he murmured, long after she thought he'd fallen asleep.

"I'm thinking this changes things," she said. "Though I'm not sure how."

He rolled over to face her, and cradled her head in the hollow of his shoulder. "I wanted you to see the possibilities," he murmured. And then he did fall asleep, leaving her to stare into the darkness, wondering if this was what it meant to be in love, to be so unsure of herself, and yet so certain that she couldn't be happier than she was at this moment.

20

When Jill woke the next morning, Mitch was gone. She frowned at the note he'd left on the dresser. *I had to go in to work early to see about something. See you later. Mitch.*

No "Last night was the most awesome night of my life," no "I could hardly bear to leave you," no "I love you."

She winced. Where had *that* come from? Neither one of them had said anything about love. Neither one of them expected it. She crumpled the note and tossed it in the trash, then got dressed. Everywhere she looked, something reminded her of last night—the empty champagne bottle in the wastebasket beside the bed, the half-eaten box of chocolates on the nightstand, his tie draped around the bedpost.

She unwound the tie from the post and brought it to her nose, inhaling the faint scent of Aramis. She'd keep this, as a memento of last night. A kind of trophy. Smiling, she went to the dresser and knotted the tie around the collar of the sleeveless blue chambray shirt she wore. When Mitch saw it, would he remember too?

Unfortunately a troop of tourists descended on the store to giggle and gawk fifteen minutes after they opened and Jill didn't have a chance to even say "Good morning" to Mitch. Between defending the store's merchandise to one outraged woman "Yes, ma'am, marriage counselors have actually recommended our store to their clients,'' and explaining the benefits of various types of vibrators to a pink-faced middle-aged couple, she scarcely had time to think for the first hour or so.

When she did finally bump into Mitch, literally, as she stepped back from straightening the costume display, all she could manage to do was blush and stammer. ''Good morning, Jill,'' he said, his hand warm on her shoulder as he steadied her. ''I see you found my tie.''

She smoothed the end of the tie. ''Oh, uh, yes.''

He looked over her head, at the rest of the store. ''Looks like we had a real rush in here this morning.''

''We did. Some tourists from Nebraska heard about the place and walked over to see it. I think our fame is spreading.'' *And how could you even think of closing the place down now?*

''I know.'' He moved away from her. ''Construction is due to start next week.''

''So you really are going to go through with closing the doors?''

He looked away. ''I don't know. I...I need more time to think.''

He didn't have much time, but she guessed he didn't need her pointing that out to him. Still, his answer disappointed her. She turned away from him, and began sorting through the thinning ranks of costumes.

''I'd better get back to work,'' he said, and walked away.

Why hadn't he said anything about last night—about *them?* For that matter, why hadn't she had the courage to speak up?

Was it because, outside of the bedroom, it was harder to see how to make things work in real life? Jill thought Mitch should keep the store open, but more importantly, she thought he should quit letting responsibility and the opinions of others rule his life. If he couldn't unbend, just a little, how would they ever compromise on anything else?

So what if he opened a restaurant? That didn't matter so much anymore, though she'd miss the fun she'd had working here. But if Mitch opened a restaurant and joined the Chamber of Commerce and got caught up in making a success of himself, would he expect her to tone down her wild ways? To attend boring business functions and make small talk to people she didn't like or respect? To become the perfect social accessory?

The frightening thing was, she could almost see herself doing those things, literally killing off part of herself, if it meant staying with Mitch. She stared at the beaded top of the belly dancer's costume she'd worn so long ago and blinked back tears. Better to give up Mitch now, and get the hurting out of the way, than to wake up ten years from now, as miserable as Jenny had been.

She'd gotten along fine all this time, hadn't she, assuring herself that she didn't need a commitment to anyone else to be happy. The difference was, before she'd believed the words. Now she knew part of her would always love Mitch. She'd given a part of herself to him she could never get back.

MITCH COULDN'T BELIEVE he'd been such a dolt, mumbling all that nonsense about not knowing whether he wanted to keep the store open or not. What the hell did any of that matter compared to what he felt for Jill?

But the moment he'd seen that tie around her neck, he'd been transported back to last night. In his mind's eye, he'd seen her lying on her bed, so beautiful and vulnerable, surrendering everything to him. The memory had left him speechless, able only to mutter inanities.

Later, he'd find a way to make it up to her. To really talk about what the future might hold for them. He didn't know if she felt as strongly about him as he did her, but he had hope. They'd probably both have to compromise some to make things work, but he thought they had a good shot.

In the meantime, he'd called the security company and learned that the alarm system had registered another silent intruder last night. Time to see if the video camera had captured anything.

He had taken the camera off the tripod and brought it into his office when he arrived that morning. Now he slipped the tape out of it and turned on the VCR, thinking again of the tape in his desk drawer of Jill and her friends. He'd have to watch the rest of that one later. No telling what other fantasies the women had confessed to.

While the tape rewound, he leaned back in the desk chair and looked around the office, at the dark paneling and dented filing cabinets, the faded posters and make-shift entertainment unit. When they remodeled for the restaurant, he'd have his office made over as well. Despite the pleasant associations the daybed held for him, he was thinking of replacing it with a couch. A very comfortable couch, with plenty of room to stretch out on.

He'd keep the chair, though. It was comfortable and masculine, and it reminded him of Uncle Grif. He felt a twinge of guilt at the thought. No doubt Grif had wanted him to keep Just 4 Play going. He didn't have any children to leave the business to, so he'd passed it on to Mitch.

At first, Mitch had looked on the inheritance as a

windfall. The capital he needed to open the restaurant. He hadn't felt any emotional obligation to Grif because, after all, he'd hardly known the man.

But that had changed the last few weeks. Spending so much time here in this room where Grif had practically lived, going through his files, learning things about his uncle he'd never guessed, Mitch had begun to feel close to the older man. He'd seen the kind of man Grif was, and the kind he wasn't.

Grif wasn't the kind of man who bowed to public opinion. He did what he thought was right and the rest of the world be damned. It was a hard line to take sometimes, requiring the sacrifice of prestige and position and maybe even money. But he'd taken it. Mitch admired that in his uncle, though he didn't know if he could be that strong himself.

He'd bought the tombstone as a gesture of respect, but he wished he could do something to show the world he'd come to love his uncle.

The tape from last night began playing, showing the darkened interior of the store. Then he heard a sound like voices whispering. Something moved in the corner of the picture.

He leaned forward, trying to make out what it was. The object disappeared, then appeared on the screen again. It was a person. No, two people. Two naked people. He hit the pause button and stared at the screen in disbelief, then began laughing out loud. His world was full of surprises so far, and this had to be the biggest one of all.

BY LUNCHTIME, JILL HAD decided that the only thing to do was to talk to Mitch and let him off the hook. She'd tell him she understood all the reasons they could never make it as a couple: their backgrounds were so different, they wanted different things in life and all that. She'd have to call upon all her limited acting ability to pull it off, but it would be for the best.

But when she knocked on Mitch's office door, no one answered, though she knew he was in there. She knocked again, then tried the knob. It was unlocked, so she peeked inside.

Mitch was sitting at the desk, turned toward the TV, bent double with laughter. When he turned and looked at her, he actually had tears running down his face!

"What is it? What's so funny?" She glanced at the television screen. At first it looked like one of the X-rated videos they sold, with a couple going at it like rabbits. That surprised her a little. Sure, guys liked that sort of thing more than women did, but why would he be watching this in the middle of the day? Especially after last night?

"Um, maybe I'd better come back another time." She started backing toward the door, but Mitch motioned her toward him again.

"No, no. You won't believe this." He paused the tape and motioned at the screen with the remote. "This is the tape I made last night of the 'silent intruder.'"

She leaned closer and peered at the screen, then her eyes widened. "Oh my gosh, it's…it's Sid." She'd recognize that dragon tattoo across his back anywhere, even if the tush wasn't familiar. She put her hand over her mouth and giggled. "Who's that with him?"

Mitch rewound the tape until the woman's face was visible. Jill gasped. "That's Lana Montgomery!" She squealed and collapsed into a chair. "Oh, this is too funny."

Mitch shut off the tape and ejected it from the player.

"Lana and Sid." He chuckled. "I wouldn't believe it if I hadn't seen it with my own eyes." He tapped the tape against his leg. "Just goes to show you never really know people."

"Do you mean you didn't think Sid could go out with a woman like Lana?"

"I mean the Lana I knew didn't have an uninhibited bone in her body. I guess sometimes, it just takes the right person to reveal that side of someone." He looked thoughtful. "Or the right place."

"What are you going to do? I mean about Sid and Lana? You aren't going to fire him, are you?" Though what difference did that make if he was going to close the store anyway? she thought sadly.

"I'm not going to fire him." He stood and slipped the tape into his jacket. "I do think I'll let him know I have this, though, and suggest he and Lana take 'play-time' somewhere else."

On his way out of his office, he stopped and looked back at her. "I wanted you to be the first to know. I've decided not to close the store. If this place can turn up-tight Lana into a passionate temptress, it must be performing a needed service."

"So seeing that tape changed your mind when I couldn't?"

He shook his head. "No, you had something to do with it, too. And Grif."

"Grif?" She looked puzzled.

"I think this wasn't just a business for him—it was kind of a statement. 'This is what I'm about, so take it or leave it.'" He shrugged. "I figure he did fine without being a darling of society and I can do the same. I guess being around this place has taught me there's all different kinds of respect and some of them are more worth having than others.''

After he was gone, Jill stayed in the office a while longer, trying to muster up the joy she knew she should be feeling at Mitch's announcement. He wasn't going to close the store. She and Sid would still have jobs. She could still come here every day and have fun disguised as work.

But she could only manage a feeling of mild relief. And a bit of pride that Mitch had found it within himself to do the right thing.

But overwhelming any happiness she should have felt was a great sadness. Mitch had reached a decision about the store, but he hadn't answered the one question she most wanted answered: What was he going to do about her—about *them?*

21

MITCH SPENT THE REST of the day on the phone, canceling contractors and breaking the news to everyone who needed to know that Ping's Peking Palace wouldn't be opening anytime soon. At least not at this location.

Chef Ping took the news philosophically. "Oh well, I think I can find someone else to build the restaurant. And I liked your store. I will come and see you there sometime."

Mort Montgomery was less pleasant. "You're making a big mistake," he said bluntly. "No respectable person in this town will have anything to do with you as long as you're in charge of that smut shop."

"It's not a smut shop, Mort. As for all those 'respectable' people, my uncle got along fine without them and he was a better man than they'll ever be."

"Which shows how little you know." Mort made a *tsking* sound. "I hate to see it, I tell you. We could have made that restaurant a huge success."

"No, *we* couldn't have. Goodbye, Mort. And good luck."

It was after six when he made the last call, to Archie, the architect. Mitch was tired, but content. He figured Uncle Grif would be pleased, and Jill, too, though she hadn't said much when he'd told her the news.

Things still felt awkward between them. He wasn't quite sure how to smooth them out, but he knew he had to try. But when he finally emerged from his office, he discovered she'd gone home early.

"Did she say why she had to leave?" he asked.

Sid shook his head. "Just said she had things to do."

He thought about going to her apartment. But he still didn't know what he'd say to her. Now that they'd be seeing each other on a regular basis at work, did she want to keep things as they were between them, or did she expect something more from him? And was he ready to give more?

He ended up staying at the store until closing, waiting on customers even, something he hadn't done before. He found he enjoyed the work. He recommended Oriental Love Potion to a college girl who was looking for something exotic. When a young man selected a package of Neon Nights condoms, Mitch was able to assure him that they really did glow in the dark.

He browsed the shelves, discovering merchandise he didn't know they carried. For instance, they had a whole section of games, including a box of plastic bubbles, each containing a suggestion, ranging from sweetly romantic to nicely naughty. The directions called for the couple to add the bubbles to a bath and take turns drawing the bubbles and acting on the suggestions. Wouldn't that be a fun one to try with Jill….

"Excuse me, I'm looking for a salesclerk who was in here a couple of weeks ago. A cute little blonde?"

Mitch turned and found a balding, middle-aged man. Slightly behind him stood a pleasant-faced, middle-aged woman. "You must mean Jill. I'm afraid she's off tonight."

"Oh." Clearly disappointed, the man turned to his wife. "She was so nice. I wanted you to meet her."

"Can I help you with something?" Mitch asked.

"I don't know." The man tugged at his collar. "I was really hoping to speak to Jill."

"Are you the manager?" The woman spoke.

Mitch glanced toward Sid, who was on the other side of the store, showing vibrators to a pair of young women. "No. I'm the owner."

"Even better." The woman stepped forward. "I want you to know your store probably saved our marriage."

"Oh?" Mitch remembered the man now. The one who'd been ogling Jill while she massaged his hand. "How is that?"

The woman looked at her husband. "Larry here is a good man, but after twenty years, he'd forgotten all about romance. The things he got at your store—the books and lingerie and candles and such—they helped both of us remember what's it like to take a little time and effort for love and sex."

Mitch smiled. "I'm glad we could help."

"So we're thinking that now we're ready to, uh, branch out." The man was pink-faced. "You know, try some new things." He looked around. "I was really hoping Jill could suggest something."

"But I'm sure you have some good ideas, too." The woman smiled at Mitch. "What would you suggest for a couple of old married folks looking to spice things up?"

Mitch swallowed. Did he dare admit he wasn't exactly an expert in this arena? "Um, I'm not sure exactly what you'd like," he stammered.

"Well, what do you like?" The woman's grin widened. "We don't want anything too wild, but we're willing to try something different."

His eyes scanned the shelves, hoping for inspiration, then his gaze landed on the bubble bath game. That wasn't too wild, was it? He grabbed the package off the shelf. "Here's something fun and...and romantic." He handed it to the woman. "You take turns selecting bubbles and acting on the suggestions."

She popped open one of the bubbles and read from the plastic strip inside. "Give partner a back rub." She glanced at her husband. "What do you think?"

He nodded. "It's a good start."

"All right." The woman turned back to Mitch. "We'll take it."

He rang up their purchase and wrapped it in the store's signature pink and gold tissue paper. "You will tell Jill we stopped by, won't you?" the man asked.

"Oh, yes, I'll tell her." Mitch handed over their purchase. "Have fun."

The woman laughed. "Oh, I'm sure we will!"

He chuckled to himself. Fun. A three-letter word he'd once despised. But Jill had been right all along; Just 4 Play was fun, and fun was a good thing. Now if he could only convince her he'd learned that lessen.

After the last customer, he returned to his office. Sid stopped by on his way out. "Thanks for being cool about that tape and all," he said. "I swear I didn't know the alarm would still register after I bypassed it."

"It's okay, Sid. Just don't do it again okay?"

"Okay." Sid lingered in the doorway, shifting from one foot to the other.

"Was there something else?" Mitch asked.

"I was wondering if I could have the tape. You know, for Lana. I think she'd get a kick out of it."

Mitch was careful not to smile as he took the tape out of the drawer and handed it over.

"So uh, you're okay with me and Lana?" Sid asked. "I mean, you two were split up and all...."

"I'm okay with it. In fact, I can't think of a more perfect couple."

"Good." Sid looked relieved. "Glad that's clear. Guess I'll be going."

"You go on. I'll lock up."

After Sid left, Mitch was restless, not wanting to go home to his lonely apartment. He could call Meg, but she was probably busy with schoolwork, or out with friends. He looked around the office, noticing once more how depressing the place looked. Restaurant or no, he intended to remodel this office.

He might as well finish clearing it out now. He'd tackle the one job he'd been putting off—that walk-in closet that held everything from the video camera to an old set of Grif's golf clubs.

He went to the storeroom and got a box. Everything to go to a storage facility could go in there; everything else was destined for the trash.

Tax records—in the storage box. Receipts for the 1996 Coors Classic golf tournament—toss.

After half an hour he was beginning to wonder if his uncle ever threw anything away. He found receipts for practically everything the man had ever bought, years' worth of old magazines and mail-order catalogs, manuals for computers and other office equipment that had been out of date for ages.

A box on the top shelf held a sad-looking black toupee. Mitch set this aside for a third category—things to be donated.

At the very back of the closet, he came upon a shoebox, filled to the brim with letters, packets of eight to ten envelopes each, bound together with thick rubber bands. Nobody he knew wrote letters anymore, so these had to be old.

He picked up one of the rubber-banded packets and looked at the loopy, old-fashioned handwriting. The envelopes were blue, made of the thin paper people used to use for airmail. The letters bore military postmarks. Of course. These would have been letters Grif received when he was serving in Vietnam.

The rest of the closet's contents forgotten, he carried the box over to the leather chair. He undid the first packet and opened the first letter. It was written in a soft, feminine hand.

Dear Grif,

You've only been gone one day and already I miss you. I thought you might like to know what I am doing with myself while you are away, so I intend to write every week. That way, we can keep in touch and maybe I won't miss you so much.

This afternoon my friend Connie and I went to the movies and saw *Cleopatra*. I think Richard Burton is the grooviest, though Connie likes Paul Newman best. Afterward, we walked down to Gold's Department Store and looked at the store windows. They had the cutest miniskirt for sale there. Mom and Daddy won't like it, but I'm going to buy it as soon as I save enough of my allowance.

Mitch chuckled to himself. The letter continued in this vein, a perfect picture of a week in the life of teenage girl, circa 1962. It ended with the word Love, in big, loopy letters, and a girlish signature: Tracy.

He stopped and stared into space. Tracy was his mother's name. What a strange coincidence.

He read the next letter, and the next. Two years' worth of correspondence. The woman who wrote the letters grew up on the page, her concerns changing from the latest fashions and music, through graduation, to a secretarial job.

By this time, Mitch knew he was reading his mother's words. She had worked as a secretary before she married his father, and the people she mentioned in her letters— her mother and father, her younger sister Sue and her grandparents in Grand Junction—were all familiar to him.

He was fascinated by this glimpse of her, as a young girl, before any possibility of himself or Meg had entered her mind. He stared at the handwriting on the page and tried to imagine her, seated at a little desk in her room, or at the kitchen table in his grandparents' house, writing these words to a young man half a world away.

But why was she writing to Grif? What had he thought, receiving them? He had obviously valued them enough to keep them, but why?

He continued to read, unable to tear himself away. The tone of the letters grew more serious as he moved deeper into the box. Tracy's feelings matured along with her, from flirting friendship, to romantic love. Mitch had a funny feeling in his stomach as he read them. This didn't fit with the reality he knew. What was going on?

The last two letters were bound by themselves with a brown shoestring instead of a rubber band. The few pages were yellowed, the writing smeared in places, as if they'd been much handled.

He opened the first of the letters and brought it closer to the desk lamp, puzzling out the faded writing.

Dearest Grif,
I can still call you Dearest, can't I? You will always be dearest to me. I don't understand why you tell

me not to wait for you. This war won't last forever and I know you'll be coming home. Don't you think it would be good to have a wife waiting for you, so you can start life fresh?

I know you say you have your mother and your brother to look after, but I don't mind. I'll help you. And it isn't as if Dickie is a baby. Why, he and I are the same age and he already has a good job downtown. I see him almost every day when I go to the café for lunch.

And I know you say you'll need to find a job and establish yourself when you come home, but I know you'll be able to find something. And I can keep working until we've saved enough money for a little house. Things aren't that expensive here and I'm sure we'll manage.

Anyway, I don't think any of that matters. I love you and you love me and we ought not think that kind of love comes along every day. I'm sure it doesn't. So please say you'll change your mind. Write and tell me you still want to be with me and I will be the happiest girl alive.

Mitch laid aside the letter, trying to absorb its contents. So his mother had been in love with Grif. But he had told her not to wait. That he had too many responsibilities to think of getting married at that time.

A shiver swept through him as he looked at the second letter, unopened on the blotter before him. Though he knew what had happened, he had to find out for sure.

Dear Grif,

I waited a long time to hear from you again after my last letter. I know you received it because my friend April Sanders's brother Alan is in your unit and he said the day you got that letter you went out and got drunk and ended up in the stockade for three days.

Then Dickie came and said you'd given him a message to give me—to stop writing you and to forget about you. I cried, and Dickie was very sweet to try and comfort me. He came by the next day and the next to see how I was doing, and after a while, he asked me out.

Since I couldn't have you, I figured your brother would have to do. And I found out he is really a good man, maybe better than you, because he wasn't afraid to tell me he loved me.

Anyway, you told me not to wait, so I didn't. The next time you see me, I will be Mrs. Richard Landry. So you see, I did what you said. All except one thing. You told me to forget about you, and I could never do that. I'll never forget you, Grif. And I'm hoping that somehow, you'll never forget me, either.

Mitch's eyes stung, and a knot rose in his throat too big to swallow. Now he knew why Uncle Grif hadn't come around much all those years. Why his mother clung so fiercely to his father, as if afraid he might abandon her as well.

And maybe he knew why Grif had left everything to him. Because his uncle knew they were alike, and he hoped he could keep Mitch from making the same mistakes he had.

He put the letters back in the box, and carefully replaced the lid, his heart pounding. He only hoped it wasn't too late for him to do what he should have done all along. To hell with responsibility and waiting until the time was right. He loved Jill and he had to tell her.

I love you and you love me and we ought not think that kind of love comes along every day. I'm sure it doesn't, his mother had written. "I think you were right, Mom," he said as he headed for the door. He only hoped Jill would listen.

WHEN JILL COULDN'T FAKE being cheerful anymore, she went home and threw herself a private pity party. She put on her flannel pajamas and went through half a box of tissues and a whole pint of mocha fudge ripple. It didn't exactly make her feel better, but she couldn't feel much worse. She didn't have much practice falling in and out of love, but from what she could tell, it was a pretty miserable business.

She was thinking of opening up another pint of ice cream when someone knocked on the door. She shuffled to the peephole and stood on tiptoe to look out, but the hallway was empty. Curious, she unlocked the door, and opened it, keeping the chain in place.

Mitch stepped out of the shadows. "Stand and deliver, *mademoiselle.*"

She covered her mouth with her hand, too startled to speak. He was wearing the pirate's costume from Just 4 Play. The one she'd ordered and built her favorite fantasy around. The tall leather jackboots clung to his thighs, which were sheathed in close-fitting tights. He wore a full poet's shirt, open to the waist and belted with a wide leather belt. A scabbard hung at his side, and he brandished a silver sword. "Unlock the door, maiden, and allow me to enter," he declaimed.

"Oh, Mitch." She sighed, and fumbled with the chain.

The door across the hall flew open and Professor Simon, dressed in a paisley smoking jacket, looked out. "What do you think you're doing, young man?" he demanded.

Mitch flushed. "I'm uh…I'm—"

"We're practicing for a play, Professor." Jill tugged on Mitch's sleeve, urging him inside.

The professor peered closer. "Oh, it's you again." He looked Mitch up and down. "You look a great deal different today. Not nearly as stuffy."

"It's a costume, Professor," Jill said. "We're uh, we're doing a revival of the *Pirates of Penzance*."

"Gilbert and Sullivan, eh? One of my favorites! *Oh, I am the model of a modern major general…*"

The professor was still singing when Jill dragged Mitch inside and shut the door. "What are you doing in that costume?" she asked.

He struck a pose, sword raised. "I've come to ravage you, my dear."

"But…why?"

He raised one eyebrow. "I need a reason?"

She sat on the sofa and pulled him down beside her. "At any other time, I might have said no, but now, I think you *do* need a reason, Mitch. Are we still playing games here?"

He sheathed the sword and sank down beside her. "No, this is no game." He took her hand. "I know you think I'm too serious sometimes, but the truth is, I am seriously in love with you. And I know I'm taking a risk here…but I hope you're in love with me, too."

There she went, puddling up again. She wasn't even sure she could get the words out, but she knew she had to. "I am, Mitch. I never thought it would happen to me, but I think I've fallen in love with you." She threw her arms around him and hugged him tightly, never wanting to let him go again.

Finally he drew back and looked down on her. "What is this—tears?" He brushed his thumb along her cheek.

"Only because I'm so happy."

He shook his head. "If you're crying, it's going to make it tough for me to ravage you."

"Then let me see if I can make it a little easier." She threw her arms around him again and kissed him for all she was worth, all the passion and love she felt focused on their lips.

After a moment, he pushed away again and grinned at her. "I think on the first day, we're only supposed to talk. On the second day, I can touch you. Or is that the third day?"

Her eyes widened. "How did you know…?"

"I found the tape from Cassie's bachelorette party—the one with the true confessions."

"That's why the whole thing the other night—with the fruit and everything—was so familiar! That was Geneva's fantasy."

He nodded. "But you said you'd like it for your fantasy, too."

"But this…" She fingered the sleeve of the pirate's costume. "This is really my fantasy."

He swept her into his arms and marched toward the bedroom. "Is it all right with you if we dispense with the first few days and go straight to day five?"

"Absolutely." She lay back in his arms. "Ravage me, *monsieur.*"

"I intend to ravage you now, and for years to come. In fact, my goal from now on is to fulfill all your fantasies." He deposited her on the bed and began unbuckling the sword belt.

She grinned up at him. "Now that sounds like a deal I can live with." Happiness bubbled up in her like champagne. "I never knew a relationship could be so much fun."

"Then you must have been in the wrong relationships." The sword landed on the floor, followed shortly by the shirt.

"I think I've found the right one now." She sat up and began removing her own clothes. "And I don't intend to let you get away. Even if it takes fur-lined handcuffs and a whip to keep you with me."

He tossed one of his boots aside and waggled his eyebrows. "Is that a promise?"

"Oh, it's a promise, my mad pirate. Now come here. I want to show you something...."

Epilogue

"SHOULD THE SEXUAL TRIVIA books be displayed with the games or with the other books?" Jill asked as she and Sid unpacked the latest shipment of merchandise one Wednesday afternoon.

"With the books, I guess. The games section is pretty full." Sid was looking like his old self these days, his Mohawk completely grown in and dyed lemon-yellow, his various rings, studs and barbells back in their appropriate places. The only real difference in his appearance was the new tattoo on his left bicep—a heart inscribed with the word "Lana."

Jill set aside the carton of books to be shelved later and opened a box of bath toys. She took out a vibrating bath sponge and grinned. Mitch would probably like this. She'd have to suggest they try it out soon.

In the three months they'd been together, Mitch and Jill had experimented with just about every other product Just 4 Play offered. For someone who'd started out uptight, Mitch was proving to be an amazingly fun and inventive lover. Oh, he still had his conservative, conventional side, but she'd come to believe that wasn't all bad. There was something to be said for a man you could count on. Jill knew Mitch was the kind of man she could depend on for the long haul. Maybe even forever. A thought that would have frightened her a mere few months ago.

She opened another box and smiled as she unfolded layers of purple and blue translucent scarves. "Seduce him with the dance of the seven veils," she read from the cardboard tag attached to the hem. Beneath the veils she found a sequin-studded bikini. "*Oooh,* this is nice," she said, lifting the ensemble out of the box.

"It's gorgeous." Tami, who had recently gone from part-time to full-time hours, came over to admire the outfit. "You should try it on."

"I think I will." Jill headed for the dressing room. On the way, she passed Lana, who had stopped by to bring Sid lunch. "Love the new outfit," she said, admiring the leather pants and jacket ensemble.

Lana smoothed her hand down the supple leather jacket. "It's my conservative, yet sexy look." She laughed. "A big change from the suits I used to wear, but I like it."

"I like it a lot." Sid came up behind her and enveloped her in a hug. "Thanks for the lunch, sweetie."

"You're welcome, tiger."

Jill hurried into the dressing room, stifling her laughter. Did she and Mitch get that silly over one another? Maybe so. She had to admit, the man really got to her.

She slipped out of her jeans and sweater and into the sequined bikini and multiple veils. The peekaboo effect of the filmy veils over the glittering sequins was sexy and fun. In other words, perfect for her. She couldn't wait to see what Mitch thought.

As if on cue, the man himself walked into the store as she exited the dressing room. From halfway across the room, he found her, zeroing in like a laser on target. As his gaze swept over her, a smile tugged at the corners of his mouth. He nodded, silently telegraphing his approval.

"Mitch, we need to order more of the Motion Lotion and the Love Beads," Tami said. "We're almost out."

"Everything's selling like crazy since you put the ad in the college paper," Sid said. "We may need to think about hiring another full-time person."

"Sounds good to me, Sid. You know I trust your judgment."

Jill made her way to him, walking with an exaggerated sway of her hips, enjoying watching desire build in his eyes. When she reached him, she stood on tiptoe and kissed his cheek. "How are things at your real estate office?"

"Boring as usual, compared to this place."

"You should move everything into the office here."

"I would, but I'm afraid I'd be too distracted." He smoothed his hand along her bottom. "Is this new?"

"Just came in today."

He nodded. "I like it."

"I thought you might." She followed him into his office, where he took off his suit jacket and hung it on the back of his chair.

"I had an interesting conversation with Chef Ping this morning," he said.

"Oh." She sat on the corner of his desk, the veils falling back to reveal her bare thigh.

Mitch glanced at her, then away, and tugged at the collar of his shirt. "Yes. He's opening his own restaurant on Pearl Street and wanted to know if I'd be interested in backing him."

"And are you interested?"

"Yeah. I think I am. It's a good opportunity for him, and it would be a good investment for me. It never hurts to plan for the future."

She smiled. That was Mitch. Always thinking ahead.

Something she never did if she could help it. Except lately, she'd been thinking more about her future with him....

He moved past her, to the front of the desk, and began sorting through his mail. "I saw Lana out front."

"She stopped by to bring Sid his lunch."

"They seem to be doing really well together. Do you think they'll get married?"

"I don't know. Sid wants it, but Lana says that's too conventional. She's enjoying being a bad girl, living with him." She shrugged. "Some people aren't interested in marriage."

"Uh-huh." He set aside the mail and drummed his fingers on the desktop, staring down at it as if trying to come to a decision. Why was he acting so strangely?

She put her hand on his shoulder. "Mitch, are you okay? You look a little pale."

He shook his head, then reached into his pocket. "I've been thinking a lot about us."

She smiled. "Good things, I hope."

"Yeah. Good things." He glanced at her. "I mean, things are going well, aren't they?"

She nodded. "Yes, things are going very well." Better than she'd ever dreamed.

"And the business is doing well." He looked around the office, which he had yet to redecorate, beyond replacing the daybed with a luxurious leather sofa. A very comfortable sofa, as she could attest. "Meg starts med school next year and I was thinking it might be time..."

His voice trailed off and he pulled a small velvet box from his pocket. Jill's heart rose somewhere in the vicinity of her throat and she scarcely heard his next words. "I know one time you said you weren't interested in being tied down to any one person, but I'm hoping maybe the last few months have changed your mind.''

Heart pounding, she took the box and opened it. A perfect diamond solitaire glinted back at her, like a miniature sun, full of light. "It's beautiful," she breathed.

Mitch shifted from one foot to the other, shoved his hands into his pockets, then pulled them back out. "If you don't like it, we could change it for something else. Or…''

"No." She put her hand over his mouth to silence him. "I like it." She fit the ring on the third finger of her left hand and admired the glow. A girl could get used to this.

She looked up and found him watching her, a frightened, questioning, hopeful look in his eyes. She smiled and wrapped her arms around him. "I love you, Mitch."

All the tension went out of him and he sagged against her, holding her tightly. "Are you saying you'll marry me?"

She drew back far enough to look him in the eyes. "I don't recall hearing a proposal."

"Will you marry me?"

She tilted her head to one side, considering. "I'm not sure I heard you right. After all, this moment only comes once in a girl's life. She likes to know it was done right."

Mitch frowned at her a moment, then understanding dawned. He stepped back and lowered himself to one knee. "Jill. Darling." He took her hand. "Will you do me the honor of being my wife?"

She grinned at him. "I can't believe I'm saying this, but yes. I will marry you, Mitch. Darling."

He stood and lifted her off the desk, whirling her around before crushing her to him and stealing her breath with a kiss. A long, deep, toe-curling kiss that promised many more of the same in the years ahead. When he finally released her, she was dizzy and giddy with happiness. Who would have thought being in love…real love…would feel so good? "I'll marry you. As long as it doesn't have to be conventional," she said. "I can't really see myself with white lace and roses."

"What did you have in mind? The Elvis Chapel in Las Vegas?"

She trailed one finger down his chest. "I was thinking maybe…the Amazon."

He laughed. "I'll go anywhere. As long as it's with you." He pulled her close once more and began kissing her neck, while his hands explored the naked flesh beneath the veils. "I like this costume. Will you wear it tonight?"

"Only if you'll wear your pirate costume."

He nipped at the edge of her bra top. "Your wish is my command."

She laughed. "And that's just the way I like it."

HARLEQUIN® *Blaze*™

GUESS WHO'S STEAMING UP THESE SHEETS...?

It's talented Blaze author Kristin Hardy!
With a hot new miniseries:

Watch for the following titles and keep an eye out for a special bed that brings a special night to each of these three incredible couples!

#78 SCORING March 2003
Becka Landon and Mace Duvall know how the *game* is played, they just can't agree on who seduced whom *first!*

#86 AS BAD AS CAN BE May 2003
Mallory Carson and Shay O'Connor are rivals in the bar business—but *never* in the bedroom....

#94 SLIPPERY WHEN WET July 2003
Taylor DeWitt and Beckett Stratford *accidentally* find themselves on the honeymoon of a lifetime!

Don't miss this trilogy of sexy stories...
Available wherever Harlequin books are sold.

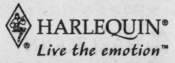

HARLEQUIN®
Live the emotion™

Visit us at www.eHarlequin.com   HBBTS

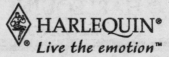

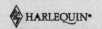

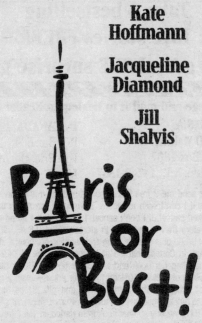

A "Mother of the Year" contest brings
overwhelming response as thousands of women
vie for the luxurious grand prize....

Kate Hoffmann

Jacqueline Diamond

Jill Shalvis

Paris or Bust!

A hilarious and romantic trio of new stories!

With a trip to Paris at stake, these women are
determined to win! But the laughs are many as three of
them discover that being finalists isn't the most
excitement they'll ever have.... Falling in love is!

Available in April 2003.

HARLEQUIN®
Makes any time special®

USA TODAY *bestselling author*

J·U·L·I·E
K·E·N·N·E·R

Brings you a supersexy tale of love and mystery…

Silent CONFESSIONS

A BRAND-NEW NOVEL.

Detective Jack Parker needs an education from a historical sex expert in order to crack his latest case—and bookstore owner Veronica Archer is just the person to help him. But their private lessons give Ronnie some other ideas on how the detective can help *her* sexual education….

"JULIE KENNER JUST MIGHT WELL BE THE MOST ENCHANTING AUTHOR IN TODAY'S MARKET." —THE ROMANCE READER'S CONNECTION

Look for
SILENT CONFESSIONS,
available in April 2003.

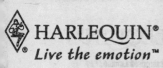

HARLEQUIN®
Live the emotion™

Visit us at www.eHarlequin.com

PHSC

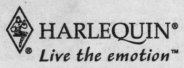